Kamal Ruhayyim, born in
from Cairo University. He is
stories and five novels. *Menorah*
twentieth-century Egyptian trilogy, that includes *Diary of a Jewish
Muslim* (AUC Press, 2014) and *Days in the Diaspora* (AUC Press,
2012). He has lived in both Cairo and Paris.

Sarah Enany has a PhD in drama and is a lecturer in the English
Department of Cairo University. Her translation credits include
works by Yusuf Idris, Mohamed Salmawy, Jerzy Grotowski, and
Kamal Ruhayyim's *Diary of a Jewish Muslim* and *Days in the Diaspora*.

Menorahs and Minarets

Kamal Ruhayyim

Translated by
Sarah Enany

hoopoe
AN IMPRINT OF AUC PRESS

First published in 2017 by
Hoopoe
113 Sharia Kasr el Aini, Cairo, Egypt
420 Fifth Avenue, New York, 10018
www.hoopoefiction.com

Hoopoe is an imprint of the American University in Cairo Press
www.aucpress.com

Exclusive distribution outside Egypt and North America by I.B.Tauris & Co Ltd.,
6 Salem Road, London, W4 2BU

Dar el Kutub No. 14801/16
ISBN 978 977 416 831 4

Dar el Kutub Cataloging-in-Publication Data

Ruhayyim, Kamal
      Menorahs and Minarets / Kamal Ruhayyim.—Cairo: The American
   University in Cairo Press, 2017.
        p.   cm.
        ISBN 978 977 416 831 4
        1. Arabic Fiction — Translation into English
        892.73

1 2 3 4 5   21 20 19 18 17

Designed by Adam el-Sehemy
Printed in the United States of America

To the people who fill my heart with joy: my daughter
Yasmine, and my grandchildren Kanzy and Selim

1

THE CAB DRIVER TOOK ME FROM the airport to the neighbor-hood of Daher, only charging me twice the fare.

I protested, "The meter says twenty! That's the government fare."

He stuck his head out of the window belligerently, preparing for a fight. "Look, mister, our fare is forty, and you should make it fifty, if you want to be a gentleman."

"But—"

"But what? Come on, now! And if you pay in dollars, all the better." I was loath to do it and hesitated, but he gestured impatiently. "Hurry up, sir, there's a good fellow. I'm a busy man!"

"All right." I rummaged in my pocket and forked over a handful of francs.

"What's this, buddy?" He stared at them. "I want my fare in dollars!"

I explained to him that francs were hard currency, just like dollars. He finally nodded, not entirely convinced. "That's for you to know and me to find out!" And he drove off, the exhaust of his retreating vehicle blasting me in the face.

The edges of the sidewalk were worn away. Some of it had disintegrated into potholes. The building gate seemed all askew, as though about to fall; the building itself seemed like an ailing man. The paint was worn away in several places; there was a crack in its wall starting from the top and creeping, crooked. The windows and balcony doors bore barely a trace of their previous paint. My pain increased when I found the ground floor apartment gone. Mr. Qasim and his wife, Hajja Samah, had always stood at the window looking out: he with his frown and white hair sticking out messily in all directions, and she, a smile gracing her friendly face, talking continuously, getting only a nod or a few words from her husband in return. She always had something for us children: some caramels, a packet of biscuits, or perhaps a candy wrapped in cellophane.

The memories came flooding back. At first, when she motioned me over, I would hesitate, overcome with shyness. With time, however, I grew familiar with her, and took to slowing down as I passed her house, hoping she might call me over. She usually noticed and, not content with merely motioning, would call me loudly by name, my candy at the ready! She'd give me some and would ask about the health of my grandmother and grandfather, while her husband inspected me and then asked her who I was. When she answered, he would look at me. I often felt a smile might form on his lips, but it never did, and his lips settled back into a frown once more. Each time he asked the same question and received the same answer. Before I left, she always asked me nicely to buy her a book of matches or a packet of tea from the grocery store, or perhaps some mastic or a quarter-pound of cumin from the nearby spice store. I would go like the wind, bringing her back the order and her change. Little by little, the old man made friends with me; he took to patting me on the head and doing as his wife did, putting a hand in his pocket and taking out a piece of candy for me, or asking me with great interest how my grandparents were.

Now, they were gone. Gone, and the apartment with them. It had become something else, a business perhaps, or some sort of warehouse. The window they used to look out of had been bricked up. Instead, a door opened from the apartment directly onto the sidewalk; people came and went through it bearing parcels and boxes. The proprietors, curse them, had cut down the tree that had stood in the entrance to make room for their delivery trucks, which were proudly blazoned on the side: Mule & Son, Building Materials and Hardware.

I caught sight of a veritable buffalo of a man sitting cross-legged on Amm Idris' old bench. God help us, he had a face like a hippopotamus and a huge body encased in a long, traditional gallabiya, whose seams were splitting at the neck and shoulders. One of his legs was folded into the recesses of the gallabiya while the other dangled free, eye-catching in its very hugeness. A pair of exhausted slippers languished beneath him, one lying some distance from him, as if it had collapsed trying to escape, while the other hid beneath the bench. This, I guessed, was the new doorman.

He did not leap to my defense as I argued with the cab driver, nor yet did he notice my approach; he was too busy sleeping, his turban falling into his face ahead of him every time he nodded off. His eyes were closed, his mouth open, and if he was aware of the fly that had settled on his nose, or its sister that buzzed around the cup of tea next to him, there was no sign of it.

There was no longer a juice store facing the building. When I turned to look, it was gone too, and in its place was a store for cassettes and VHS tapes, a trio of young men loitering around in front of it. In short, it was time to say 'rest in peace' to the street I knew—no, rather, time to say, 'Be gone, evil spirits,' for it was as though demons, not humans, had taken possession of it!

I took my bags—one in my hand and one over my shoulder, to say nothing of the massive burden I lugged behind me with my other hand—but scarcely had I reached the doorway of the building when the doorman's voice yelled after me, "Hey, mister! Where do you think you're going?" He didn't even give me a chance to answer, but snapped obnoxiously after me, "Hey, you there, mister—yes, you, just barging in like that!"

Turning, I found he had taken off his turban and laid it in his lap. It was a huge turban of the sort they wear in deepest Upper Egypt; if unfurled, it would have been the size of a boat sail. He stared at me, feet feeling about on the floor for his slippers; when the search proved fruitless, he leaned back at the shoulders.

I said a silent 'rest in peace' for old Idris, the Nubian doorman who had always filled our building with life and movement. Bustling in and out, up and down, he had had a smile that never left his lips, his broom leaning against the wall of the building's tiny service courtyard, at the ready to catch any speck of dust foolhardy enough to float in on the wind. And here sat this great buffalo, staring at me, drinking his tea, waiting for me to approach.

I came up to him. Lord, the stench of the man! And me unable to protect my nostrils, for my hands were full of luggage. "Are you the new doorman?"

"Who're you calling 'new,' mister? I've been working here for seven years! Who are you, that's the question, and where are you off to?"

A simple question, with a lifetime for an answer! I said simply, "I'm going up to Umm Hassan's."

"Umm Hassan, who lives on the third floor?"

I nodded.

"She's away. Been visiting relatives in Abbasiya for two days now. The apartment's closed up."

"I've got the key. I'm the original tenant, you see."

"The original tenant!" His eyes widened and he leaned toward me, staring. "You wouldn't be one of the first residents, would you?"

"Yes."

"The ones who're away in foreign parts?"

"Yes."

"The family of . . . "

"Yes, the family of . . . "

His eyes gleamed. "You can't be Galal!" He jammed his feet into his slippers, which he had located at long last, and reached for my bags, taking them from me. "Why, they say that no one's seen hide nor hair of you for ten years or more!"

Forbearing to comment, I asked instead after old Amm Idris. "Dead, may he rest in peace."

"What about Sitt Shouq, his wife?"

"God only knows."

He began to hawk deep in his throat, preparing to spit. I took a step back, just in case, swearing hearty oaths for him to hand back the suitcase he had taken out of my hand and go back to his bench, as I knew my own way. "But why not let old Bashandi, here," he said, referring to himself, "carry your bags upstairs?"

I didn't reply. For answer, I pushed a ten-franc note into his hand. He examined it in excitement. "What's this? Dollars, then, or what?"

"Something like that."

I left him busy stuffing the banknote into the folds of his turban, and said a silent prayer for the soul of old Idris, who had only ever known the twenty-five piaster note and that President Nasser was the Leader of the Arab Nation.

2

I passed through the building gate with Nadia on my mind: Nadia, the daughter of the family who lived upstairs.

I still remembered that day. She had been coming home from school, and I had been barreling down the stairs. It was here we had met, in the entranceway that separated the outer door from the start of the stairwell.

In those days, I had been quite the young imp: I'd never climb downstairs like a normal person when I could take the steps three at a time. That day, though, I'd lost control: my arm swinging desperately for some purchase to save myself a nasty fall, I shoved her down hard with my shoulder on my final leap, just as she set foot inside the door.

She had dropped all her things, supporting herself, small and soft, against me with a little gasp, and we had knelt together on the floor, breathing hard, picking up the things that had fallen. Her lashes had drooped to half-mast over her eyes, concealing her shy glances, and I had moved closer, giving in to her completely. She had left her hand lying pliant in mine; when she rose, I remained standing there staring after her as she ascended the stairs, until she disappeared in the curve of the stairwell.

Here was the door to Abul Saad Effendi's apartment. How many times had I come knocking on his door when I was having trouble with my history lessons? He would always greet me with a smile, and I would follow him into the sitting room. His eyes would look brightly upon me from above his glasses, perched low on his nose, while I pointed out the part I found hard to understand.

I could still remember him on one occasion, leaning back with a smile. "Really, Gel-gel! Who could confuse Ahmose I with anyone else, my dear boy? Ahmose, of all people! Really, you can get mixed up about anyone's name, but not this fellow. He's one of the most important kings of Ancient Egypt. Why, it was he who conquered the Hyksos who had invaded our land."

Noticing that he hadn't offered me anything, he paused as was his wont, and called to the maid, "Saadiya! Fetch us two bottles of Spatis from the fridge, straight away!"

Then he turned back to me. "There are two men, my boy, who are unique: Ahmose, and President Nasser." Whereupon he forgot what I had come for completely, and started to wax lyrical about Nasser. I eventually brought him back to the subject at hand. "Oh!" he said. "Oh, that's right. Lord, we've digressed. Right, back to our old Uncle Ahmose, then. Look here . . . "

Three more steps, and I would be at Umm Hassan's old apartment.

The lights in there were on; from behind the door came the sound of shrieking children, and I could see the shadows of things being thrown and caught through the frosted glass of the small panes set into the old-fashioned door. "Ah, Hassan," thought I. "Even now you may be inside, sitting on some chair or other, having tea or busying yourself with a cigarette, letting things degenerate into chaos all around! You old devil, you got the apartment all to yourself, didn't you, after the Papa died and the Mama got sick of you, and so she moved upstairs to live in our apartment."

I caught myself: "'The Papa' and 'the Mama' isn't the way people refer to their parents here! That's what you say in Paris in the company of your mother's Jewish relations."

Hassan and I were brothers, having been nursed by his dear mother; it was true that he was the companion of my

8

childhood and my youth. How our young feet did wear away the steps of this old staircase, going up and down in each other's company, or racing to see which of us would get to the rooftop ahead of his brother!

But I would rather not meet him right now—for this is a moment in time unlike all others, and I want it to be mine alone, all to myself.

"Just one more step, and another, and then, Galal, you'll be at your apartment."

The first breath was drawn here. The first exhalation. The first smile. The first laugh. The first everything . . . .

A seedling, not a few months old, wrapped in swaddling clothes, helpless, incapable of doing a thing for itself, there I lay in my mother's lap, clinging to her presence and the tones of her voice, losing myself completely in her, all, all in her embrace, finding my ease in her heartbeat as though it beat for me and not for her.

Different hands picked me up: my grandfather Zaki's, tenderness overcoming wonder as I wrapped my tiny hand around his finger, my grandmother Yvonne, my uncle Shamoun, my aunt Bella, and our neighbor, Hassan's mother, called Umm Hassan, who offered me her breast to nurse at to make up for my mother's, whose milk had dried up.

Here I was born and grew up, played and loved, left and returned. . . .

I reached out and touched the metal bars on the traditional window set into the door of the apartment. They were damp, cold, no trace of warmth coming out or in. Their corners were rusty; one of the heart-shaped tips that adorned their uprights was missing, another crookedly leaning into its fellows, and the rest had their edges eaten away. For some reason, the little window itself seemed smaller to me than I had thought it was.

There was the scratch I had made at the door hinge one morning. My mother had been running toward me as I tied my shoelaces, yelling at me and pushing me with a hand to hurry up and get to school before the bell rang, and I remember my grandfather, who had just come out of the bathroom, telling her to go easy on me. Now that was a journey that had wearied my little feet. There I was, a small form like something out of a Disney cartoon: huge schoolbag strapped on its back, traversing street after street, alley after alley, under the merciless early-morning wind that stung my nose and neck, my mouth blowing plumes of warm vapor into my palms that begged for relief.

The schoolyard; the morning lineup; the fluttering flag; the classroom they packed us into like chickens in a coop; a chalkboard black as the robe of some evil spirit. The Venerable Headmaster, in a safari suit and dismal shoes; the physical education teacher, of whose stick we were very wary; and the little boys, some yawning, some crying or dreaming of mommy back home, and playing and fighting with hands and rulers and copybooks and anything at hand.

It was as though the whole world held its breath.

The stairwell was still, not a soul ascending or descending. The walls were silent, the apartment door staring silently at me.

It was the first to recognize me, after all. It asked me to come inside and meet the others: the carpet, the armoire, the bed where I used to sleep, the table where I used to sit with a copybook or book. . . .

It looked at me, and I looked back.

It asked me questions, and I asked back.

But neither of us had any answers.

3

EVERYTHING WAS JUST AS WE had left it.

There was the sheepskin on the floor outside my grand-father's room, the sewing machine, the two patches on the left-hand side of the kilim rug. My grandmother Yvonne had taken off her shoes and felt its threadbare weft with her feet, sighing and bending to peer at it, her glasses taking up half of her face, needle and bundle of yarn in hand. Since she had grown older, she was no longer able to mend anything—she couldn't even thread a needle. I remember her holding the needle and thread out to my grandfather, who looked away; my mother took on the challenge, only to struggle unsuccessfully with the task; then along I came, to thread the needle for her in the blink of an eye. I'd expected a word of thanks or a pat on the shoulder, but she gave none; she turned her back on me, and crouched to the kilim, poring over it with the needle.

Here was the couch where my grandfather used to sit, magazine or book in hand. The frames of his spectacles were discolored from the sun's merciless rays and from the salinity of his sweat, especially at the tips of the arms and at the points of contact with his nose and eye sockets. From behind the lenses, his eyes seemed sleepy and fatigued. I would often get the sense that he was not reading: the book or magazine would remain open at the same page before his staring eyes for an hour or more, and when his eyelids relaxed and slipped shut completely, my suspicions would be confirmed. What he had been reading would slip from his hand to rest in his lap, whereupon my grandmother would notice and urge him to leave the couch and go to bed for a nap before dinner. He would always receive her words with obvious astonishment, insisting he hadn't been asleep, then raise the book or magazine to his eyes once more.

He would spend the entire weekend at home, like most of the people in our street, reading something or other, or flipping through television channels. His pack of Belmonts was always at his side wherever he sat, with a matchbook on top, and the cigarette never left his fingers. Not even once did he notice the long, fragile cylinder of ash that grew longer and longer, falling with the first move of his hand and sprinkling his clothing with grey particles.

Rest in peace, Grandfather!

How I used to cling to him whenever I saw him going out, especially if I knew he was going to Abu Auf's café. He would put his arm over my shoulder, and we would set off, among cars that mostly bore the state-sponsored Nasr Auto Company logo, bicycles with a cast-iron frame that could carry two men and a suitcase if the need arose, and advertising and movie posters: I remember the one for the iconic Sixties movie, *al-Nasser Salah al-Din,* about Saladin repelling the Crusaders, and another for Kina Romany, touted as a power drink that gave you energy and strengthened the muscles.

There had been no shortage of things reminding us of our Great Leader, President Nasser: a photograph on a wall or a lamppost, a live speech floating over to us from some nearby radio, or two passers-by speaking of him, one singing his praises and the other chiming in with enthusiastic agreement.

None of this, however, caught my attention. All I cared about was the little things: a cat lying against a wall, a toy that jumped out at me from a shop window, a boy my age walking with his mother, with whom I exchanged glances, or children playing at marbles, rolling the small green glass globes with inner stripes and swirls of black coloring. They looked like eyes.

We would arrive at the door to the café. I would stare at my grandfather, who always scanned the patrons, searching for his friend, Hajj Mahmoud the spice merchant, Umm Hassan's husband. One of them would catch sight of the other soon enough, and they would then repair to a table in the corner. I would follow them, inhaling the scent of Hajj Mahmoud's gallabiya, which bore a perfume like incense.

They would get ready and sit on two opposite chairs; before sitting, Hajj Mahmoud would take off his abaya, folding it over the back of his chosen seat. They would start with black Turkish coffee. My grandfather would hold his cup like regular folks, with both hands; as for Hajj Mahmoud, he would hold it by the handle, fingers splayed and extended. I used to stare down the wide sleeve of his peasant-style gallabiya, and look at his ring with the blue stone that encircled his finger. At the arrival of the water pipes, pleasure would spread across their faces. The smoke would fly up and around in thick clouds, and I would follow the patterns it made in the air. From time to time, my grandfather would look at me from the corner of his eye; when he noticed that the clouds of smoke had become thick around me, he would wave them away with a hand or motion to me to change my seat.

The only thing that would take my attention off them was the old man with the pointy beard and the beret. I had long seen him seated alone in the bowels of the café, drawing with a thick pen, talking to himself without pause, avoided by all and sundry. The only thing that could distract me from him was the waiter in the white apron, appearing before me with the cups of coffee, tea, and other orders, especially when he yelled at the fellow manning the preparation station with his long, melodious calls. To my young ears back then, they sounded as though they, too, had a flavor, like the flavors of the beverages. I salivated over the sight of a man sipping a certain red liquid in a transparent glass, whereupon my grandfather unfailingly called the waiter over and ordered me a hibiscus tea as well. I would always look on in amazement when he and Hajj Mahmoud unfolded the wooden backgammon board, and the enthusiasm of play transformed them into creatures not unlike fighting cocks.

This particular café was my grandfather's favorite. He was familiar with the patrons, and he felt at ease there. He only stopped going once, when war broke out in 1967 and the shock turned everyone somber and gloomy, walking around in a daze as though the Apocalypse had arrived. His cautious nature prevailed, and he stayed home, contenting himself with listening to the news on his small radio, never once turning his feet toward the café to share the space with its patrons, following events on the large radio set there. His grief was their grief, his suffering their suffering; but he was overcome by the feeling that if he were to express how he felt among them, his words would be, as it were, tainted; that anything he might say was capable of being misinterpreted, or that some muddy-thinking or racist ignoramus might insult him by word or deed. After all, was he not a Jew, one of those for whom Palestinian lands were so unjustly taken? Even my mother and grandmother quit going out. I was the only one who was free to come and go, bringing in the news from outside.

When Hajj Mahmoud realized what was in the wind, he stood by my grandfather and comforted him. He said as he always did, "Don't let your fears get the better of you, Abu Isaac! You're one of us, those others are Zionist curs!"

Then he took my grandfather by the hand and brought him to the café, where everyone greeted them as usual, imputing Grandfather's absence to some illness, business, or perhaps some occurrence that had claimed his time away from them, nothing more. He chatted with them gladly, thinking how silly he had been to stay away for an entire month, drowning in fears and delusions.

4

UMM HASSAN HAD CHANGED NOTHING in the apartment. Even my grandfather's photo still hung on the wall in its old frame, my grandmother's portrait facing it on the opposite wall. She was seated in a leather armchair, my aunt Bella standing next to her in school uniform. The laughter of my two-year-old self resounded throughout the apartment as I ran from room to room, chased by my mother or grandmother for some mischief I had committed, or perhaps as I sat on the floor in a corner of the hall, legs stretched out in front of me, playing with my treasures: an old whistle, some bottle caps and empty containers, or a broken watch my grandfather no longer needed. I had a child's small awareness that I was a Muslim living among Jews: mother, grandfather, grandmother, aunts and uncles. But they were all I had; moreover, I was my grandfather Zaki's favorite, dearer to his heart than any of his pure Jewish grandchildren.

They were all I had. My father's family, farmers and landowners all, were wary of getting too close to me; when one of them patted me on the shoulder, I would find him staring deep into my eyes, as though asking whether I really was one of them or some strange alien creature? Was I their true flesh and blood, worthy of a place among them, or a curse foisted upon them by Fate to eat their food and usurp their name? Was I a son of the countryside and the Muslim of my father's heritage, or a city boy and the Jew of my mother's influence? They were all suspicious of me: aunts, uncles, and all their children.

The only exceptions were my father's parents, my grandfather Abd al-Hamid and my grandmother Umm Mahmoud. They recognized me from their hearts, not from any birth certificates, calculations, or deductions. My grandfather recognized that I was his flesh, sent to console him for the loss of his son, killed in the Suez war. My grandmother scented in me the traces of her own son, the son she had lost. I came to them as a blessing, and Umm Mahmoud's heart broke open to admit me. However—as the proverb goes—only the evil cattle stay at the trough! My grandfather died, and my grandmother soon after, and with them the ties that bound us to my father's village in Mansouriya. All that remained was the few pennies my uncle Ibrahim would send my mother every month, to clear his debt of honor, since he had promised my grandfather before the latter died that he would continue to send us money.

In time, I fell in love with Nadia; I still remembered my mother watching us, plotting ways to prevent me getting too attached to her, so that we could join my grandparents in Paris. She succeeded, and I left Nadia behind when we left the country together. I spent years there, only to return, after so many deaths: my grandfather Zaki, my grandmother Yvonne, Khadija, the Tunisian girl I had married in France, who died suddenly on a trip we had taken to Nice. My mother, though, was still living, although a part of her had died in my heart the day she married Yaqoub Abul Saad, an Egyptian Jew who had settled in Paris.

I rose and walked over to my grandfather's armoire. There was nothing in it; it was lifeless, the air in it still and heavy. The shelves were filled with emptiness: only a bottle of medicine relieved the vacancy, wrapped in an old sock, stiff with age. On closer inspection, I espied a pair of glasses with a broken arm and a shoelace. There was also an empty razor-blade wrapper with a drawing on it of a crocodile with a broken back.

I stared at the portrait of Abu Hasira, the Jewish saint, that my grandfather had clipped from a newspaper one day, and attached with pins to the inside of the wardrobe door. One side of it had come off and was drooping, the whole yellowed and ancient. His face was darkened, not the same face we had left. I wanted to reaffix it with the pin from which it had come loose, and return it to its former state, but refrained: what would be the use? The man who had sought its blessings morning and evening was no more.

A cockroach the size of a match head ceased its scurrying: it must have sensed me, and froze so as to remain inconspicuous. I made to crush it, but refrained. I closed the door of the wardrobe on it, as well.

What I had brought of my grandfather's things, I placed in the wardrobe: his old tarboosh and his grey shirt. As for the wedding ring I had taken off his finger the day he died, I could find no more loving place for it than my own finger. His Jovial watch was no longer running; I wrapped it in a handkerchief, and tucked it away in a drawer, in case I should come back to it one day.

I spent the night alone, accompanied only by the shades of those who had once lived there. We haunted one another; we spoke with one another. They came and went, as though I were living in another time: a time just created, where I was subject and object all at once.

5

THE NEWS OF MY ARRIVAL spread, and Abul Saad Effendi was the first to come and welcome me.

How he had changed! His hair had receded and was mostly white. Wrinkles had settled in the region of his neck and around his eyes. He had filled out: layers and layers of fat sat about his waist and hips, in addition to the higher regions of his shoulders and chest. This increase in girth had ruined his figure, for he appeared shorter to me now than he had before. In spite of all these changes, his face was still fresh, and his loud laugh was just the same. He still wore the old safari suit I was used to seeing, and I could have sworn that the glasses he wore were the same old pair I knew.

He flung his arms around me, voice ringing out on our doorstep. "Welcome back, Gel-Gel! We've missed you, you little devil! It's been so long, you rascal!" He tut-tutted sadly when I told him of my grandfather's death. We moved to the couch in the hall, where he sat, looking somber and patting me by way of condolence, my grandfather's portrait opposite us on the wall, looking down at us. "Rest in peace, old Uncle Zaki. You were the sweetest man who ever lived. You never said a word against anyone, nor hurt anyone's feelings." He drew nearer. "You, er, buried him there, of course."

I nodded yes.

"O Lord, have mercy on his soul! Praise be to Him who lives forever." After a pause, he said, pushing his glasses up on his nose with a fingertip. "And how's your grandmother, Madam Yvonne? Well, I trust?"

"She's passed on."

"Her, too? O Lord have mercy on her soul."

He hesitated, then asked after my mother, clearly fearing that she, too, might be among the deceased; but I reassured him. "What about the others, Galal? Your uncle Shamoun and your aunt. . . . " He hesitated, as if he'd forgotten my aunt's name.

"Aunt Bella?" I smiled.

"Yes, yes, her!" he jumped in. "How is she? In good health? How's she doing? Well, I trust?"

The smile in my eyes grew. "Smooth, Mr. Abul Saad!" I thought, "acting like you don't remember my aunt's name!"

Aloud, I said slyly, "Oh, if you could see my aunt Bella now! She's the only one of us who has conquered Old Father Time! The older she gets, the younger and more beautiful she looks."

"Oh, Bella," he sighed, giving his tongue free rein. "How you're missed! Where are the good old days!"

I drew him out. "She's not doing so well, you see. She and her husband weren't getting along. Why, she used to leave the house for a month or more, and come stay with us at my grandfather's."

I paused, quite deliberately. He craned his neck toward me, face begging me for more. "And then? And then, Galal?"

"What can she do? That's her lot in life. Sometimes, when she was crying, she'd say, 'Why did I ever tie myself down to this miserable brute, why did I make this match? I never loved him, I never wanted to marry him. You were the ones who made him seem like such a catch. It feels like you forced me into it,' she'd say."

"Is that what she said? She has every right. Every right! Ah, Haroun, you lowlife, you don't know the value of the jewel you possess!"

Struggling with all my might to keep a straight face, I said to myself, 'Oh, so you remember Haroun's name, do you? And here you were, pretending that Bella's name had slipped your mind.'

He appeared to realize that he had revealed more than he should, and fell silent, eyes on me, fearing that I had guessed or noticed. I played dumb. I knew about the romance between him and my aunt Bella: he was one of the first inhabitants of the building, and had come to live there before I was born. Back then, he was a bachelor, newly appointed as a history teacher at the Nuqrashi Secondary School. He caught sight of my aunt, who was two years older than my mother, and the die was cast. What happened with my father nearly happened with him, too: he would have married my aunt, but for the fact that he was loose-lipped. News of the romance leaked out. The news flew to his father back home in their village via an itinerant juice vendor in our street. His father and mother arrived posthaste, and dragged him by the collar back to their village, Osim, a suburb of Giza. He only came back two months later, with Sitt Nazira, the respectable Muslim match his family had made for him, in tow.

My grandfather had been aware of what had occurred, and many was the time he tried to comfort my aunt Bella. Back then, she had been a fresh-faced girl, not yet even fully rounded into womanhood. And along had come Abul Saad Effendi into her life, with his white shoes with the buckles, a carnation in his buttonhole, and his hair parted in the middle with a spoonful of oil poured over it for a brilliant shine—in the style of the Don Juans in the movies in the 1940s and 1950s. My grandfather tried to console her, telling her that one so quick to abandon his love and careless of his affections was not worth crying over. He had encouraged her to marry the first man who asked for her hand, who, unfortunately, had been Haroun, an accountant at Shell Oil Company, the son of a Jewish acquaintance of my father's. The poor girl had never liked him, and was unhappy in her marriage to him, both in Egypt and after they emigrated. My grandmother, Yvonne, sided with Bella and called him Old Elephant Trunk, because of his unusually large nose and to get back at him because he was so unpleasant and ill-spoken.

Captain Farid came calling, a large watermelon under his arms by way of a welcoming gift, followed by Bashandi Effendi, the doorman, panting under the weight of a crate of 7-Up. He placed it at the door of the apartment, then loitered, clearly hoping I would give him some of what the Lord had given me, as the saying goes. I waved him off with the back of a hand, indicating that he should leave and let us alone. Seconds later, Hassan rang the doorbell. He flung himself into my arms and showered me with kisses, then carried the packages he had brought into the kitchen. But I noticed something odd in his eyes: a question, some kind of disquiet. It was only later that I realized what my arrival meant for him: would his mother, Umm Hassan, remain with me in the apartment, or leave and go to live with him now that I had returned?

Our number increased by one with the arrival of Magdi, son of Muallim Habib, one of my grandfather's old friends. He used to own the juice store on the corner that I had seen when I arrived, now transformed into a store for videotapes, cassette tapes, and the requirements for young men's nocturnal entertainment.

I said a prayer for his father's soul. He bowed his head and crossed himself. When I asked, he told me they had accepted a lump sum to transfer the lease on the store, and that he had changed his profession, and opened a store that sold imported products on al-Geish Street. Now, every month he went to the port city of Port Said, which had been designated a duty-free zone by Sadat after the ban on imported goods was lifted, to bring back his wares: perfumes, canned goods, women's underwear, chocolates, and baubles. He kissed the back, then the palm, of his hand, as lower-class folk do to give thanks for the money that crosses their palms, then said, "And I make a living, thanks be to the Lord."

He had been my schoolmate in preparatory and secondary school; I know he used to dream of becoming somebody, an ambassador or a professor at university. He had been meant for great things: he was always top of his class. He had earned his high-school degree, with marks that qualified him for medical school; however, he had declined that sought-after college in favor of the College of Economics and Political Science, under the delusion that this was the path to the Diplomatic Corps, and that he would one day become an ambassador.

"I graduated with a general grade of Very Good, that's the second highest mark you can get! And then, after waiting for something like four years, I finally got the promised government appointment, in my case, at the Ministry of Agriculture. After a couple of years of that, I realized I just wasn't going to make a living that way. So I sold my father's store, and used part of the money to finance a new store, and part of it for the stock from Port Said."

"Dad's spice store is still in business," Hassan added, "but I thought I'd try my luck, too. Sometimes I go there with Magdi and stock up on goods to sell." They launched into anecdotes of the tricks they used to get through the customs at the gates of Port Said with their stock without paying duty. Sometimes they hid the goods in a secret compartment in the car; other times they had the stock brought to them in the nearby town of Qantara West by female smugglers who did this for a living; or else they smuggled it out in a government vehicle, or even an ambulance!

"And we know how to deal with each of the customs inspectors, too. For this one guy who always wears a yellow jacket, you have to throw yourself on his mercy and tell him how you haven't a penny to your name and that you have a dozen children to feed. The fat guy in the baseball cap, you have to arrange with him in advance. As for the one in the black pants, Heaven protect us from him! He wants to be Mr. Straight Arrow, and collect every penny for the government."

Abul Saad appeared displeased, waving a hand, "This is all we've gotten from that weakling Sadat and his foolish open-door policy. Bunch of thieves and robbers, one and all! As if it isn't enough what we hear about every day, our own boys have taken to working as con men and smugglers." Sounding hopeless, he continued, "No, no, never! These aren't the same boys who sat at their desks in my class, not the boys I used to talk to about the Ancient Egyptian pharaohs Thutmose III or Rameses, or President Nasser or Saad Zaghloul."

Captain Farid lived in our building too. Although he was over sixty, we still called him Captain, rather than the more traditional Amm, because he had been the physical education teacher at Ismail al-Qabbani Secondary School, and now ran a health club dedicated to muscle-building. He adored politics, although his knowledge of the subject was extremely limited. He could be classed loosely as a tenth-rate politician: all he was good for was repeating and praising the words of important men.

As he sat among us, he listened, watching whoever was speaking. When Abul Saad finished speaking, he said to him, "Forget Thutmose and Nasser, man! Sadat's done well! Take off your dark glasses; you'll see that things are all good! Turns out peace is better than war, and there's money being made, and people are doing well."

"Captain Farid, do shut up; there's a good fellow," snorted Abul Saad.

The telephone rang. It was a call from Paris, from my ex-father-in-law, Sheikh Munji al-Ayyari, the father of my deceased wife. With him on the line was my Lebanese business partner, Akram Abul Shawareb. They congratulated me on my safe return, and Abul Shawareb asked when I was coming back.

"What's the rush, brother Akram?" I objected. "I just got here yesterday, and I don't know yet how long I'll be in Egypt."

When I had hung up, Abul Saad said, "They can't wait to have you back over there, eh?"

I conveyed to him that Akram and I were partners in a business worth millions of francs, and that each of us had his own specialty, and that I had promised not to be away too long. "Galal, my boy," Captain Farid said, "there's money to be made in piles over here. Since you're worth some money now, pack your things and go into business here. We've never had it so good! If you're up to it, you can rake in money by the fistful."

Abul Saad shot him a dirty look. "Oh, really! Rake it in by the fistful, eh? Rake it in from who, Captain Farid? From our blood, and the blood of the poor people, or where from?" He jumped to his feet. "I'll be seeing you. It's just about time for noon prayer." And he walked out.

6

Apple of my eye, oh where are you,
Whose image comes unbidden?
Where is the path that leads to you?
Tell where your heart is hidden.

I lay on my bed reading the national newspaper *Al-Ahram*, when my heart was stolen away by the old familiar song floating in through the gaps in the shutters.

They said 'Forget her, live alone,
For love should not be felt';
I said, find me a heart of stone,
A heart that cannot melt.

I laid my paper aside, singer-composer Mohamed Abd al-Wahhab's voice wafting up to me amid a cacophony of street sounds and people's voices: vendors calling, cars rumbling, and an infernal car horn whose owner seemed bound and determined to overtake everyone else. Little by little, I calmed, until I could hear only the song, ignoring all else, and dreamed, overcome by the melancholy, yearning melody from the nearby radio. I could almost see Nadia before me, in her school uniform. Her face was tranquil, as God had made it, innocent of any makeup; she held her bag of books and pens up to hide her chest. She gathered up the hem of her skirt as she descended the wooden steps of the tram. I had been wait-ing at the tram stop for some time.

I saw her in my mind's eye, standing on the platform. Her figure was perfectly formed, her mouth beautiful in smile or pout. Her eyes roved here and there, as though her heart were seeking me out, telling her I was there, waiting.

She never stayed for too long. She crossed the street as I watched from behind. Her feet fell with measured step; her coal-black hair was smooth and glossy, teased by a gust of wind. She sensed me as I caught up with her, and we matched our steps without a word, until my feet led her to a slim street that was not as busy.

One day I was closing the door to our apartment as she went downstairs, I asked her to stop, and she paused, looking around, afraid that someone might see us. My breath came hard as I approached her. She stilled, receiving me, her eyes distant. I felt the softness of her lips between my own, her body pliant beneath my hands, giving herself to me, and I to her.

It was our first kiss. Afterward, we looked into each other's eyes, stunned by the taste of its nectar, and the effect it had had upon us. Her scent was primal and instinctual, born of her urges and her pores: in that moment, it was more fatal than any poison brewed and bottled by art or artifice.

It lasted but a moment, an instant snatched from time. Then she pushed me away, her reproachful eyes unable to believe what had taken place. She paled, dew breaking out on her cheeks and forehead, I knew not whether as a result of what had just transpired or out of guilt and shock.

We spent long, long days together, dreaming, dreaming and building castles in the air. When we fell silent, the silence itself tasted better than words, sweetness without end.

She was married now. Married when I was abroad, snatched from me by her cousin.

*

I went to the balcony. This was not the street my heart had loved, not the street my feet had trodden. Abu Auf's historic old café now bore a sign proclaiming its new name, Morgan's Café, the place having been bought by this Morgan from Abu Auf's heirs. On your left as you came in was a wooden billboard bearing a colorful poster depicting a black gentleman's hat, next to which stood an empty glass with a cigar lying on top. They hadn't stopped there: they had removed the ancient wooden door, with its eight panels and thick ornamental stained glass, and replaced it with a sliding aluminum door, cold and inimical to anything approaching charm or beauty. The chairs from the good old days, made of strong wood, padded with straw and bamboo, capable of bearing the heaviest of weights, had been discarded, and all I could see were soft seats that were bad for your back. As for Hassan, that gormless idiot, he hadn't so much as repaired the front of his father's store! The sign was in a deplorable state, all color washed away, the smog of the road making a home in its many cracks. Hajj Zenhom's butcher shop had lost its honor, defiled by a new refrigerator filled with chicken breasts and thighs, and dark, frozen meats shipped here in crates from Australia and Brazil.

The street had lost its gentle, welcoming feel. Not to mention the trees we knew, and that knew us in turn, that used to embrace us in their shade when we drew near, who looked down at us from above and whose branches smiled upon us from on high, were now gone. They had greeted each sunrise along with us, as though it were the first light for us, for them, the first light in the world.

An ululation of joy filled the air. Long, cheerful, joyous, and shrill, it announced its author's joy in no uncertain terms. I looked down in surprise at the door of our building, to find Umm Hassan stepping out of the taxi that had brought her. She must have looked up to see me at the balcony, and burst into ululations, while the taxi driver leaned out of the window, clearly gearing up to claim double his fare!

I ran down the stairs three at a time, as I used to when I was a boy. We hugged each other as the doors to the other apartments opened one after another, disgorging women who greeted her, and me: some older, who knew me, and some new tenants, who seemed to have heard about me and about my story. We ascended in a procession to the door of the apartment, as though I had arrived just now, this minute, and not a few days ago!

Umm Hassan was half the size I remembered. Gone was the fat, the flesh, the sturdy frame. Her life-giving, bountiful breasts, into which I had sunk my fingers and which had dripped milk into my mouth, were now drooping and withered. The feet that had walked through the apartment like a sentinel, coming and going to the butcher's, the poultry man's, and the grocery store, were thin and wasted. "Diabetes, my boy, destroyed my health. It's wrecked me, God wreck it!"

"But you must take better care of yourself. You are like a mother to me."

"Your mother is still alive, my boy. May God give her a long life for your sake, hear my prayer, Lord."

But, since she counted as my mother, she took the black veil off her head, which only made her appear even more frail and feeble, as her hair was thin, white, and translucent. From time to time, as she reached or gestured, I detected a tremor in her hand. When she laughed too long, the laughter was followed by an attack of coughing so severe I would rush to her aid, urging her to sip from a tall glass of water.

We talked for a long time. I told her my story, all of it. I told her my tale of life in a strange land, in the diaspora. She told me of her troubles after the death of her husband, Hajj Mahmoud the spice seller: she had become like a stranger in her own home, in the midst of her son Hassan and his wife, for nobody listened to her, and she had no function other than caring for their young children. She had preferred to go upstairs and live in our apartment until such time as I should come back. When the talk turned to my grandfather, she took out her handkerchief to wipe away a tear. "We were neighbors for a lifetime, my boy. Only an evil person forgets old times!" She took a breath. "He confided in us, and always had an ear for our troubles. Many's the time your old uncle, Hajj Mahmoud, sat with me when he was still alive, and we'd think of you all and say, 'I wonder what they're doing abroad? How are you faring, Uncle Zaki, and you, Mrs. Yvonne? What's kept you away so long, Camellia, you and your boy Galal?'"

She asked after my mother. I told her she had remarried. "Married?" she muttered. Then she caught herself, hiding her disapproval. "It's her right, after all, my boy. She has every right."

"Her right?" I retorted, thinking of my father, faithful in his grave, and barely keeping my anger in check. "Why didn't *you* remarry, then?"

"What, me marry? Marry again, after Hajj Mahmoud!" With this, she seemed to sense my resentment toward my mother, and said, "You see, my boy, marriage is protection for a woman like your mother. She suffered a great deal, raising you. She spent long, long nights alone, all by herself. Don't ever resent her, Galal." Her curiosity getting the better of her, she asked, "Who did she marry?" I acted as though I hadn't heard her. "Was it someone Jewish?"

I nodded.

"God bless her union." She said it in a way that made me feel that she would have been happier if my mother had married a man who was Muslim as we were.

She went into her own bedroom. When she had been inside for a long time, I knocked at the door. When I opened it, I found her stacking her clothes into neat bundles in a row on the rug, and placing her small personal effects into a handbag on the bed.

I rushed in. "What do you think you're doing?"

"Thank you for all you've done. It's time I was leaving."

"Where will you go?"

"Home." Her voice dropped, and she lowered her head. "To Hassan's."

"Hassan's! Your home is here!"

We started arguing, if that's what you want to call it. It was pro forma at best; she was already disposed to yield and gave in to my argument. In truth, she hardly made any protest beyond what she had already said; she merely gazed at me without speaking as I returned her things to the armoire. I felt she looked upon me as a son, preferring to stay with me rather than go to Hassan's; it was the same for me. I wasn't insisting upon her staying out of some sense of chivalry or gratitude, but out of the feeling that she was a mother I had made and chosen for myself, in consolation for the mother who had given birth to me.

She had taken as her bedroom the room that my mother and I had slept in when we used to live here; as for me, I moved my things into the room that had belonged to my grandfather.

7

UMM HASSAN SAT ON A chair in the balcony, a table before her bearing a tray with a glass of water and an empty coffee cup, turned upside-down. Sensing my approach, she said, "Come here, dear."

I drew nearer, bearing my own cup. I took the last sip of it, then placed it, bottom-up, next to hers. She looked at me while I leaned on the railing, looking down at the street below and the people coming and going. From time to time, I glanced at her to find she had lifted her cup and was gazing deeply into it, reading the coffee grounds within, like some good-natured young woman you might see in a café, laughing with her friends over some dubious prognostication. Her expression vacillated between confusion and disappointment, as though she had not yet found the answer to some question that was puzzling her.

When she was finished divining the secrets held within her own cup, she took up mine. First, she glanced at it quickly, then moved it away, then brought it up close to her eyes, scrutinizing the wavy lines and runnels created by the coffee grounds. After a few moments, she called to me.

"What's the cup have to say?" I asked, leaning forward.

"Just something to pass the time," she said. "I never used to read coffee cups or know what they said. I only took to it when I came to live alone."

"I want to know how she is," I said.

"Your cup is full of good luck. Joy surrounds you and happiness lies before you."

"But what about the one who's in my heart?"

She understood, but refused to get drawn into what I wanted to speak of. "Leave off listening to the devil's whisperings, and come here, next to me. I want a word with you."

I sat by her while she returned the cup to its original position and opened the snuffbox that lay in her lap. The smell rose, sharp and stinging, to my nostrils. I let out a slight cough, so she changed her mind and recapped the box. Turning her tired eyes to me, she said, "It's my heart's desire to go on the pilgrimage to Mecca, my boy."

"Pilgrimage?" My enthusiasm was apparent in my voice. "Of course! I'll cover the costs, every penny, from the moment you set foot on the plane till you're back home again."

She silenced me with a gesture. "That's not what I meant. I get an income from the store, and I've got more than enough money, praise the Lord. I was just waiting to see what you think."

"What I think?" I said, astonished.

"Of course. Aren't you my son? Aren't you my man, now, and responsible for me?"

I laid my hand on hers, lying on the chair arm, a hot wave surging through me. "Does Hassan know?"

"Hassan?" she snorted, and said no more. After a moment, she resumed. "You see, some of the women in our street are planning to go on the pilgrimage together. I want to go with them. I didn't give them my final agreement, though, until I asked you, to see what you would say."

Our conversation was suddenly cut short by a commotion: people were screaming and shouting in the street. We leapt to the railing to see a paddy wagon, the policemen pulling a young man up its steps. He had wild, unkempt hair, his shirttail was untucked, and one of his shoelaces was untied; it seemed they had arrested him so suddenly that he had not had time to finish getting dressed. He was docile, offering no resistance. Wedged in among the men arresting him were a man with white hair, still in pajamas, and a woman still in her house gallabiya. In her haste and panic, she had thrown some old thing over her hair to cover it—some sort of rag, or perhaps a baby's blanket.

The white-haired man was livid, asking questions angrily, his arms protectively shooing everyone away from the boy willy-nilly. One of the policemen shoved him away repeatedly, but he was insistent, and his increasingly loud questions and increasingly desperate attempts at protecting the boy almost caused them to come to blows. The woman was sobbing and crying, pulling the makeshift scarf over her hair with trembling fingers whenever it came untied. A large crowd had gathered, but they were ineffectual.

Traffic had ground to a halt by this point; motorists began to stick their heads out of their car windows, asking what was going on. Some, not interested in finding out, began to honk their horns, calling out for whoever was blocking the street to make way.

Finally, the paddy wagon drove off. The woman's wailing filled the street, and she craned her neck after the wagon until it disappeared around a corner.

Umm Hassan pressed her forefinger to her brow. "Poor thing! It's young Islam, Hajja Taqiya's son. Every few days they come and pick him up, him and another boy in the same street, by the name of Khalid. . . ." She trailed off, leaning out to watch the wagon on its way, to see if it would stop outside the house of this boy Khalid as well. When it failed to do so, she returned to me, telling me Islam's story. "He's just a student at university, his father and mother don't have much, they're poor folk. And poor thing, he's just a boy, as you can see. They're saying he's part of the extremist Islamist organization al-Gamaa al-Islamiya, and you'll soon hear of what's going on between them and the government!"

After a pause, she asked, "Why would a boy like Islam and his ilk want to fight the government, anyway?" I didn't have an answer. "Just like that, without any provocation? Are they crazy? It doesn't make sense!"

We moved on to another topic. "What do you plan to do, Galal? Are you here for a visit, or do you mean to stay with us for good?"

"I don't know where I'm going to end up yet in this world." I fell silent for a while. "I wish I could live here always. I'd like to have my career in my own country, because no matter what I achieve abroad, I'll never be somebody, and I'll never be recognized by anyone. But part of me still wants to pack up and go back! Tomorrow, even! To do what, I have no idea. And my business is there, what'll I do with that?"

Her simplicity coming to the fore, she said, "Is there only business in foreign parts, then? Move your business here, among your kith and kin. What's so great about staying out there? Do you like living among foreigners? They're not like us; their habits aren't our habits. Everyone minds their own business; they don't know how to be neighborly or help one another or care for each other like we do." She looked deeply into my eyes: "Your late grandfather is gone to his Maker. Your mother is married. Who do you have to stay there for?"

I fell into deep thought. She resumed, trying to make it seem easy. "Just make a decision, put yourself in God's hands, and you'll find the doors of fortune opening over here. With time, you'll find a nice girl to keep you company and make you happy."

Without meaning to, she had led me back to Nadia. I asked about her directly.

"She's fine," Umm Hassan said shortly. Scrutinizing whatever she saw in my face, she went on, more gently, "Didn't Hassan tell you her news in his letters? Besides, who cares about Nadia now? Just think of yourself and your own best interests." I looked away, but she wasn't done. "Nadia's a married woman now. As you know full well, she's married to her cousin Fouad. He's an army officer: he's made her comfortable. They have a beautiful little girl." Her tone somber, she added, "Although he's a sick man, poor fellow."

My eyes went to her: I was suddenly filled with satisfaction, as though getting news of the death of some enemy. It must have shown on my face, but she didn't notice.

"He's got liver trouble, and he has to stay in the Military Hospital for a month or two at a stretch. Nadia has a time of it, going to and fro to visit him."

I asked her if Nadia was still living in the building. She said she was, noting my silence when she said it.

She contemplated me with a kind look in her eyes. "Everyone gets what the Lord has ordained, my boy, and He who created Nadia created many women, better women, much better, than her. Look forward, son, and don't lend your ears to the Devil. To covet what's on another's plate is to hate the will of God." She looked firmly at me for a moment, then away.

"Anyway," she said, very conspicuously changing the subject, "don't you have land in your father's village? What are you going to do about it, just leave it like that? Not only land, but a sister as well. My dear boy, go and see how she is, and pay them a visit, your family over there."

I spent a restless night, asking myself why I had come. Was I going to go or stay? If I stayed, what was I going to do? It was true that I was back in my own country, but where would I find my homeland? In a lost love? A sister I did not know, nor yet knew me? Or in an uncle who frowned when he saw my face? Or in a land where I had eaten, drunk, and played; in the memories that still lived within me, or in an old woman I imagined to be my mother?

8

"I AM EGYPT, WITH ALL that is fair and foul!" says the Rod al-Farag Produce Market. In the month or so since I'd arrived back in Egypt, I'd acclimated to the climate and the people and the pace; however long I'd trod the streets and pavements of Paris, my body and soul knew this as home. It was with great difficulty that I arrived at its gates, not unlike the gates of a fortress; no sooner did I step across the threshold than I was lost in the crowd. All manner of people were there: from towns, villages, and from Upper Egypt, bareheaded, in caps, turbans, and gallabiyas. There were effendis in shirts and pants, women in black wraps with children in tow, and ladies in expensive clothing followed by servants carrying their shopping. There were older boys and powerfully-built men in traditional waistcoats and breeches pushing handcarts, or carrying God's bounties upon their shoulders in wooden crates. There were trucks and mule-drawn carts, unloading their burdens of watermelons, melons, zucchini, and cucumbers.

Being shouldered aside was something you quickly grew familiar with, as was stumbling over the refuse, empty bottles, and cartons underfoot, unless you were vigilant, with a thousand eyes in your head! From a nearby radio, someone was reciting the Holy Qur'an; from another, the older singer Abd al-Muttalib sang, "You who give the evil eye / Why so covetous, oh why?"

There were shops and stalls of every size: small, large, and no bigger than a matchbox. All had floors carefully covered with smooth sand, to form a soft surface for the fruits and vegetables. The proprietors' names were mostly Upper Egyptian: The Zidane Family, Haridi Sons, al-Marzouqi, al-Sohagi, and so on and so forth. People trooped in and out, some buying in bulk for themselves and their neighbors, some choosing only the freshest of produce, some accepting squashed or rotten fruit as long as it was deeply discounted and within their budget. Beggars in rags reached out toward passers-by; some picked up whatever they saw, stuffing it into bags or sacks: half a watermelon, a rotten mango, or remnants of food.

Along the back wall of a shop ran a water pipe, ending abruptly in a tap. Before the tap stood a pair of men: they had both hitched up their gallabiyas to mid-thigh, the excess material pulled inside-out through the inside of the garment and out through the neck opening, to keep it out of the way. One was bending over the tap, lathering up his face with soap, his fellow waiting his turn. It seemed they had spent the night at the market, and were just now waking up. A whale of a woman, steps away, appeared to have just finished washing her head. The veil over her shoulders trailed in the dirt, dripping water mingled with sand and mud, as she wrung out her dismal locks with her hands, a thin stream of water issuing forth. She pulled her hair back so hard that the skin of her face was drawn tight, and her mouth had come open to reveal two gold front teeth.

There was hubbub and commotion, hustle and bustle, buying and selling accompanied with kind words and pleasant smiles, and occasionally with yelling and squabbling. Voices called down blessings upon the Prophet, and others were moved by frustration to curse everything, including religion itself. It was a world that captivated the eye; an admirable though incomprehensible method to its madness.

*

I walked all over the market, back and forth, in search of Leithi's shop. Leithi had been a classmate of mine: I say it loosely, for he attended, at most, a day or two of classes every week, spending the rest of the days in his father's store in the produce market. The poor fellow had spent seven years in secondary school to no avail: he could not parse a sentence in Arabic, pronounce a word in English, or solve a trigonometry equation, although I had to admit that there was no better nor more helpful fellow to his friends and acquaintances. I would be a character witness for him in a moment, provided it had nothing to do with learning or study.

I had come here desirous of seeing him and rekindling our old acquaintance; I also hoped that it would be a visit that mixed business with pleasure. Umm Hassan's words had fallen on receptive ears with me, and who knew? Leithi might be able to help me start a business venture, or I might be able to go into some form of partnership with him.

Finally, I asked a passer-by where his store was. "Oh, you mean Leithi and Muftah's?" I wasn't able to answer, but the man continued undaunted. "That'll be him; it's got to be. There's only one Leithi in the market, you see, and his brother's called Muftah. Straight ahead that way and you'll find it on the left."

I turned my face in the direction he had pointed out. He was bareheaded, wearing a gallabiya, sitting on a wooden chair outside his store. They pointed him out to me. He lifted up his Persol sunglasses as I approached. He scrutinized me for a long moment, then surged up from his chair, yelling, "As I live and breathe! Galal?"

We embraced and sat down, which heralded the start of a stream of soft drinks, coffee, and tea. Leithi motioned to a vendor passing with a container of hibiscus juice on his shoulder; I remonstrated, to no avail, and he then insisted I take a puff of the water pipe he had with him, and flatly refused to converse with me unless I accepted this hospitality. I did as he asked, and took one puff, then another, until I burst out coughing. We talked of matters old and new, the good old days when we were schoolboys, in Mr. Busrati's class, which soon turned into a circus. Then there was Mr. Kharboush, the biology teacher, perfumed and smartly dressed with his white mustache and shiny shoes, who seemed to us in those days like a veritable Minister of Education, the Big Boss of Everything, the other teachers mere schoolboys compared to a man of his stature.

We moved on to what was new: I told of my long absence, and he of his father's store of which he was in almost complete possession, only a small portion belonging to his brother Muftah. The brother had taken a different path in life, content with his income from his share in the store and his name on the sign. "And I'm doing all right. I drive a Mercedes and I smoke Marlboros"—American cigarettes, whose importation had been banned in Nasser's time, were a status symbol nowadays—"and I bought an apartment for my wife Umm Fathi in Nasr City, and an apartment in Mohandiseen for my wife Umm Hussein."

Encouraged, I launched into the topic I had come to broach. He fixed me with a stare, looking serious. "Look, Galal, old man. All I know from is fruit and vegetables. If you want to go into this line of work, I'll welcome you with open arms; just tell me how much you've got."

"Does that make a difference?"

"Does it make a difference, he says. Why, that's the very heart of it!" He gave a grunt that indicated he was thinking, then, asking me to wait a second, he bent to pick up a copybook cover that lay by my feet, and waved it energetically back and forth, to fan the flames of his water pipe. Taking a deeper breath than before, he exhaled, heavy smoke flowing in even, successive plumes from his mouth. "Listen to me, man. This market's days are numbered. In two or three years' time, it's going to be moved away from here altogether, to a suburb called al-Obour. I'm planning to book two big stores there. If you like, I can make them three, and you can be a partner. But you need a respectable sum for that, my brave man. Down payment, installments, commissions, and redecorating—not to mention some money in advance to the growers. You see, my fine fellow, if we don't get in line in time to reserve stores direct from the government, we'll have to pay double, because then we'd be buying from the early birds who've already booked their turn."

I stared at him, listening, nodding instead of speaking.

"But listen! I only deal in traditionally farmed produce, stuff from old-fashioned growers. No hothouse stuff, nothing grown out of season or puffed up with hormones and what-not. That's my system. And to be plain with you, that's what's causing trouble between me and Muftah." He leaned closer. "Or are you going to tell me you're back from abroad, eh, and technology this and technology that? If you tell me that's what everybody's doing nowadays, then I'll say no, thank you, and each of us can go his own way in business. I may be old-fash-ioned, but I'm straight. I only deal in what's right. Ask the whole market about me. If you want to join hands, you're welcome, just know what I'm like, and honesty is the best pol-icy. I like to set down rules and be clear, man, that's what I always say."

I let him go on and on without comment. "That's just the start of it," he went on. "If you want us to expand, and grow, I've got the cash. We could find a plot of land around Beheira and have it cultivated for us specially, and use the crop for stock. But that'll really take outlay, maybe too much."

The idea appealed to me. "Why look for land?" I jumped in. "I've got land." Then I told him about the plot of land I owned that was in my uncle's possession, land we could use for our business venture.

"Where's this land, then?"

"In Mansouriya."

"Is it ready for planting?"

I wasn't sure of the answer to that. Finally, I said, "All I know is that it's my inheritance from my grandfather, but the exact location of it I don't know."

"But is it ready for planting immediately?"

"I don't know that, either."

I spread my palms. He stared at me, astonishment growing in his face. "And you want to make it part of the venture?"

No sooner did I nod than he cut me off. "Look here, Galal. Right from the start, I'm telling you, keep this land of yours out of it. What you're telling me means that it's a long story, and you may never see this land of yours until you're old and grey." He let another plume of smoke out of his mouth, then pushed his shisha aside. "For heaven's sake, my good fellow, how could you be so naïve! What shall I call you—a foreigner who doesn't know what's what, or a man gullible as a child!"

I made to interrupt, but he forged on. "You don't seriously think you're going to get this land, do you? Or, if you do get it, that you're getting it without a fight?" He pointed to a miserable peasant man sitting on the dirty ground some distance from us, selling a pile of watermelons, counting something on his fingers. "You see that fellow bending over his wares, the pitiful one?"

I looked to where he was pointing. "That guy, the one you'd think so miserable and dumb, he could trick the Devil himself! As the proverb says, he could lead you to the river and bring you back thirsty. And if you don't learn your lesson and try to do business with him, he'll take you to the river again and bring you back thirsty a second time!" He made a sweeping gesture. "Forget it, just forget it! Anything but land. You'll never be able to get the land from them without a fight to the death." He turned away for a moment to yell at one of the shop boys, then turned back to me. "I'm of farmer stock, you know, born and bred, and I've been dealing with them all my life. They're good-hearted and harmless, I won't say anything against them. But let them catch someone setting foot in the land they're tilling, and they turn into wolves." He spread his hands. "I never heard of anyone getting the better of them in matters of land."

"What are you saying, get the better of them? It's my due! I'm just going to get my due, the way everyone gets what's coming to them!"

"I respect that. But that's not the way they'll see it. All they'll think is that you've come to snatch the food off their plates."

"It's my land, Leithi!"

"They're going to say it's their land, too."

"Even my uncle?"

"Even your brother, born of your father and mother. So long as you're away from the land and from them, with no roots in those parts, kiss your land goodbye. The most you'll get out of them is a few pounds by way of settlement."

The conversation ended. As he said goodbye, his parting words were, "Well, we'll see what comes of it. About our business, just get your capital together, and you'll find me here waiting."

9

I left Leithi's, thinking of what had passed between us, especially what he had said about only dealing in traditionally-grown produce. As far as I was concerned, God had created the fruits of the earth for us, pure and chaste, to fill our stomachs, nourish our bodies, and protect us from illness. It could only do us injury and bring us disease when His creatures ruined it with pills and injections, creating unnaturally huge gherkins swollen to the size of Armenian cucumbers; strawberries, devoid of their rich flavor and scent, puffed up to the size of sycamore figs; and watermelons whose size struck awe and admiration into one's heart, yet proved void of goodness when you cut into them, useless even to fill your stomach, less a meal than a drink of plain water.

Leithi labored under the misconception that 'they' liked 'that kind of thing' in 'foreign parts.' Some did, of course, but he was unaware of the significant number of French folk who refused to eat fruit and vegetables injected with hormones, and were careful only to eat healthy and wholesome natural produce; indeed, they valued such goods and displayed them in special racks in their stores, and at a premium price, to boot! Why should I not put my hand in his hand, and export these good fruits together to the wholesale produce markets of Paris? This might be the business venture that would link me to my family and my homeland, and give my feet a chance to be planted in both countries, that I might go back and forth.

The other thing, which I found worrisome, was the seed of doubt he had planted in my head, about my land back home in my village. Would I run into trouble with my relatives over there if I went to claim it? It was true that I hadn't remained in contact with any of them, particularly the children of my uncle Ibrahim. But what had the one to do with the other? The one was my right; the other, ties and loose ends left behind by my father's marriage to my Jewish mother, and I rather thought they had dissolved with time. Would I be kept from my land? If I were, would it be for the sake of some old disputes, or for the reasons Leithi was citing now?

When I arrived home, I made a telephone call to my uncle Shamoun. He had called me from Paris twice: once to congratulate me on my safe arrival, and the second time a month later, to see how I was and ask me to arrange a visit to Egypt for him, as he wanted to see the old place and meet his old friends. I had not paid his request much mind, to be honest.

This time, he asked me again, and I told him I would do what I could. Then he suddenly asked me a question he had asked the last time: Was the branch of Dawoud Ades' department store in Azhar Street, the branch he had been manager of before he emigrated, still standing? What about al-Malki's Dairy, the one opposite al-Hussein Mosque? Was that still in business? He had, he explained, taken breakfast there often.

I had not been to the places he mentioned, nor even asked what had become of them as he had instructed, but I assured him that they were still there. I told him all sorts of things I knew nothing about, inventing answers out of whole cloth, not out of a desire not to disappoint him in me—having ignored his requests—but just to make him happy and not to kill the hope that remained alive in his heart: the things he wanted to be still there *were* there, that he might visit one day and see them again. His persistent longing took me by surprise and my tongue ran away with me, and I told him what they tell a child overcome with longing for his dead father: that he is still alive, just away on a long journey.

I resolved to go to the places he had told me of the very next day, after which I would be able to see how things went. He had asked after other places and people: the Khan al-Khalili market, and a particular store he knew on al-Moski Street, as well as Amm Idris our old doorman, and Amm Marzouq who used to walk from building to building bearing a wooden tray on his head, selling homemade yogurt in small earthenware containers. What about Abu Auf's café? Did I sit there as he had done in the past? I played along with him, telling him what he wanted to hear. I loved him. I knew he was the only one of my mother's family, now that my grandfather was no more, who still clung to the old world and felt lost without it.

When I asked him how my mother was, he said, "Didn't she call you?"

"She did, once."

"She's in Israel now with her husband Yaqoub. They'll be back in Paris in a few days."

We hung up. A dark cloud hung over my head, because of my mother who seemed always in Israel, not Egypt, the land where she had been born and raised and had thousands of memories.

10

ABUL SAAD EFFENDI SAT IN his usual seat in his living room, the prayer rug still unfurled before him, reading from a copy of the Qur'an in his hands, having just finished the noon prayer. Behind him on the wall was a framed proverb in Arabic naskh script: "Patience Is the Key to Deliverance." On a nearby table was a folded copy of *Al-Ahram*. What showed of it was filled with repetitive accounts of what the US Air Force had done to us a couple of days ago, cutting off an EgyptAir commercial flight in mid-air. After closing the holy book, he reached for the radio, which was next to the newspaper. He turned it on, listened to the news and commentary, then turned it off. Silence spread throughout the apartment, but for some clattering about from his wife, Sitt Nazira, standing in the kitchen at her pots and pans.

"Nazira," he called. She came out, a squat, thick-set woman with fleshy buttocks, who smelled strongly of boiled meat and soup. "Do your best today!" He smiled at her pleasantly. "Don't let us down today of all days, I beg of you!"

She smiled back, bursting with confidence in herself and her cooking. The doorbell rang and the maid came in. She bore a tray upon her head, wafting the perfumes of rich local ghee and coconut. He craned his neck curiously. "What's this, then?"

"A tray of basbousa I was having cooked in Umm Nabil's oven," answered his wife, pulling a rag out of the pocket of the apron she was wearing and supporting the maid's burden as both women took it into the kitchen. "Our stove's all full up and the oven's small, as you know." She turned back before disappearing into the kitchen. "Couldn't you have gotten us a new one? One of the big imported ones?"

As she disappeared, he called after her. "What's wrong with the Military Factories cooker? Local made, and we can't afford fancy stuff!"

Bashandi, the doorman, came in, bearing loaves of fresh bread and bagfuls of fruit. Abul Saad rose and went to him. They quickly took up their standing dispute, Abul Saad losing his temper and telling him to keep a civil tongue in his head, and not keep harping on the subject of a tip. In this resentful mood, he started to search through the bags of fruit, accusing Bashandi of having eaten one or two pieces at least out of each. After his burdens had been surrendered, the latter turned and marched out full of righteous indignation at having his honesty so impugned.

When Sitt Nazira was done with her cooking, leaving the maid to clatter about with the pots and pans, she returned in fresh attire: a clean house gallabiya, and a pair of made-in-China slippers with a red rose on them. She appeared to have combed her hair as well as she could, although it was unruly, clearly not holding the waves she had attempted. "When are the guests coming?" she said, seating herself opposite him.

"Oh, not for a while yet. We said three o'clock." He gave her the look of a man plotting something. "What do you think of Galal, Umm Hadeel?"

"He's a good boy. No one's ever had anything bad to say about him. There's only that thing, you know."

"You mean the thing with Nadia?"

"No, no! That was just puppy love."

He was thinking of Galal's aunt, Bella. One day, as a boy, Abul Saad had lain in wait for her and tried to snatch a kiss, but she had run away from him and rushed up the stairs. Abul Saad was pensive as he went on to Sitt Nazira, "We all have things like this in our young days, but they pass with time." He paused, looking down and pretending to be absorbed in flicking a speck of dust off the sleeve of his pajamas. "Wouldn't he be a good match for Hadeel?"

"Hadeel? Our daughter Hadeel?"

"Why not?" He turned his gaze back to her. "Find a fiancé for your daughter, after all!" He was referring to the old saw, 'Find a fiancé for your daughter, not for your son.'

She seemed genuinely shocked. "But she's got a B.A. in agriculture! She's all we've got! And he's, well. . . . " She paused. "I remember clearly that he only finished high school, and then left the country right after that. Umm Hassan knows everything about him, and she's with me all the time, and she never said a word about him going on to college or anything like that."

He wrinkled his nose. "My dear, loveliest of all women! Did our old Sultan Mohamed Ali Pasha have a university degree, then? Or Abbas al-Aqqad, the famous novelist? What about Averroes, and al-Ghazali, did they sit on benches while a teacher pointed to them with a finger, writing with chalk on a chalkboard?"

"Who are they? Are they from the city? Are they important people?"

He rolled his eyes, muttering, "No, never mind, my dear. Pretend I didn't say anything!"

She rose to go to her room, but turned halfway through the hall. "Did he talk to you about wanting to marry her? Or did he show any signs?"

"The boy hasn't said a word. I just think it's a waste."

She turned and went back to her seat, recalculating. "I heard he's got a proper pile in the banks in foreign parts." Her husband said nothing. She folded her hands in her lap. "But what about the other thing, then?"

"You mean his Jewish mother and uncles?" She craned her neck toward him. "Look, Nazira, dear, we're in no position to forbid what God has permitted. The boy's a Muslim, as you know, and that's the root of the matter. But talk of his mother, and his mother's relatives, that's just unnecessary." He waved a hand. "The main thing is that he has to ask for her hand, though!"

She remained silent, heart vacillating between 'yes' and 'no.'

At exactly three p.m., as per our appointment, I found Captain Farid waiting for me on the steps, where we met and headed for Abul Saad Effendi's apartment. He met us wearing a robe over his pajamas, something like a nightcap on his head. We went immediately to the table, and from there to the sitting room, where my eye was caught by a bookshelf in a corner. It had glass fronts through which books beckoned. I took to leafing through them. Some were leather-bound, some with covers of thick cardboard; some were tattered, and some lacked a cover at all. Dust filled the cracks and spines, and pressed between the pages were tiny insects that had clearly been dead for a long time. Most of the books were history books, especially about Ancient Egypt and the history of the pharaohs: Cheops, Thutmose, Rameses, and Akhenaten, and *Pearls of Wisdom on the City of Memphis* by Ahmed Kamal Pasha. There was *The Encyclopedia of Ancient Egypt,* by Selim Hassan, and books about our kings, sultans, and rulers, such as Muhammad Ali Pasha, and Khedive Ismail, and the great leader President Nasser, and the book *Autumn of Discontent* by famous intellectual Muhammad Hassanein Haykal, which criticized President Sadat and for which the president had put him in jail. On the higher shelf was a bound copy of the Holy Qur'an, next to which were two books by the great intellectual Taha Hussein, *The Mirror of Islam* and his autobiography, *The Days.*

I went back to my seat with Captain Farid. We would talk for a quarter of a minute, then fall silent for three, until Abul Saad Effendi came in, holding a radio the size of the palm of one's hand, put it on a high-legged table, and launched into conversation. We talked of anything and everything; eventually, the conversation turned to me. I told them of my visit to Rod al-Farag, and my conversation with Leithi. Abul Saad Effendi, seeming well pleased, said, "Excellent. That means you'll be staying on with us!"

I nodded.

"It would be great, Gel-gel, if you and this friend of yours didn't just go in for business and shops and so on. What a good thing it would be if you really did get into farming, and got into desert reclamation for agriculture—it's all the rage now—and reclaimed twenty or thirty feddans!"

Captain Farid looked at Abul Saad. "If that happened, we could always do with the experience of our dear daughter, Hadeel, the agricultural engineer!"

"Hadeel?" Abul Saad Effendi's stare grew vacant. Almost stuttering, he said, "Right, yes . . ." and looked at me, not seeing, naturally, any change in my expression: I didn't even know who Hadeel was, and thought, in fact, that she was Captain Farid's daughter. I didn't like Captain Farid much, so I didn't pursue the conversation nor was I curious at all.

Abul Saad scratched his wedding ring with a fingernail, then reached for the radio and turned it on. Leila Murad's voice flowed forth, smooth, pure, and lilting, laden with the perfumes of the good old days, which I had never forgotten nor stopped yearning for. "Doctor of the heart," she crooned, "darling of my heart, you left me bereft, and cleft my heart in two!" It was our song. As Leila sang, I heard Nadia's voice on the phone, singing the same song the day she had called to let me know she had achieved high marks in her high-school leaving exams. I had been making preparations to enter medical school. "It's Friday!" she'd said. "Quick, turn on the radio! Leila Murad's going to sing right now on the request show!"

"What's she going to sing?" I asked. She remained silent, seeming shy. When I insisted, she responded, singing what

Leila Murad was singing now. "In my eyes are words for you, if you could read their song! In my heart is passion true, I've hidden it so long!"

Loud voices roused me. Captain Farid and Abul Saad were noisily discussing the relative merits of my proposed business venture, opining that I might lose everything if I sank all my money into the project. I went back to feeling sorry for myself. I had not become a doctor, nor even, in Leila Murad's words, her darling. I noticed Captain Farid looking at me, expecting me to take part in the conversation which was, after all, about me, or at least respond to what he said. I just looked perplexed.

"Galal!" he said, grinning. "Galal, where have you gone? You must be thinking of your good mother. Don't tell me— you miss Paris and the high life there!" I nodded. Seemingly satisfied with this explanation, he went on, "Wouldn't it have been better to save your money and effort and hop over to China instead? Get some stuff from there, and sell it here? The profit in this kind of business is guaranteed, son!"

"Good Lord, Captain Farid!" Abul Saad slapped his knee in annoyance. "What's this nonsense? China indeed!" The radio rose in volume suddenly, drowning him out: Leila had reached the end of her song. The music was followed by an interview with a prominent politician. The interviewer was asking what he thought of Uncle Sam's actions against the EgyptAir passenger aircraft, and he answered in measured tones about the US administration's loss as a result of its rash actions, and Egypt's gains as a result of its wise and magnanimous restraint, as though we were listening to a referee at a soccer match, or some politician from Tanzania or the Philippines—not someone with our own blood running through his veins!

Abul Saad grew even more irate. "So these sons of Uncle Sam, or Uncle Mud, overstepping and insulting us in such a way, and this ass saying that by standing for it, we're mature adults in the eyes of the world?"

"What could we have done?" retorted Farid. "It's America, sir—America!"

"What could we have done, he says!" Abul Saad turned to me, dusting off his hands in a gesture of disbelief.

At that point, I excused myself and went upstairs, leaving them hot at it, still arguing.

11

". . . And then, after you're done at the grocer's, you can pass by the bakery and get me a kilo or two of breadsticks, dried biscuits, and some kaab al-ghazal date cakes."

"I will."

"But, Galal, tell him to give you the fresh stuff! And please, nothing too hard, my teeth are hopeless!"

"All right."

Umm Hassan was busy as could be: the day after tomorrow, the plane would take off, bearing her to Mecca. She sat cross-legged on the bedroom floor, beads of sweat on her brow, her sleeves rolled up, an old-fashioned trunk open beside her, and her things strewn all about: gallabiyas, white veils, a prayer rug, a pair of slippers, and underthings, small bundles tied at the top with string or strips of cloth. She reached out and picked up a small copy of the Qur'an off the bedside table and stuffed it into an inner pocket of the suitcase, together with a rosary with a green tassel. Then she looked up at me. "I asked you to get me a dozen jarfuls of cooked beans? Make it two. And the tuna and sardines, instead of five tins, make it ten."

I listened without a word. "And the limes, make it a kilo. And the corned beef, six tins, no change, just like I told you."

"Anything else?"

"Yes! Dozens. Just go get that stuff first, there's a good boy, and when I remember something else, you can go get it too. It's hours yet till our old friend Zaghloul the grocer closes."

My eye was caught by the immense belly of the trunk, to say nothing of its iron jaws, hasps, and padlocks. As if that weren't enough, it had a belt with buckles. I gestured to it. "Surely you aren't taking that monster of a trunk? You'll have a terrible time carrying it. As far as I know, they won't let it on the plane, or even put it on a scale."

"You just get the groceries, and never mind the bag."

"It looks like the crates they used to load onto caravans in the processions, in the days when you had to go on pilgrimage by land and they rode on camels!"

"Galal! I won't hear a word against this trunk! It's a lucky trunk, and it's been to Mecca dozens of times!" She dropped whatever she was holding, and took to counting on her fingers. "Your uncle Hajj Mahmoud, God rest his soul, took it on Hajj in '56, and then again ten years later. Abu Nabil took it on two umra pilgrimages. And quite a few people from our street borrowed it when they were traveling, too."

I turned to go without a word. Before I left, she called, "Oh, that's right, I've just remembered something! Find me a leather belt that's nice and broad, son, with pockets, and snap closures, so I can put the money in it and wear it around my hips."

"Wear it around your hips?"

"Of course, wear it around my hips! How else will I keep my money close by and safe?"

I left her for the street, resolving to return with her groceries and make myself scarce, for she would give me no peace, and I would be running up and down the stairs all night.

The street knew me by now. Bashandi the doorman; the one-armed man who stood selling his beans out of the large pot; the boys at Abu Agwa's bakery; the waiters who served the drinks at Morgan's Café. Amm Zaghloul the grocer, who had known me since I was a little boy, and was all smiles whenever I arrived, listened patiently to me and set out my orders on the counter. "Here are the cans of tuna and sardines. What else, Mr. Galal?"

"Hmm. What else, what else . . . ?"

As I stood thinking of the list of things Umm Hassan had asked for, the grocer looked past me at a man who had just walked in, and was now standing next to me. "Well hello, Mr. Fouad! If you'd wait just a second, please."

I followed his gaze; the newcomer nodded at me in greeting. Zaghloul, surprised, said to both of us, "Don't you know each other? Why, you're neighbors!" He motioned to me. "Galal Effendi's from the street here. He's been away in foreign parts, and he's been here for three or four months now." Then he turned to the other man. "And this is Mr. Fouad. He's married to Sitt Nadia, who lives two floors above you."

I looked at him cautiously, heart beating fast. His gaze met mine, and we reached out to each other and shook hands. Encouraged by his friendly demeanor and the warmth of his greeting, I shook his hand as vigorously as he pumped mine; I couldn't quite control my eyes, though, which looked him up and down. I could not get them to do my bidding, as they moved from his military-seeming shoes to his puffy pants, descending without a crease to keep them in line, taking in even the belt around his waist and the color of his shirt. On the whole, he appeared to be suffering from some kind of wasting illness; his face was grey, and there were dark, puffy circles around his eyes.

A little girl burst in, flinging her arms around his knees. She lifted her eyes to him. "Don't forget the chocolate and the chewing gum!" she piped up. I guessed that she was his daughter.

He patted her tenderly. "Where's Mommy?"

"She's at Abu Agwa's. She'll be right over."

"This is Reem, my daughter," he smiled at me. "I'd be honored if you'd join us for a cup of tea one afternoon."

His invitation pleased me, for it laid to rest any fears that he had any inkling of what was between me and Nadia. His daughter was whining because he was ignoring her, so he picked her up and added, "And where were you living abroad, then, sir?"

"In France."

"Were you there long?"

"About ten years, a little longer."

"My word." He raised his eyebrows. "That's a lifetime."

Amm Zaghloul was listening. He looked at me out of the corner of his eye as I said in a low voice, "One does what one must."

"What one must? In any case, you bring light to our street," he said in the old-fashioned phrase, "and you're most welcome home."

I realized that he had never heard of me before. "Shall I wrap up your order, Mr. Galal?" asked Amm Zaghloul.

I nodded. Fouad said, "I'll expect you anytime, then. But don't forget to bring Reem the chocolate she likes!"

Reem pointed to one of the bars on display. "This kind."

"How much will you like him if he brings you some?" he asked.

She spread her arms wide. "THIS much!" We both laughed.

Nadia came into the shop. Startled to see me, she paused in the doorway, then took a step forward, eyes on me. I didn't know where to look, and ended up staring at my feet, then quickly glanced at her husband Fouad, then at a shelf of canned goods high up on the wall, then to the boxes of tea and packets of matchbooks next to those. Amm Zaghloul didn't notice, engrossed as he was in shooing away a cat that had poked its head in the door.

Her skin had lost some of its tautness, and she wore a hijab now. I didn't notice anything else; my eyes did not dare, either to devour the sight of her face, taking everything in, as they had just done with her husband Fouad, nor to drop to her breasts or neck, nor to areas that had once been my holdings. Her husband interrupted, saying, "This is Galal, your old neighbor. You must remember him."

I held out my hand and shook hers, then took my leave. Naturally, I forgot all about Abu Agwa's, and about the kilo of limes, and even about the things I had bought at Amm Zaghloul's, merely hurrying upstairs to Umm Hassan to tell her what had happened while she interrupted me with exasperated cries of, "Well, I never! Where's the stuff I asked for, then?"

12

FROM THAT DAY ON, I resolved to stay in Egypt.

I did not think of leaving my old apartment for somewhere smarter, such as Heliopolis or Mohandiseen; the old
place was dear to me. It was nothing but stone, but it had a
home in my heart. In all fairness, I might even say that it was
part of me, despite being stone, and I was part of it, although
in human form. I had crawled upon each of its tiles on my
hands and knees; from this balcony I had first looked upon the
world; on this bed I had been covered with my first blanket;
at this sink, how often had I stood on tiptoe so that my small
hands could reach the tap.

These dear walls, with their peeling paint; these photographs, hangings, and scratches, this old furniture! This small
radius, two rooms, the hall, kitchen, and bathroom, were my
home. Here I had laughed and cried, at this door my friends
had knocked, this was the home that had sheltered me when
my father's family had, in those early days, not thought enough
of me and my mother to even find out how we were.

The problem now was this: How would I raise the money to
allow me to start my business venture in partnership with Leithi?

I started with what was easiest: I rang up my business partner, Abul Shawareb, in Paris, letting him know what I intended
to do. "What's this nonsense, Galal?" he said. When I proved
insistent, asking him to send me a sum from the company

coffers, he sounded angry. "Money! Where am I to find you money, Galal? I don't have liquidity in the account, and I don't have any francs. All our money is in our wares, in the market."

We argued heatedly. Finally, he said, "If every time you're going to come to me with nothing to say but money, money, let's dissolve the partnership between us. Each of us can take his money and do what he wants with it."

We launched into another round of accusations, and memories of the old days. He ended the conversation in a voice filled with emotion: "Galal, my brother. You're a good young man, and you've a special place in my heart. Be wise, and don't ruin the business we have going, the business we've been building for long years. Don't listen to everyone who gives you advice over there in Egypt! Not every idiot needs to have an opinion." And he finally told me to dismiss the idea from my head completely and come back at once; it was enough that he had done X, and Y, and Z in my absence and that he'd had to move the autumn stock all on his own. The holiday season was coming and we had to meet and plan what we were going to buy, and work out which stores and which closeouts to buy. I promised to think of what he was saying, my mind searching in the meantime for another source of cash.

There seemed to be nothing for it but to ask my mother's family for money. The first to come to mind was my uncle Shamoun, but he was poor as a church mouse, with not a penny to his name. Haroun, the husband of my aunt Bella, was a rat, and everybody knew it. My uncle Isaac was an equally fruitless proposition: he hated me and I hated him. There was no one left but my mother.

I picked up the telephone receiver. As soon as I started to talk to her, she interrupted me mockingly. "Melons and vegetables? What foolery, Galal! You want to peddle melons on a cart through the streets? Sell zucchini to passers-by?"

"Mom!"

"After the lifetime you've spent in Paris, and all your friends there, and your business in Givenchy, Chanel, and Dior, you want to open a stall and be a fruit seller, a vegetable man? Come back to your senses, darling, and pack up and come home. Come on, I'll be waiting."

When I finally gave her to understand that the crux of the matter was not in melons or zucchini, but that I wanted a business venture that would give me some link to my own country, a venture that would give me a foothold so that I could come and go as I pleased, she drawled, "Your country? If it's all about your country, as you say, we're planning to invest in Egypt as well. But my smart boy, we don't till the land or build factories, and we don't want a stall in the farmers' market."

I bit my lip. She talked on, machine-gun fast. "The permits for the gambling casino we applied for in Sharm al-Sheikh are almost approved. Sell your land in the village and liquidate your assets in Paris, and come in as a partner."

"Gambling casino?" I exploded. "Mother, I won't sink my money into something sinful! I'm not going to do anything but follow through on the plan I've made."

This, of course, led to a heated and exhausting argument. "All right, all right," she finally said. "You're free to do as you please. And we don't need your money either, and we don't need you to start a business. But I feel sorry for you, with these silly notions. I'm trying to open a door to a respectable source of income for you, and it's something in your home country, like you said you wanted, instead of running about with a basket on your head, hawking spinach and cauliflower!"

Whereupon we launched into another round of arguments. "Come back to Paris," she coaxed. "Egypt is no home for us any more. It'll do us no good to invest too much of our money there, or seek to put down roots there."

I was as gentle with her as I could, until I lost my temper. "Speak for yourself! Don't say 'we'!" Other words clamored to be said, rising to my throat: words heavy as stones, with the same power to injure. But I swallowed them, choking them back down; she was my mother after all.

My mother, Umm Galal, was no longer the daughter of our street in Daher, the street I had come and gone through so many times, nor the apartment whence she had gone to school every morning and returned. No longer was she like a sister or an aunt to the many ladies among her neighbors with whom she had been friends, who had loved her and she them, who had always said how polite and demure she was; the ladies who had respected her for not remarrying after my father's death to protect me, her son, from being lost forever in-between, without a family I could call my own. Gone was the girl who had grown into a woman on our pita bread and the cheese and olives of Amm Zaghloul the grocer, on falafel and beans. How often had I seen her dreaming, listening to the songs of Abd al-Halim, Leila Murad, and Umm Kalthoum! "Let's go to the cinema, Galal," she used to say, "to watch a movie with Rihani in it, or Omar Sharif!" Or "Let's go to Umm Hassan's, she's invited us to her house for iftar on the first day of Ramadan!"

Now she was someone else entirely. Day by day and year by year, she had changed, and now the transformation was complete: she was a businesswoman, with enterprises and bank accounts, and had turned into a ravening wolf. She was a different person.

I didn't exempt myself from blame, either. More than likely, she was thinking the same thing of me: that I, the child she had borne in her womb and dandled in her lap, had become a prodigal, forgetting that because of me and as a consequence of my very existence, the best years of her life had been erased by Time.

There was silence on the telephone line. It went on for so long that my mother, thinking that the connection had been cut off, called, "Galal! Galal, where'd you go?" When she heard my artificial cough, she said, in the tone of one ending a conversation, "I've told you where I stand. Think about it, and give me your answer later."

"I'm not going to think about anything, and I'll have no part in gambling or anything that offends God. I'm buying fruit and vegetables and I'm not leaving."

"Offends God!"

"Yes, offends God!" I had raised my voice by now. "Gambling's a sin in our religious law, and in yours, too! If you didn't know that, go ask any rabbi!" She made to interrupt, but I cut her off, determined to have my say. "And don't think I don't know that you and your husband Uncle Yaqoub would have opened your casino in Israel if you could, but you're well aware that things like that are against the law over there! There isn't a single gambling casino in Israel!"

"Whose religious law? What's this talk of your law and our law?" she scoffed. "This is business. Trade. Money making money on the market. Money knows no creed or religion, my boy, all it knows is how to grow and multiply. Save your fine talk and keep to your fruit and vegetables. With or without you, we're coming to Egypt in a few months anyway." Her tone grew even more mocking. "Is Your Highness going to come and see us when we come to Egypt, or is that a sin as well?"

Then the line cut off.

13

Umm Hassan was relentless.

She sent me out for a box of pins, then for a needle and thread—a piece of clothing might rip after all, and a stitch in time saves nine, as they say!—and now she was asking me if they had snuff in Saudi Arabia.

"I'm sure I don't know!" I said, baffled.

"Well, since you don't, go out and buy me two packs, and by the way, the breadsticks were too dry. The only thing fresh enough to eat was the kaab al-ghazal."

"There's nothing for it," I said to myself, and put on my shoes, readying myself to go out. Meanwhile, she heaped blame on her son Hassan, who had bought her Saudi riyals at higher than the going rate, and asked me to look out of the balcony to see if the store was still open, and if it was, if that ill-bred boy Hassan was still in it?

The final straw was the arrival of the neighbor women. Nine of them in veils and gallabiyas, one with two children in tow. Umm Hassan held court from her perch on the couch in the hall, coffee cup in one hand and prayer beads in the other, while I shuttled back and forth, dancing attendance on them all. "And bring in the chairs from the balcony, there's a good boy, for the ladies who're still coming. And put an extra cushion on the chair for your old auntie Umm Nabil, because she suffers from, well, it's not polite to say." And she didn't. "And Galal, look down on that lazy lout Bashandi and yell at him to bring up the crate of Pepsi right away!"

The talk turned to what each of them wanted brought back from abroad: open-door policy or no, the availability of things was still limited back then. One of the women reminded her that she wanted a coffee-grinder-cum-blender, but when she made to reach for her purse (in the neckline of her gallabiya), Umm Hassan would have none of it. "For shame, Hajja Samia, for shame! I have plenty of money, and when I get back there'll be time enough to speak of things like that! You in particular I won't take a penny from! Have you forgotten the last time you went to Mecca? You bought me back six meters of duoline and flat-out refused to let me pay for them, and I had to fight you to make you take the money."

One of the women had changed her mind, and decided that instead of the white velvet gallabiya and the shawl, she would prefer a ring in twenty-one-karat yellow gold. Another wanted incense—"Not any old incense, mind you! Incense with the perfume of the Kaaba, or nothing at all."

There were other requests: a prayer rug, henna, veils and shawls, and toothpick weed. Finally, she called, "Come over here, Galal, and start making out a list of orders. For each order, write the name of the one who wants it in the opposite column, and set down how much she paid."

The women exchanged glances in code, realizing that Umm Hassan meant to collect the money for the purchases in advance, or at the very least, a down payment. Some of them held back or changed their mind, while the ones who had really meant it pulled out their purses and started counting out money. "Listen, Umm Hassan! I'm going to make you promise, and a promise must be kept," one woman insisted, patting a drop of sweat off her forehead with a tissue, "that you stand by the Holy Kaaba and recite the Fatiha seven times, praying that my wish come true." She looked about her for a place to throw the tissue away; finding none, she repeated, "My wish, the Fatiha for my wish."

I looked up at Umm Hassan. "Shall I write that down as well?"

"What?" she said, "write that down! You don't write that kind of thing down. One Fatiha for everybody and that's it, thank you very much!"

"No, listen here, sister," grumbled the woman. "I want my own Fatiha all to myself. And especially for my wish. Not just any old Fatiha!"

"All right, all right!" Umm Hassan said with a sweeping gesture of her hand. "Make a note of what she said."

I dutifully took up my pen, murmuring, "And a Fatiha seven times for Sitt Umm Labib for her wish to come true." I looked around at the women, wondering what request was going to come next.

After they had finally graced us with their absence and Umm Hassan succumbed to fatigue, I rushed to bed. The moment I laid my head on the pillow, I thought of Nadia. She came to me, skinny eyebrows arched over her eyes, her dress bright blue, a ring around her finger. Freckles dusted her cheeks, invisible to all but the closest inspection and scrutiny. She came to me looking as she had earlier that day at Amm Zaghloul's. Where had all this detail been, how had it come to my eyes? And here I had been thinking that I had only caught the most fleeting glance of her! I must have been looking at her with one eye calculating and pretending, the other working in secret! Is there, then, something with ironclad sight that works in us independent of ourselves? It sees for us what we do not see, and when it comes time for contemplation and remembrance, it shows us what we had not seen before. Or was I raving now, spewing crazed imaginings aimed at filling the empty pathways of my heart?

Her husband Fouad approached me. He came clothed in the garb of a good man, looking and speaking kindly. I saw him in my mind's eye, inviting me warmly and enthusiastically to come over for tea. He came closer, and paid me pleasing compliments; I, who had been looking at him with one eye, and with the other at his wife, not a few hours ago.

Exhausted with my thoughts, I finally dropped off. My late wife, Khadija, came to me in a dream. The dream came in two scenes: in the first, Khadija knocked at my door in the garb of a pilgrim to Mecca. The moment she saw me, she hid her eyes from me and looked away. It was only later that I realized that I was naked, and had opened the door to greet her in this embarrassing state.

In the second scene, she was in mourning, leading me to the cemetery where we had buried her, one day in the suburbs of Paris. "Who died?" I asked her.

She pointed to a gravestone that said: GALAL, THE NEIGHBORS' BOY.

I slept till late morning, and only woke up when I heard Umm Hassan dragging her bags to the door. Seeing the old trunk, I said, "For Heaven's sake! Are you still determined to take that monstrosity with you?"

Filled with beatific joy, she smiled. "Just put your trust in Him."

Finally, D-Day dawned. The omnibus belonging to the Hajj and Pilgrimages Travel Agency arrived, to take her and four other women on the first leg of their pilgrimage. Ululations rang out, and women came out at the windows and balconies to wave them goodbye. As for Umm Hassan's closest friends, they had gathered outside the door to the building, previously agreed upon as a meeting and departure point. There were about seventy women, maybe a few more; there were automobiles whose owners had insisted on accompanying the would-be pilgrims to the very gates of the airport, and children clinging to their mothers' clothing and holding lollipops, or, overcome with sleepiness, starting to cry. Some sat on the steps of the building, leaned their heads in their hands, and fell asleep. If it had not been shortly after dawn, we would have dealt the morning traffic a fatal blow, blocking our street and one or two more besides.

Umm Hassan looked down at us from the window of the bus, instructing Sitt Nazira and her husband Abul Saad Effendi to take good care of me till I returned. "Galal will be perfectly all right, we'll take care of him, you just take care of yourself." Abul Saad Effendi warned her to stay out of the noonday sun, and drink as much water as she could. She remembered her water flask, and bent out of sight looking for it. "What on earth are you looking for, Hajja?" he called. "It'll be under your feet, or stuck somewhere between the seats—the strap's around your neck, my good woman!"

Finding out he had been right after all, she straightened up, laughing at her own panic and befuddlement, looking at us. Meanwhile, my eyes widened at the stunning beauty who stood by Abul Saad Effendi. I couldn't help staring. He noticed, and said, "This is my daughter Hadeel, the agricultural engineer."

I shook her hand; she lowered her eyes shyly. Sitt Nazira was looking at us with about a quarter of one eye, while Abul Saad Effendi let out a fake cough. Umm Hassan was paying close attention from her window seat, watching, pleased with the turn of events. At the sight of her son Hassan coming out of the building in his house gallabiya, she shrilled, "Only now you come to say goodbye to your mother, you shameless, feckless boy! Where's your wife then, and the kids? You'd think I was going out to buy pickles or get some beans or falafel! I'm going up into the air, to cross the length and breadth of the sea!"

"Calm yourself, dear," another lady shushed her. "From this moment on until we return, the Prophet is with us!" She went on to quote the verse from the Qur'an that said that Hajj should be free of wickedness and wrangling and nothing should be spoken that might displease God.

The scene was cut short, finally, by the bus driver, who took off, bearing the lady pilgrims, followed by a raft of vehicles that honked their horns incessantly; I went upstairs to collect myself and get ready for my own journey.

14

WHEN I ALIGHTED IN MY village, I found no trace of the place
that lived in my memory. The old mill, from which puffs of
steam had once risen, was gone; so was the square before it,
once filled to bursting with women carrying baskets of grain,
and others bringing it in bales on the backs of donkeys. The
hustle and bustle, the spacious atmosphere, and the joy in
the bounty being milled for them by the old steam-powered
device: all gone. Gone, too, were the old women who used
to sit before the mill, selling their modest wares of sprouted
beans, lupine beans, and the groundnuts known as hab
al-aziz. The tea tent on its northern side, where the mill
workers drank tea and smoked, was gone too; often had I
seen them, when the sun was at its zenith, spread out a straw
mat for a quiet siesta in the shade of a tree or alongside the
wall, resting their bodies from the strain of arguing and haggling with the women who unceasingly talked and bargained
over the milling fee.

Gone, too, was the one-armed man who used to stand at
the scale, moving its weights right and left with bent arm and
raised shoulder; gone was his comrade of the spectacles stuck
together with glue, who wrote down what each bale weighed
with a quill pen on scraps of paper and handed them to whoever had his turn. Perhaps they had passed on to their eternal
reward, along with the owner of the wooden table with its
wares of cigarettes, packs of shisha tobacco and tea, and the

old man who used to sit beside him with his sheaf of bamboo rods, which he sold to those who needed to punish their beasts of burden or drive them to go faster.

Where the mill had stood, there were now four buildings, whose style screamed 'low-cost government housing.' Women from the town, who had made the village their home, sat on the balconies in their nightgowns: some dangled straw baskets to vendors who placed their vegetables and other wares inside, calling down and bargaining from above. Others gabbed with each other loudly, or stared at passers-by with a bold-ness that no peasant woman would dare display. Inside the building were a grocer, selling cheese, pastrami, and cooked beans in containers; a man who sold grilled chicken; and other small shops of all varieties. One had American-style clothing hanging in its window; another displayed Marlboros, gaudy keychains, and cigarette lighters behind the glass. Women's clothes had their place, too: blouses, perfumes, high-heeled shoes, and lingerie pulled tight over mannequins of disem-bodied breasts and thighs.

I looked around, seeking a seat upon which to rest. There was a café, chairs and tables scattered about outside, and a waiter in a smocked gallabiya and a white apron moving about among his customers, a mix of city men and peasants. Some distance away, next to a side road leading to the fields, was an enclosure ringed with braided reeds, empty but for a few men who were rising from their seats and preparing to leave.

I headed for this, my eye following a boy with a hitched-up gallabiya, splashing water on the ground to settle the dust, using his hand and a bucket of water in his other arm. An old man was inspecting the empty stone benches, lifting the reed mats off them and cleaning off the dust that clung to them. A stone's throw away from him, the blade of a plow split the earth, manned by a man in a traditional waistcoat and breeches, mopping the sweat off his brow with the shawl that hung from his shoulder.

The old man left off his task, watching me approach. He must have thought I preferred not to sit on stone, for he hurried to fetch me a seat made of palm branches, placing it in the shade of a thick willow a few paces away. As soon as I sat down, he said, staring at my attire, "Sorry, we don't serve anything but shisha and tea, sir."

I looked up at him without comment. He added, eyes flickering to the bus stop, "You'll find soft drinks, backgammon and salep, and everything a city gentleman might like, at the foreign-style café over that way." He inspected my dress again. "Is that all right, sir?"

"It's fine. Tea."

"That's a man after my own heart!" He called to the boy to prepare the order. Then he sat down by me, feeling the trunk of the tree we were using for shade, and whittling away some of its sharp protrusions with a pocketknife he took from a pouch sewn into his gallabiya.

His presence didn't bother me at all. I left him to what he was doing, and lost myself in memories of the all-too-brief days I had spent here in the village as a boy. My mother had been fearful of all around her, hand tightly clasping my own: I had been enchanted by the world of the countryside, with its winding roads, the one- or two-story buildings of raw brick, the abu qirdan—cattle egrets—that flocked in to circle the branches at sunset, seeking a foothold to rest and sleep, the cattle with their long, lazy lowing, and the little lambs panting after their mothers with incessant high-pitched bleating. I had come back one time, in my early youth. I had come alone, and only stayed for half a day: I had come to meet my uncle Ibrahim, and tell him of my intentions to leave for France, and join my mother's family there.

Uncle! How I feared meeting this uncle of mine.

"Have you just moved here, sir?"

The old man's question brought me out of my reverie. I turned to him, indicating that I had not moved there.

Meanwhile, the boy approached, carrying a small wooden table bearing a cup of tea, set it before me, and left at once; then he returned with a lit shisha, which he handed to the old man. He wiped the tip of the mouthpiece with his palm, and tested it with his mouth, emitting two puffs of smoke. Then he leaned back against the tree trunk, crossing his legs, the pipe in both hands, bubbling monotonously, the water gurgling in its glass jar whenever he took a puff, the lumps of coal flaring brightly as he did, some popping and bouncing in place, then subsiding into ash.

After a few moments, he turned smoke-teary eyes on me. "The town's full of strangers now, as you can see. They come from all over the suburbs of Giza: Imbaba, Warraq, Bulaq al-Dakrour; they built them apartment houses, and the rents are sky-high!" He waved his arm, shooing away a stray dog. "What's your name, then, sir?"

"Galal."

"Long life to all names, as they say, Mr. Galal. We never had any truck with rent before, you see. Everyone, rich or even poor, had his home—two rooms, a barn, and a court-yard for the poultry, and a gate that closes, protecting him and his things and his kin. That was all. If a stranger set foot in here, the whole village knew. They'd know who you are, what's your story, where you're going—not what goes on nowadays." He took a long puff of his pipe, followed by a fit of coughing. He went on, voice a bit choked with coughs at first, to make fun of the strangers who had come here seeking refuge from the high prices and limited housing in the big city: he mimicked their smooth tones when speaking, spoke disapprovingly of their women who had no shame, and their men who were like great oafs, walking out in the public street with their see-through gallabiyas, that showed their legs and their breeches—"Breeches no bigger than the palm of your hand, sir. And no shame, no shame at all! Horsing around, off-color jokes, and talking bold as brass about things no well-mannered man should speak of. And our ill-bred brats are happy to do as they do."

I let him finish, then asked him, "What became of the old mill?"

He sighed, waving a disparaging hand. "They pulled it down, didn't they, son! And the poor farmers like us, who don't have much, we've got to buy flour from the government now. But the rich folk, and even the so-so farmers, they don't bake at home any more. Just look at them! They're all transformed into fancy folk and they buy ready-made bread, just like the newcomers." Another sigh. "Where have you gone, Hajj Kassab? Oh, for the good old days!"

Probably anticipating that I would ask the identity of this person, he added before I could ask, "Hajj Kassab owned the mill. He was something! In the morning, he'd come cantering by on his mule, Umm Shnaf by name." He fell silent, looking at me. Seeming to glimpse some surprise in my expression at the idea of a mule with a name, especially a name such as that, he added, "Yes, Umm Shnaf! That was her name. And Hajj Kassab would get off her, from his baize saddle, and what a gallabiya! And he'd have his umbrella under his arm, and his turban double-height, and it was all, 'Out of the way, boy! Out of the way, girl!' And they'd rush to set out his bamboo chair, and him, with eyes in the back of his head! He'd point with his bamboo stick to any woman who wasn't waiting her turn, or any man standing there staring at the women. He'd call out to a random woman coming out, and take a feel of the flour on her head. If it wasn't smooth enough and good enough quality, he'd go into the mill and yell the place down at the men working there."

Another long pull on his shisha, and he resumed his tale, smoke pouring out of his mouth as he spoke. "Bounty, coming and going! If a woman didn't have the money for the mill fee, he would grind her grain for free. If a man had money troubles, he always put his hand in his pocket and gave him money. Everyone went home satisfied a hundred percent."

I listened, his words kindling a memory. I could feel something inside me struggling, struggling to remember—until finally, from the deepest recesses of my mind, I extricated the remnants of a man who looked like the description, a man I had seen outside the mill when I was young. Short and fat, with a mustache punctuated with white hairs, waving a stick of bamboo, gallabiya sleeve flapping each time he did so. His plump arm was covered with yellow hair, and on his hand was a ruby ring. Was this description slumbering within me, or was my imagination playing tricks on me, adding a touch here and there to the storehouse of memory? Was this the Hajj Kassab of the old man's story, or was it the image of someone else? A hybrid, partly from my own imagination and partly from this old man's tale?

I found welcome company in the man's conversation, no less so when he paused in his tales, and a companionable silence fell. We would look at each other without speaking, or each look at what was going on outside: farmers cutting stalks with sickles, two donkeys kicking at each other, some distance away, even the sunbeams slanting through the willows and dappling all around with intricate patterns, little spots of light and shadow shrinking and expanding on the fabric of my pants with every movement of the leaves and branches.

It occurred to me to ask the old man if he knew my uncle. He gave me a look out of the corner of his eye, taking the top off his water pipe and knocking the dead coals out into the dirt. "Sheikh Ibrahim? Know him, he asks! Do I know him!" He paused, pushing his headgear back to scratch the front of his head: I could see an ant, disturbed by his fingers, slipping through and making good its escape. He turned back to me. "No offense, Galal, but are you coming to see Sheikh Ibrahim himself, or one of his children?"

"Sheikh Ibrahim himself."

"For what reason? Is there business between you?"

I refused to satisfy his curiosity.

"Right," he said, disappointed.

And he rose too, telling me the way to my uncle's house.

15

My uncle's house overpowered the houses alongside it. It was four stories high, with a stone wall around it topped with bars with heads like spears, to say nothing of the iron gate. It looked like some great skewer, sticking out in the middle of the peaceable, amiable houses beside it, all of which barely rose out of the ground. Their mud-brick structure harked back to the good old days, their windows blessedly free from decoration or ornament, from bars and padlocks. There were women, of course, lurking behind them, but they were not so conspicuous and forward as the women from beyond the village: these were experts at stealthy observation. The women born and bred in the village, by dint of experience, could scrutinize you from head to toe from behind their windows without letting you see so much as a finger or a turn of the head. The doors were ajar, with birds and children coming and going across their thresholds, guarded by dogs whose teeth were blunted by a long tradition of friendliness and welcome.

My uncle's house had been built on the ruins of the old house—the sprawling home that had opened its arms to me as a child, and whose features were still etched into my heart even now. The gate with the drawing on the right-hand side of a five-fingered palm, to ward off the evil eye, and a crescent, for blessings. The ancient dog lying alongside the door, who cared for nobody and listened to nobody but my grandfather, Abd al-Hamid. The garden path, where my old grandfather used to like to sit on a wooden bench, inspecting everyone who came in or went out. At the end of the house there used to be a silo, an elderly farmhand leaning at its door, a fly buzzing forever around his face. He shooed it away mechanically, eyes closed. From time to time, he would yawn loudly and go back to sleep.

Here was where I had slipped past my mother and gone out into the courtyard, with a healthy respect for the turkeys strutting proudly about, each of them with a long chin and a beak like a knife. I avoided them. I did not want them to gobble in my face: one had done that once and then attacked me; it was a miracle they managed to save me from it. Here were the brick ovens that would be filled with pots, their covers rattling with the pressure of the steam within: before them, my grand-mother and her daughters would be seated on bricks. I would approach, and my grandmother would see me and beckon me closer. She would jump up, taking the lid off one of the pots. The hot steam would surge up into her face; she would tilt her head and fan it away. Then she'd pull out a piece of meat for me, or perhaps a piece of goose liver. She would blow on it until it cooled, then placed it in my palm, urging me to eat it at once before my grandfather's dog snatched it out of my hand. The dog would be watching, readying himself to come near. Meanwhile, my aunts, including the wife of my uncle Ibrahim, would look at me oddly, as though I were no son of theirs, but a strange creature who had dropped out of the sky.

Gone was my grandfather's house. Gone, like my grand-father himself, like the old mill. My uncle had cursed us with this huge frame of steel and concrete: I had never in my life imagined having any connection with such a structure.

I must have spent a bit longer than I should outside my uncle's house, for I seemed to have piqued the curiosity of some boys playing. One of them, little gallabiya hitched up to his upper thighs, a long stick-horse between his legs, came up to me. "Is this Amm Ibrahim's house?" I asked him. He nodded and galloped off, making a sound with his lips like a car horn, running here and there, kicking up dust with his bare legs.

A great brute of a man with a thick mustache came out to me. I told him who I was. Still looking me up and down, he said, "You're my cousin?"

I said, "Yes."

He stood there, clearly still taken by surprise. "So you'll be Leila's brother, then. The one who's been abroad for years."

In a completely neutral tone, he invited me in. I followed him through the gate, up a broad set of steps; on the right was a small raised platform, below which were two cane chairs. On the left, where there was more space, were rows of sacks, stacked high. A wide room faced the stairs, where he bade me have a seat, and left.

The walls were gaudily painted; the second hand of the clock that hung facing me was broken. The clock itself indicated a completely different hour from the actual time. The room was furnished in a mélange of my late grandfather's old couches and gilded couches still new, and on the walls were two photographs of my late grandfather Abd al-Hamid and Uncle Ibrahim, side by side. Both wore turbans and abayas tightly closed about the neck, concealing whatever they might have been wearing underneath. My grandfather's face was frowning, his pupils large, perhaps focusing on the camera. My uncle had a smile on his lips, his eyes twinkled with mischief. In a far corner was a fridge, its handle black with dirt. On top of it stood a bottle of medicine and a deep dish. When I bent to retie my shoelace, I caught sight of an orange underneath the couch, a single sock keeping it company.

My cousin arrived with a tray, a glass of some yellow drink on it. It tasted sharp; I choked, but forced myself to drink it down at one go, like medicine. My cousin, sitting opposite, stared at me without comment. He gave a small cough that sounded false, then leaned back, crossing one leg over the other. My eye alighted upon his foot, sticking out from the bottom of his gallabiya: the toes were all thickset, and his feet were flat, without normal arches. He had an infection in his big toe. I looked away at once and raised my gaze to his face, whereupon he, too, took to staring at the mug of this accursed visitation that had descended upon him out of the blue. We spent no little time staring at one another. Finally, I asked him, "What happened to the old house?"

"You mean my grandfather Abd al-Hamid's house? It was pulled down years ago!" He added, more enthusiastically, "It was a miserable old house, rotten at the core. Look how the house is now—like a palace! A room to receive guests, a floor for my father, and a floor for me, and two floors for my brothers, Farid and al-Shahhat."

I suddenly wanted to pee. However, I held it in and kept on listening to this big lummox, letting him gesticulate left and right, until a fly came buzzing toward me. I shooed it away, and it escaped in his direction, settling on his shoulder. I watched it follow the weave of his gallabiya, then circling again, buzzing around him in flight, then coming to rest safely on the crown of his head. "What about the silo?"

"The silo! It was pulled down as well, to be part of the new house." He smiled. "The couch you're sitting on now, no offense, is where the donkeys used to sleep."

I said nothing. Suddenly, I was overtaken by a violent fit of sneezing that I couldn't control: it burst forth in powerful explosions from my mouth, producing a copious spray, some of which landed on my cousin's gallabiya. He grimaced at me and started to brush it off in disgust. When he was done, he added pointedly, "And the window you're leaning your arm against was where the great fat ox used to lean. Now we've none of that in the house, no silos or anything like that. The cattle spend the night out in pasture and there's a man to guard them."

I looked my cousin over for the twentieth time, then looked up at my uncle's photo. "Your uncle's not too well," he said. I tut-tutted sympathetically. "He's really ill; we've taken him to doctor after doctor, but no change." He had probably realized it was past time I was meeting my uncle, so he hastened to say, "I did go in to see him and tell him you were here, but poor man, he was sound asleep."

The door opened to admit a woman in clothes that told nothing of whether she was from the country or the city. This must be my sister, I said to myself, as she called out in delight and ran toward me with open arms. "Welcome, welcome! Greetings, my dear! Everyone else has their troubles, but today is my day to celebrate!"

I was struck dumb, unable to find a single word. My feelings would not allow for a reaction, nor for any impression, nor did any way out of my predicament present itself. I stood there, blank, frozen, stiff in her arms, face expressionless. I was completely unprepared for this outpouring of affection, and I was unsettled. I didn't know her as a brother knew his sister, had only ever seen her once or twice. Her image had never come to my mind—how could it, indeed, when I knew nothing of her face nor form, nor did I recognize her voice? All I knew was that I had a sister on my father's side, who inhabited a world other than my own. A sister who had her own life as I had mine, no more and no less. I had thought that what lay between us was as silent and arid as my relationship with this cousin who sat before me: distance and separation had caused me to forget that we shared the same father, the same blood, the same bereavement.

But it seemed that some part of me was moved, bringing me back to myself, and I flung myself into her arms, as she had done moments ago, kissing her cheeks and her hands and the parting of her hair that showed through her black chiffon veil. We gave ourselves over to each other completely, and our embrace was like the healing of a wound: flesh and blood knitting together. She swore a thousand oaths that she must take me to her house immediately. She swore as men do, my cousin bleating, "Just rest and catch your breath, won't you, Umm Galal!"

Before I had fully absorbed the shock, she smiled, "I named my son after you. There's no name dearer. My husband has my father's name, and my son has my brother's."

I exited in her wake, without a word from my cousin asking me to stay.

16

THE BED IN MY SISTER Leila's house was comfortable; the gallabiya lent me by her husband, Mahmoud, was wide-sleeved,
openings everywhere. His family came from a place near the
governorate of Kafr al-Sheikh, but they had made our village their home for decades. They were humble, simple folk,
with no money to speak of: his father owned a grocery store,
and his uncle a store for veils, kohl, snuff, and other ladies'
things. The third brother had bought a small Toyota truck
and worked day and night making deliveries so as to make
the payments on it. They had no knowledge of farming, nor
any powerful friends or family, except for some unimport-
ant relations by marriage. For this reason, the marriage of
Mahmoud to Leila, daughter of a prestigious clan, had been
considered odd, and, as I found out, the talk of the town for
a number of years.

Leila and Mahmoud had gone to prep school together.
Mahmoud's courtesy and reticent manner had, it seemed,
been the key to Leila's heart, which had beat for him from
afar. He had gone on to secondary school, then the Faculty
of Commerce; she had gone on to stay at home. They had
parted, but their hearts still communed. "After he graduated
college, and got his appointment at the Agricultural Co-op,"
Leila told me, "he came with his father to ask for my hand."
She told me she had seen him that day, standing at her window, as they knocked on the metal gates: his father in a freshly

ironed gallabiya and new footwear, Mahmoud in a white shirt and bell-bottoms, as the fashion was in those days.

"You still remember the color of his shirt and the style of his pants?" I asked.

She smiled, looking down shyly, then resumed her story. Our uncle hadn't offered them so much as a glass of water, nor turned them away tactfully or gently. He had been savage, he'd attacked Mahmoud: "Who are you? Whose son are you, that you want to marry into my family, you overreaching nobody! Didn't anyone teach you any manners?" Pointing a finger almost into Mahmoud's nose, he kept on yelling, "You, you lowlife, you want to lie in the same bed as a girl of a good family? Good God! Go ahead and marry whatever scum you like, but not our daughters! Try the bean vendor, or the guy who sells rope and baskets—that's where you'll find a bride who suits you!"

When his father tried to ward off the attack on his son, my uncle glared him into silence, then turned and gave him a few poisonous words in his turn, the man bending over to put his slippers on so as to rise, putting them on the wrong feet in his haste. Apparently, though, my uncle, not feeling he'd humiliated them enough, followed them to the gate, yelling loud enough to be heard on the horizon. "Have you no shame, Abd al-Raouf? Have you no idea of what's not done, you lowlife? You want the daughter of a high-born family to be a shop girl in your store, selling soap and sugar and oil?" They ran, the father looking behind him for fear my uncle might throw a slipper at him, and Mahmoud in disbelief that the world still held men like this brute.

My uncle's yelling filled the house afterward; Leila's mother, God rest her soul, hid her from his sight while he searched from room to room, a two-tailed tawse in his hand, a few strokes of which were sufficient to reduce a grown man to a compliant, blubbering wreck who agreed with everything you said.

*

It didn't end there. A few months later, one of my uncle's sons caught the house's old servant, Umm al-Kooz, with a letter for Leila in her bra. This old crone, eighty or older, was Cupid's little helper, bringing her perfumed notes and flying like a dove to Mahmoud, while the household knew nothing. Naturally, everyone blazed with rage, especially the cousins, who considered it an insult that could only be avenged by cutting Mahmoud's throat. Their father urged them to control themselves, though, so as not to mar the girl's reputation in the village; he started working in secret. First, he paid a number of his men to pick an apparently unrelated fight with Mahmoud, and they took him by the back of the neck and tried to drown him by dunking his head in the cattle trough. But for the crowd of bystanders who intervened, Mahmoud would have been dead by now, or maimed at the very least.

Three years went by. Everyone thought the romance was dead and buried. That was, until Leila had her maternal uncles come and talk to her uncle Ibrahim about the hitherto unmentioned matter of Leila's right to a share of her dead father's and grandfather's estate. Leila's mother, too, was from an important family, though not as strong and powerful as Uncle Ibrahim's. Their family elder was a sagacious man: tactfully, he spoke to the uncle, and dangled the carrot of not insisting on her full share, if Ibrahim in his turn made the concession of agreeing to Leila's marriage to Mahmoud. The uncle drooled at the proposition, and the deal was struck. He got Leila's land for pennies, in return for not standing in the way of Leila's marriage to "that Mahmoud."

Leila's heart held nothing but hatred and resentment of Uncle Ibrahim. True, they met on special occasions, and said things like, "Hello, Leila," and "Hello, Uncle Ibrahim." Sometimes he might even grind out, "And how's that boy, Mahmoud?" And she, sucking at her lips in disapproval, would respond, "He's fine. He sends his greetings." But there was no love lost between them, and my sister had no recourse but to pray to God for his ruin.

"And was all your land lost?" I asked my sister.

"It would have been lost anyway," she said. "Does anything come back up out of the lion's mouth?" She sighed, "He didn't even give me the rent. When I asked him for it, he played deaf, and when I insisted, he always said he had it for me in safekeeping."

Dinner that first day was mouth-watering. It reminded me of the meals my late grandmother used to prepare for us when my mother and I had come to the village for the first time. In those days, Umm al-Kooz, who was charged with our care, used to roll the low tabliya into the middle of the room we were staying in so we could sit around it and eat; then she would make her exit, only to return with the tray on her head, laden with food and drink, while I tried to guess what surprise they had prepared for us today. Boiled meat? Two pairs of pigeons? Or had they finally tired of us, and thought it enough to give us a couple of loaves of bread and some moldy cheese?

Ever more eager, I would watch through the keyhole. If the tray was late, I would slip past my mother and step a few paces outside the door to reconnoiter after Umm al-Kooz. Next thing I knew, I would feel my mother's hand, dragging me back into our room by my shirt collar, and poking me here and there. If she felt me trying to squirm away in order to catch a glimpse of the tray, she would pinch my ear or punch me in the back.

In hindsight, I believe my mother had treated me unfairly: my transgression was no more than child's play, a release of pent-up energy. She and I were always in that room like prisoners back then; we never left the room, and no one spoke to us beyond a few measured words. My cousins, the sons of my father's brothers and sisters, growled at me whenever I tried to play with them.

So many years ago!

Here I was, twenty years later, eating country food once more. A table with chairs, true, not the low table of yesteryear; facing me hung a still life of a basket of fruit with an empty plate next to it bearing a crossed knife and fork.

My empty plate had a knife and fork on it, set out just as in the painting, in addition to a spoon, with a white napkin next to them. My sister's husband, sitting opposite me, got none of this; all he got was a plate with a chipped border. My sister, in her house gallabiya, pushed all the dishes closest to me, while her son Galal crawled in her wake, but whenever I bent to him, he would crawl away, overcome with shyness.

There was still good in the world. I was filled with contentment, my heart gladdened by this unexpected outpouring of tenderness from my sister, and the dozens of kindly pats on the shoulder from her loving hand. And as for the dishes she placed before me now! Duck fricassee was nothing to it, or turkey with peach stuffing, or duck à l'orange, or any of the delicacies I had sampled in Paris. The rice with nuts she had prepared for supper tasted better to me than candied chestnuts, or Black Forest cake, or Gâteau Maréchal. "And what's this, Leila?"

"That's oxtail."

"And this?"

"That's testicles, with some kidneys mixed in."

"If only we'd eaten at the tabliya, though!"

"That's old hat," she smiled, "those days are over!"

Days passed with Leila taking care of me. There was nothing she wouldn't do to make me happy or make me stay. However, whenever I mentioned someone I had known as a boy, her responses were clipped and curt. Once I asked her what had become of old Imam, my late grandfather's valet. "Imam! You don't still remember him, do you? He's an old wreck now, his back's all bent and he never goes out."

I sat up, wanting to hear more, and asked after my uncles, aunts, and cousins. It had been a week since we had seen hide or hair of them, and not even a messenger from them to ask where I'd disappeared to. I was struck by the leisurely rhythm of life in the country: the sense of 'why not put off till a couple of days later what you can do today,' and what we were planning to do tomorrow would do perfectly well delayed a week or even two. Umm Hassan was on my mind: I thought of her ululating with joy the day of my return, sitting with me on the balcony, embracing me with her eyes, and only saying what she thought was good for me, as though I really were the son she had brought forth into this world from her womb. Who, I wondered, was closer to my heart: she, or my mother who had given me life? And which of them held me closer to her heart?

I called Abul Saad Effendi, who asked if I had made any progress. I told him, disappointed, that I hadn't even seen my uncle yet. "Goodness!" he said, "Five days, and you still haven't met him? Why, you might as well be requesting an audience from King Cheops, or Khedive Ismail." He urged me to be patient, however, and pay attention to every word that was said, for "Country folk like your uncle aren't as simple as they seem! They're experts at the art of talking rings around you, and if they mean to say something, they'll twist it all around in conversation, and make you swallow the sword of their cunning!"

After the conversation with Abul Saad, I recalculated. So far, I had not taken any clear stance with regard to the land that my uncle had in his possession. I had not found out what was better for me: to demand it from him, or offer to be bought out? And if he did hand it over to me, what was I to do with it? And if I offered to be bought out, how could I be sure he would not pay me a mere fraction of the price, as he had done with my sister?

17

I SAT WITH MY BROTHER-IN-LAW drinking mint tea. Leila was telling me about this uncle of ours. Our grandfather, our father's father, that is, had left him thirty feddans, a house, and a vacant lot, and told him with his dying breath to treat his sister, nephews, and nieces fairly. "And as soon as your grandfather died and we were just starting to breathe again after the funeral, he up and sold the vacant lot, and used the money to build a new home on the site of your grandpa's old house, that mansion you saw." She watched the effect of her words in my face. "He did what he absolutely had to in terms of parceling out the land among his brothers: gave each a third to farm and harvest. Then he sat down cross-legged on his bed putting on the airs of a rich man, and sure enough he soon had people coming to him from far and wide: consulting him, asking him for favors, and it was all 'Sheikh Ibrahim, come and perform a reconciliation between two friends who have had a fight,' or 'Sheikh Ibrahim, come and grace our wedding with your presence today.'"

She rubbed her knee, scratching it lightly over her gallabiya. "Year after year, he and his sons have thought that all the land belongs to them, and that if there's a decision to be made, it'll be made by them. And they're the only children my grandfather Abd al-Hamid had!" She waved a hand, looking at me. "Farid's the best of the bunch, I suppose. He's had schooling, and everyone says he's a decent sort. He doesn't know a thing about farming; he doesn't even know where his land is! Sultan, his elder brother, takes care of everything for him, and makes sure his land is planted."

"Sultan?"

"Yes, that's his name. That big lummox you met when you first arrived."

I noticed her foot moving about in search of its slipper, indicating that she was preparing to rise. I held her back. "Go on!"

"On about what? That's all there is to it."

"But what about my share? And my aunts'?" I asked, open-mouthed.

"Your aunt Nefisa died young, poor thing, still a virgin, even—she never saw land nor even a husband. That leaves only two: Hanem and Umm al-Kheir. He gave each of them a bit of money and that was that."

My throat felt dry; I reached for a glass of water. She went on, "Your aunt Umm al-Kheir's a sick woman, with no energy for fighting. She took the money and didn't make any fuss. Hanem kept butting heads with him for close on two years, but it still wasn't any use. She finally gave up, and said 'Get me out of this mess'—and wouldn't you know it, she got the exact same pittance as her sister. When she asked for more, he said, 'Am I a man with two faces? What your elder sister got is exactly the same as what you'll get.' She said, 'Have some compassion, brother. Heaven knows, that's not the price of the land!'

"You know what he said? He said, 'Did you show any compassion to me, for me to show any to you? You showed me up in front of everyone, and caused a scandal and set every-one's tongues wagging!' And," my sister said softly, "as for my land, you know all about that."

She refilled our glasses from the teapot and drew breath. "Women have nothing for it. We're in the hands of Fate. If her brother or uncle is a God-fearing man, then the gates of heaven will open and shower blessings on her. If he's anything else, well. . . . You see the result." Her voice rose. "Even his daughters, Aida, Samia, and Zinnat, didn't escape his injustice. He said to them, 'When I'm dead, each of you will get twenty thousand pounds from her brother, and is free to come and go in this house as she pleases. Each Ramadan, you'll receive a visit from a donkey with a basket on its back, loaded with good things. On the Bairam feast, you'll get a live sheep and the customary tips.' And that ear-pinched good-for-nothing thinks that he's done his duty by them! And the three of them, the fools, bend over his hand and kiss it, and say to him, 'All we want is your long life, Father, and to have you in the world hale and hearty! And when you're gone, may it never come to pass, our brothers will take care of house and land, too!' Silly idiots."

"I once heard my father say," said my brother-in-law, "that when they were living in a village on the outskirts of Rosetta—this was a long time ago—it was the same old story. A woman or an orphan child had no chance of getting what was rightfully theirs, unless there was some miracle or intervention by some prophet or saint!" He turned his eyes upon me, and then on Leila. "But Leila, there's still good in the world, and honest people in it. There's Hajj Hassanein Abu Auf, now there's a man who's never let a penny into his house or into his family's mouths that was stolen from anyone. And Hajj Abd al-Ghaffar al-Minshawi, he's related to you—you know him. Didn't he say, 'Bear witness, everyone! Each of my sisters will get her rightful due, and her share in the house, too, even before her share of the land? And over and above, their mother's gold jewelry and everything that was hers personally.' That's what he said."

"I'll tell you what. That one and the other one you mentioned, I count as saints, holy saints of the Almighty," she retorted, looking from me to him. "Point out to me some more people who did as they've done. That's the way of our village.

Girls never get what God ordained for them, or else get it with a bit missing." A tear escaped her eye. "Not one bit, either. More like two or three." Her face darkened suddenly. "And you're to stay out of it, Mahmoud! Don't you dare poke your nose into my and my brother's business!"

He looked at me; I looked at Leila. She didn't seem to mind having embarrassed him. He busied himself with adjusting the shawl that lay across his chest, pushing it out of place, then adjusting it into its previous position. After a few moments, he left. "Call him back and apologize," I urged Leila, but she gestured her refusal.

"He'll be back in a bit. I've my own way of dealing with him."

I made no comment. She pressed my knee. "What are you planning to do, then, Galal?"

"Planning? I'm planning to take what's coming to me, down to the last penny!"

"Perfect!" Her eyes shone. "Bless you, brother! Now you're talking!" Her breath came faster. "Right, listen. We're three shares. He had a share; your late father had a share; and your two aunts, that was one share, since each sister was entitled to half a share. Each share was ten feddans. My share was swallowed up by him, may he never prosper. Find out how much you're supposed to have left."

She kept on encouraging me. She warned me to be wary when I went to meet my uncle, and be careful of his convoluted words. "He'll say things just to see your reaction," she said. "He's cunning. He'll throw something out, just to see your reaction. He says it so you'll swallow it, then he will build on it after some time has passed. He'll lead you up the garden path, twisting and turning, until you're exhausted. Then he'll pat you on the shoulder and bring you out to where *he* wants you to go."

Her tones were sharp and loud: occasionally, overcome with enthusiasm, she would start yelling. It started to seem to me less as though she were giving me advice, and more as though she had forcibly taken possession of my ears, commanding me what to say and do, as I sat listening. It floated through my mind that her enthusiasm might not be entirely disinterested and altruistic; she clearly wanted to get back at this uncle of hers, who had cheated her out of her inheritance long ago. She seemed to burn with enthusiasm for my sake, yet the flame seemed less for me than for herself. Part of Leila, maybe the obvious part, worked for me at this moment; the still, buried part worked for herself and sought to satisfy her own resentment against this uncle of hers. Each handful of earth taken from his hands to return to mine was a drop of water to cool the flames of her own grudge. And who could blame her? The entire family was against her except for one, and I was that one.

Her husband Mahmoud, it appeared to me, carried no weight and was little more than a yes-man, offering her the protection and comfort of a husband without the command. She clearly wore the pants in the family, and had been the groom, rather than the bride: she had desired him, taken his hand in marriage, and led him by the hand, as men do with women, to her home. The poor man could do naught but submit; it seemed to be his specialty, for he was a doormat.

Her relatives on her father's side, as I understood, seemed to have supported the uncle's monkey business: most of them, it appeared, were afraid that if any part of the Minshawi family land fell into the hands of Leila's no-account husband, it might set a precedent for the rest of the women of the house. As for her mother's side, they feared the powerful uncle; they might have told each other: "Since the land, which is after all the point, will never come into our possession, but will go to a stranger anyway, why get into a quarrel with this loose cannon of an uncle? Meanwhile, the exchange that's taken place has the blessing of both parties. He got the land, and she got Abd al-Raouf's son."

Leila's only recourse now was me, so she did her utmost to puff me up: meanwhile, I asked myself whether I would do her proud, or fail as she had, and return with my tail between my legs.

Suddenly, Umm al-Kooz knocked at the door, accompanied by Sitt Bahana, Mahmoud's mother. This Umm al-Kooz was a veritable miracle: pushing ninety, she had wrinkles on her face crafted so finely that they would be the death of any artist who tried to copy them, for no brush could hope to emulate them. You could only find her eyes with great effort and dedicated scrutiny; that their owner could see you was a wonder in and of itself. As for the hand that reached out to shake yours, it belonged to a skeleton, dead for decades. The odd thing was that she stood straight and erect, moving and whirling like a woman just turning sixty. The old crone recognized me as soon as Leila told her I was Galal, her half-brother, and when I pressed a banknote into her hand, she called out blessings upon me in a quavering voice, from a mouth with only three teeth left in it.

I reached out to shake Sitt Bahana's hand. You would never think she was Leila's kin; she was something else entirely. Her gallabiya was made from cheap velveteen; the black veil on her head was wrapped in the style of lower-class women that made it look like a turban. The lobes of her ears were almost entirely cleft in two, tin earrings dangling from them. Her gallabiya was short, a little above the ankle; around one of her ankles was a silver anklet, thick and crude. The skin of her heels was red and rough around the edges, cracked from rubbing. She wore no expensive malass, the fabric rich country women wear over their clothing like a cloak; no gold bracelet encircled her wrist; there was no jeweled ring on her finger such as those worn by women of noble houses who did no work, nor did she even wear perfume, smelling instead of bread dough. But her face was kindly and gentle, and in her voice was a motherly tenderness. She and I began to talk, and were soon on friendly terms. I was especially pleasant to her so as to erase the sting of Leila's words a little earlier: "Welcome, Aunt, have a seat. This is your home, after all . . . I suppose."

18

I WAS FINALLY GRANTED AN audience with my uncle.

I entered a room like a meeting hall, with a bed in the middle big enough for three people to lie very comfortably. Its brass posts appeared to have been recently polished: they were brilliant yellow, flashing brightly where the daylight caught them. Above them was a canopy of light fabric, then snow-white mosquito netting tied back in an elaborate knot fastened to the corner of one of the bedposts. It was positioned directly over my head where I sat, and I felt it might fall into my lap every time a breeze moved it, coming in from the open window.

I recognized the bed at once. It was my grandfather Abd al-Hamid's four-poster, the one I had so often contemplated in awe as a little boy. I still remember the time I had climbed onto it to play and roll about, as though on a lawn and not on a bed.

The four-poster had figured prominently in my mind when I crept into my grandfather's bedroom at siesta time, finding him stretched out on the bed. The pair of them seemed to me in those days to have been made for one another: the bed larger than any bed ever made, and my grandfather larger than any man ever made. Now my uncle was lying in it: his head was covered with a white cap, his face skinny and dull, his neck emaciated, lost in the neck opening of the gallabiya. The rest of him was covered up, except for his toes, which poked out occasionally from the end of the quilt. He tried to rise, but I rushed to stop him, ill as he was. He looked intently at me, extending a hand to me in a position that indicated I should kiss it. Not wishing to subject him to the embarrassment of a refusal, I did so, then bent to his head and kissed his forehead, and tasted the salt of dried sweat.

He leaned back against the bedstead, and bent his knees beneath the quilt. A girl arrived, with a tray of thick, dark grapes. My cousin Sultan, who had ushered me in, invited me to have some. "It's a new variety. A gift from the Basha, the owner of the farm next to ours."

I obliged. My uncle reached for a grape with two fingers, and placed it in his mouth. He didn't like it, though, and spat it out into his hand. He looked up at my cousin. "Isn't this the stuff planted by those Jews? The ones the Basha brought in from Israel?"

"Yes, it is, and it sells for a ton of money, by the kilo, in Cairo, to say nothing of the exports." He added admiringly, "Those smart sons of a so-and-so speak Arabic as well as we do! One of them, called Ezra, sometimes puts on a cap and acts just like the peasants."

"Oh, really!" The uncle scowled at him. "So what?" My cousin fell silent, but my uncle kept going. "That great idiot the Basha's a fool, and his sons are too. These grapes are sour enough to give you a sore throat! What are these compared to Fayoum grapes? Or the ones we call the Goat's Tit?" He gestured dismissively. "Grapes aren't even in season. They've mixed everything up, may they always be mixed up, and confused winter with summer!"

"But I'll be straight with you, Dad," said my cousin, "they're good at what they do. And the Basha's made good money by bringing them in."

"Good?" My uncle looked daggers at him. "What's this good at what they do, you ox? Aren't those the same ones who killed your uncle in '56?"

We looked into each other's eyes. He sat up straighter. "You're welcome, my boy, I'm sure."

He started to talk; I contented myself with nods and gestures. He spoke of the passage of time, of his declining heath, and reminisced about my grandmother and grandfather Abd al-Hamid, and about the world that had gone topsy-turvy. Here were the lowest class of peasants, who owned no land to speak of—a few qirats or a single feddan at most (folk who had once hastened to dismount when they saw him coming and clear the road for him!)—here were their sons becoming judges, doctors, and architects, thinking themselves equals to the great houses, thinking nothing of standing against them in elections or asking for their daughters' hands in marriage!

His talk led him to Leila; his face darkened. "I raised her like my own daughter—and then what? She goes against me, marries this no-account peon, less than nothing in the marriage market."

He fell silent, slipping a hand underneath the quilt. I could see it moving, and a moment later, heard the sound of his fingernails scratching what appeared to be the calf of his leg. He noticed me watching, and stopped, looking closely at me; I tried to appear absorbed in something else, bending my head and fiddling with the top button of my shirt, undoing and redoing it. He pulled his hand back out, resting it on his chest, and launched into a monologue about farming: tomatoes, peas, beans, and the onion crop that had all been devoured by worms, losing them their entire profit for that year.

His voice sounded weak and feeble to my ears: it was monotonous, unemotional, without highs or lows. It seemed to run on a straight track, never stumbling, stopping, or encountering any bumps in the road. His body might be frail, but he kept a level head: he moved from one subject to the next with no confusion or hesitation. President Nasser, President Sadat, and the newly formed Engineering and Plowshare Company that had raised the price of tractors.

With all this gabble, he never once moved to the subject of my land that lay in his possession, asked after my mother, or showed any desire to know what I had been up to in all my years abroad. He talked until he was tired out, and I sensed that he was on the verge of falling into an exhausted sleep.

Suddenly, he stopped, eyes going wide, a bead of sweat falling from his cap and creeping down his forehead, leaving a visible trail. Then he stretched out his legs and pulled the quilt tight over himself up to his chin, so that only his face could be seen; his sleepy eyes entreated me to leave. I rose and excused myself: he watched me until I was through the door.

19

LEILA WAS ASTONISHED TO SEE me return empty-handed, with no news. "Ill? What sick man has the energy to talk nonstop for two hours?" And, bitterly: "He's faking it, Galal."

A day went by, then another, and the days became a week, and no word from the uncle's house. I went to him, egged on by Leila to do something final, as they say.

In point of fact, I went many times. Every time I knocked at the door, the house would fall silent as the grave. One would think it was abandoned. I would stand there helplessly, looking around me: I would look up to see shadows, fleeting, behind windows, as though a thousand eyes were staring at me from above, taking in every detail. Should I stay too long at the door, convincing them of my insistence upon entry, they sent out a little cross-eyed boy to me, in sandals and a smocked gallabiya, who, I must admit, was a real pro at leading you up the garden path. He would meet me with a scowl and ask what I wanted, taking in my appearance with his good eye; I could never tell whether the other was doing the same or looking at something in the distance. I could never get a straight answer from him: when he let me into the waiting room, he told me by turns that the uncle was asleep and that only the women were in the house; that he was seeing the doctor; or some other excuse that would never have occurred to me.

I would bite my tongue, saying only that I wanted him for something important.

"I told you, sir, the doctor's in there with him. You want to go in and see him undressed and being examined?"

"Shall I come back in an hour?"

"He'll have gone to sleep."

"Shall I stay then?"

"It's up to you, but it'll be ages before the doctor comes out."

I cursed him all the way back to his great-grandparents in my head, and waited. He waited on the couch, picking at his decayed rear molar with a straw. When I had had enough of waiting, and told him to do something, anything, he suggested I go back to where I had come from before it got dark.

The final time, I happened to find Cousin Sultan standing at the door, the servants preparing a mount for him. I hurried to him, sticking out my hand in greeting. He jumped, then tried to hide his displeasure. When I asked him where my uncle was, he said, "He's shaving. The barber just went in to see him. After that, he's going to take a bath. And I was going on an errand, as you can see. What do you say, cousin, to going home and giving us the pleasure of your presence another day?"

"No other days! I've had it!" I fumed.

"Had it?" He hurried inside, to the room with the couch where their nasty cross-eyed boy had made me sit. We sat for fifteen minutes, saying nothing but platitudes:

"How are you?"

"Fine, thanks."

"Our home is your home."

"Thank you, I'm sure."

My cousin was lugubrious company. The fly that had joined us last time buzzed helplessly around the glass of a closed window. I watched it fail for the thousandth time to fly through the glass. When the maid arrived with the tea, my cousin snapped at her for her tardiness, saying that she had made him late for his appointment with Hajj Lamloum, the beans trader. It was no secret that this was meant for me, and for the household to do the necessary in case I didn't get the message.

I awaited the barber's departure, but it was an idle dream! I sat, my only company deaf ears. He was between a rock and a hard place: he couldn't openly acknowledge his displeasure at my presence, nor did I mean to budge off the couch where I sat. Time passed cripplingly slowly. The poor fly was getting increasingly desperate, its buzzing fading in exhaustion. The household, who had been on the line with us, seemed to have gotten the message: they never ceased to offer the cousin assistance, at which they proved resourceful. After a short while, a little boy came in, saying, "Saadawi Abu Kaff wants you outside, Uncle Sultan."

He answered, eyes on me, "Have him wait. I'll be right out."

Another moment, and the boy came back in, saying, "The men have finished plowing. They want their pay so they can go home."

When they grew weary of my lack of common decency—for that was how they must see it—they stepped up their attack. A servant burst into the room, screaming, the wrath of God on his face: "Our bull just butted someone on the south way! The man's dying! Quick, Mr. Sultan, before the police come!"

My cousin jumped up, glaring at me. I got that he had exhausted all peaceable methods, and that this was my final warning to get out if I knew what was good for me.

My resentment began to grow. I felt as though a war of nerves was being waged against me, seeking to tire me out and make me turn back, so that when I finally got in to meet my uncle, I would be already exhausted, whereupon they could dictate their own terms. However, they didn't realize that what they were doing was actually accomplishing the reverse of what they intended: instead of weakening my resolve, it only strengthened it. More importantly, it put paid to the hesitation from which I had suffered: where before I had vacillated, unsure where to start with my uncle, whether to offer him my land at a reduced price to just have him buy it and be rid of the headache, or demand it as my birthright and then do with it whatever I saw fit? Now that they had done all this, I completely put out of my mind any thoughts of selling my land to the uncle, and resolved to take it from his hands, after which we would see what we would see.

I consulted Abul Saad Effendi by phone. "That's the right thing to do!" he said. "As long as the land is in his possession, he'll buy it for a pittance. Go in to him, sink your claws into the land, and create a scandal. This might take a while, though. But let it take as long as it takes! It's not as if you've urgent business to get back to!"

"But what about my venture with Leithi?"

"All in good time, Galal."

20

THE ROAD TO MY FATHER'S grave was not the same road it had been before. Back then, the gravestones would not become visible until we had left the populated area, and walked for quite a while through farmland, until there was nothing but fields as far as the eye could see. The path itself had been soft beneath our feet and we'd walked at a leisurely pace: I clinging to my mother's skirts, my grandmother alongside us, and before us, my grandfather on his donkey. All around us, farmers walked to the fields to start work for the day, hoes over their shoulders, small bundles of tea, sugar, and their daily smokes in their hands or hung about their mounts.

How the road had changed! It was depressing and strange. It was no longer unspoiled; the corner-cutting contractors and workmen of these modern times had violated it with asphalt and paving, no doubt without properly preparing the roadbed for their handiwork, and the road was cracked and mercilessly uneven. My sister and I were forced to walk at the edges, in the fields that bordered it: fields upon which those who had the resources had erected boxy buildings utterly lacking in any kind of taste, neither formed of mud brick like the houses of our ancestors, nor homes designed like the ones in towns and cities. They were a different breed, characterless, borrowing the ugliest and most unappealing from here and there. She and I got off the road entirely to make way for the tractors that rumbled past, the bicycles carrying containers of milk on either side, and trucks loaded high with all kinds of produce. There were boys wearing an odd hybrid of clothing, American-style jeans below, and traditional waistcoats and long-sleeved white tops above. They played without any regard for common courtesy, and yelled out at the top of their lungs to each other: obscene jokes and lines from comic plays, learnt by heart from the television.

What had become of the towering eucalyptus trees, whose branches I had watched waving and playing against the sky? The old drainage ditch, in whose waters the boys of yore had waded or swum? Before the sun slept and turned its face to the west, they used to come in their gallabiyas and cluster around it with fishing rods fashioned from reeds. Now, the ditch was dry, its bed cracked and filled with the detritus of the wind: dust, tumbleweeds, and dead leaves—that is, but for a few places where the women dumped out their washing and bathing water; those places were still damp and filled with some water that swirled forlornly for a few moments before being swallowed up by the cracks. Some of it was still there, standing and stagnant, foam on its surface, filled with green algae and fungus, and speckled with manure in various stages of decomposition.

The scene as a whole depressed me, filling my heart with decay and desolation. Rats and small reptiles had made a home there, swarming here and there unchecked. The rats, in particular, ruled the roost: chasing each other playfully, sticking their heads out of their holes and squeaking. As I watched, a particularly experienced rat slipped past the cat lying in wait for him, and sneaked around her from behind, right past her twitching tail, and crouched, readying himself to pounce.

As it happened, that day was Friday, the traditional day for visiting the recently departed. There were flocks of women in black gallabiyas, hems trailing in the dirt and kicking up dust. The older ones were shrunken and small, wrinkles reshaping and unifying their facial features, making them look more or

116

less identical, their arthritic legs forcing them to shuffle along slowly, and causing the younger ones to slow down in order to keep pace. The old women, to tell the truth, were sensible and reserved, only speaking when necessary, and were treated with the most respect. The young women were curvy and healthy, baskets on their heads covered with old rags or towels, filled no doubt with bread cakes, dried dates, and menein buns for alms. A few of these were silent. The rest didn't have much reverence for the occasion, winking and nudging one another, bursts of laughter ringing out followed by sudden silence.

When their noise reached the ears of the elders, an old woman would turn to glare at them; they quickly moved away from each other, keeping their balance by means of judicious touches upon their baskets, eyes front or on the path, the picture of respect and good manners, as if to say 'I'm not like those other noisy girls!' The canny old women, not buying the innocent act, would dispense a speedy tongue-lashing made up of insults and reproaches, or wag switches at them that they had picked up on the path.

Our procession was accompanied by stray dogs: some were entranced by the contents of the baskets, and determined to follow their trail, even if it took them to the mythical lands of Wak-Wak in the *Arabian Nights*; others, wearying of the long walk, or nervous at approaching the territory of other dogs, grunted unhappily and left us, stretching out on the path, watching us move away.

My sister was worried about me. She walked arm-in-arm with me, in defiance of the custom of the countryside that dictated that men and women should walk apart. She never turned away from me, talking all the while, but I must admit I heard very little: my ears followed her talk, but my heart was still lost in the memories of that long-ago day when my grandfather Abd al-Hamid sat on his high perch of reeds. I approached him: his hand closed around my shoulder, and he pointed with his other hand at my father's grave. My mother and grand-mother were leaning back against the wall of the cemetery. As their tears flowed, my grandmother hid her face in her black veil, while my mother dried her tears with a handkerchief she held in her hand. I was swept away by the solemnity of the occasion and overcome with awe. Something greater than us was overtaking us all—at least, that was how I had felt. I stared intently at my mother's face, hoping to understand, then at my grandfather's, and grandmother's.

The women noticed my sister's demeanor, not to mention the stranger in their midst, as I undoubtedly seemed with my Western attire. They devoured us curiously with their eyes, girls leaning closer to their companions to whisper about us. The women behind us quickened their pace, overtaking us with fleeting, but expert, glances, doing their level best to appear, to us at least, as though they were not trying their hardest to find out everything about us, but just glancing at us in passing.

As soon as we crossed the threshold of the graveyard, the murmurs increased, new life surging into everybody. The old women moved apart, each looking behind her in search of her daughters. Some were already crying, and started rum-maging in their bras for a tissue or handkerchief, or wiped their eyes with the hem of their headscarf. They began to call upon the girls who were still lagging back, busy chattering and fooling about. The calls grew louder and louder; when there was still no response, the yelling began to be accompanied by irate waves of the hand. One of the girls noticed suddenly, and hurried to the woman waving angrily, followed quickly by the next, and the next, until all were hurrying to catch up with the elders, still, however, treading carefully, so as to main-tain the equilibrium of the baskets on their heads. One or two things fell out, for all that: a pie, a piece of bread, or a few dates, the owner hesitant whether to let them lie where they had fallen and continue on her way, or bend to pick them up. The dogs solved this issue: a bold one quickly snatched up the pie, another the bread, and others the other fallen treats, and they trotted with their bounty to the bottom of the dry ditch, followed by several other dogs getting ready to do battle.

Suddenly, we heard screaming, wailing, and traditional chants of mourning. One woman started it, and the others quickly followed suit. Some, transported by grief, drew great arcs in the air with their arms, holding their shawls; one removed her veil and stood bareheaded, an odd, lone figure with a wild shock of hair, half-white, half-dyed with henna, face pale and bereft.

The young girls had stronger lungs than their older companions: their wails were more like ululations, ringing loud and long and cleaving the air. The elders had more expertise: their mellifluous modulation, repetition with variation, and careful insertions of 'gaps'—their voices breaking and cracking at calculated points—made their mourning more expressive than the raw power of those younger than they. The cries of old and young mingled as we made our way between the graves, so that they appeared all to be mourning one person, not a number of dead.

I felt my sister's tug on my hand. My eyes followed where she was pointing, to the grave where my father lay. The women around us filled the air with whispers, each reciting under her breath the prayers she knew. There were babies in their mothers' arms. One started to crawl away in a moment of motherly inattention; alerted by a companion, his mother rose with a shout of annoyance to scoop him up, but only succeeded in catching hold of his legs, while he whined, wriggled, and kept on crawling on his hands alone. A crone, as old as Umm al-Kooz, sat at the grave next to ours, staring at me, the odd man out among all these women. I endured her scrutiny, staring right back. Embarrassed, she looked away.

There were Qur'an reciters, in a great rush, sitting before each grave and barely reciting the requisite quarter before hurrying on to the next tomb, sometimes not even finishing the quarter, constantly on the lookout for anyone who motioned to call them over!

I sat on a brick at my father's grave, facing a Qur'an reciter brought by my sister. He was a small man, his turban the largest thing about him, who cast curious glances at me from time to time. When I caught him doing it, he ducked his head, feigning engrossment in his reading. He was reciting the al-Rahman Chapter; he blurted out the verses so fast I couldn't follow him, not to mention that his eyes never stopped creeping toward me. Before the chapter was properly over, he suddenly lifted his head with a conclusive, "Thus spoke the Almighty," indicating that he was done.

"Finish the chapter!" I said, dusting my hands off in disbelief, while my sister urged him similarly. But he jumped to his feet, swearing a dozen oaths that he had recited the whole thing just as dictated by God Himself, and it was we who hadn't been paying attention.

Resigned, Leila handed over a small banknote. "No, no," he demurred," I wouldn't dream of accepting money for my services!" Meanwhile, his eyes invited me to intervene and offer a more respectable sum. I pulled a few notes from my wallet and he fairly snatched them out of my hand, almost falling on his face in his haste to reach a nearby grave, where a family was looking around them in search of a Qur'an reciter.

I stared at the marble plaque on the grave, pensive, unable to find expression for all that was in my heart. My life unspooled before me: the sweet and the bitter, certain scenes weighing heavy on me, passing slowly. I asked myself, "If he had not been untimely killed, this man beyond the wall, would my life have been the same? Or would I have gone to college, and become a doctor, and married Nadia, and maybe have had children by now? I wouldn't have emigrated with my mother, nor would she have married the Jew, Yaqoub."

My childhood flashed before me: boys walking in the company of their fathers, but my grandfather Zaki, not my father, signing my school documents. He showed me kindness, which I took for pity. A hand—oh, that the owner of that hand were still alive!—a hand on my brow, encircling my wrist, soothing me.

No one knows what it is to grow up without a father, except those who have experienced it. A sense of vacancy, as though you are a drop of water sinking into the sand. A plant uprooted by the wind, left to fall where it may, to be trod underfoot, licked by a dog, or urinated on by some passer-by. I was struck with a sudden longing for my mother who was abroad. A vast gulf separated me from her as well: countries upon countries, and guards who stood at borders.

"Where is my grandfather buried?" I asked my sister.

She said that he was buried in the same grave as my father and grandmother, pointing at the grave, and explaining that the woman was separated from her son and husband by a brick wall. As was customary, my family members were not buried in the earth, but placed in a cubicle built below ground, which was then bricked up until the next person was buried there.

We rose and started on the long walk back, accompanied by women who had come with us, leaving other women still sitting on the ground talking among themselves. One was scolding her little son, who had relieved himself ("Just like that? Have you no shame?") in front of the gravestone.

Another was haggling with the same reciter who had played at refusing Leila's money to take mine. He seemed less piously willing to refuse this fee, spittle flying from his mouth as he gesticulated, swearing oaths on the Holy Book, that he knew all about people like her, who thought nothing of taking advantage of poor hardworking folk like himself, taking another oath that he wasn't budging from this spot until she filled his sack with loaves and gave him two pounds.

I could detect no trace of grief or tears on the women. The fits of emotion that accompanied their arrival had cooled, and they were starting to collect their things in preparation for leaving. When we reached the top of the road, I saw donkey carts all in a row. Their owners, who had been lying in the shade, leapt to their feet. Some women went to take the carts home, while others preferred to return on foot. Others went to get onto mules and donkeys that were waiting especially for them. I noticed some young women, a way ahead of us, chorusing the refrain of some popular ditty, led by a girl with a sweet, melodious voice.

Gradually, the crowd thinned. In a couple of hours, all would be over, and people would approach no more.

21

OUT OF THE BLUE, A messenger arrived at my sister's house, inviting me to come and visit my uncle.

I had been lying down; Leila burst in, bearing the news. She rushed to the wardrobe, rifling through it to find my best clothes. She offered these to me with an unceasing stream of advice: "If he says so-and-so, you're to say such-and-such. And if he tries to change the subject by saying this, you're to say that. . . ."

When I was dressed, she looked me up and down and took a step backward, staring intently at my attire and figure, as though I were a lowly employee at the bottom of the organizational ladder, granted a golden opportunity to meet an important executive to plead a favor or beg for a reprieve. I left, her piercing eyes following me.

It was no longer daytime, but night had not yet fallen. The light had gone, leaving its remnants at crossroads and above the houses. The night lurked on the horizon, but its path lay clear: it was only a single, sinuous pounce until it arrived. It was the end of the lunar month, and there was no sign of a rising moon. The sunset prayer had finished a short while ago; the streets were vacant of people and beasts of burden. A tardy goose shuffled its way along a path, and a man jogged out of a prayer nook, having finished his prayers ahead of everyone else. A finger-sized lizard scurried down a wall, and disappeared into a woodpile in the blink of an eye. Whispers and faint hints of movement came from behind the windows and doors left ajar.

It was kinder and more gentle this time. My cousin Farid stood at the door; thank goodness that this time I had not had to meet his brother Sultan, nor that accursed cross-eyed boy. He welcomed me in and took me straight upstairs to the third floor, where he lived, and where my uncle awaited me in his sitting room.

The only thing of particular note in the room was my uncle, and a wallpaper mural that covered a large area on one side of the room. It depicted a green pasture disappearing into the horizon, with a flock of bright, white sheep grazing. In the foreground were two foreign farmers in jeans and straw hats: one stood with a leg bent forward, while the other pointed with his whip. The picture caught my eye, but I looked away when I noticed the uncle's eyes following me. He was shrunken, ravaged by illness. It showed on his body, which had been covered up by the quilt the day I had paid him a visit. It was without fat or muscle, barely taking up space on the couch he sat on.

"You like it?" he said in a low voice, as soon as we had looked at each other. He gestured to Farid. "He likes pictures and hangings and singing and music and all that nonsense that goes on in Cairo." His tone grew mocking. "He keeps a violin, and plays on it all night long."

I gave Farid an encouraging glance; he looked back gratefully. "Did you go to college?" I asked.

"I went to the Conservatory of Music," he replied.

"And when he got his degree," said the uncle, "we thanked God, thinking we'd heard the last of the lute and violin, but now we have him working as a singer, and every night he's in a chorus backing up some crooner."

Farid, clearly used to the way his uncle spoke, didn't seem in the least embarrassed. Smiling, he said, "I'm a member of the Arabic Music Choir."

My uncle slipped his left foot out of his slipper, resting it on the rug. His toes had the remnants of some black tincture on them: it seemed to itch, for he rubbed it against the carpet several times in irritation. He talked of inconsequential, unrelated things, then came to the point. "What is it you want, son?"

This was the very thing I had come for, yet when asked so bluntly, I was taken aback, seeming to him—and indeed to myself—unprepared for the question. My confusion robbed me of words to ease into the subject, so I came directly to the crux of the matter. "The land that belongs to me."

"Yes, I know you've come for the land. But what do you want with the land?"

I fell silent.

"Look, son. If we go by the documents, we owe you six or seven feddans. God's law says that's your share, and who are we to contradict God's law?" He rested his chin on his hand. "But what will you do with land?"

Taken aback once more, I hemmed and hawed. "Do with it?"

I looked to Farid for help. My uncle eyeballed me, then said, "Yes! What will you do with it? What I mean is, in plain Arabic, what binds you to it?"

Farid made to speak, but his father gestured to him to be silent. "Mind your own business. And while you're at it, go see why our tea hasn't arrived yet."

Alone with me, he asked me again. I said, "It's mine, and I want it. It's my due, and I've come for it."

He looked down, pretending to be occupied with returning his foot back to his slipper, muttering, as though to himself, "Due? Due, indeed! What due?" Then he looked back up at me, scratching his earlobe. "What are you thinking of doing with this due of yours? Do you want to sell it, rent it, farm it, what do you want to do with it exactly?"

My cousin returned with a tray of tea, followed by a small child on all fours. He crawled a few paces, then stopped, having lost his little slipper. He sat on his haunches, trying to put it on, but failed. He punched it, then continued in Farid's tracks. Meanwhile, my cousin was bending to pour us tea.

I took up my cup, my eyes fixed on my uncle. He took up his own cup, and tilted his head. Our eyes met; we quickly looked away. I tried to control my eyes; they went back to him, and I saw his eyes, planning some maneuver to lure me into a trap. They moved slowly over what was before them, and came back to me. I was waiting: they moved away once more. The infant would not stay still, and kept tugging at his father's gallabiya, until the latter scolded him, whereupon he took to crawling rapidly back and forth across the room, peals of laughter issuing from him for no apparent reason. Farid's father indicated that he should get the child out of the room; sensing the threat, the child tried to get away, but his father picked him up, still screaming over his shoulder and flailing at the little slipper lying on the floor.

After they had gone outside, my uncle turned to me. "Don't take offense at my questions, son. But when a stranger arrives out of the blue and says 'Give me my land,' it's inconceivable that I wouldn't ask and find out what's what."

The word 'stranger' offended me, and I let my displeasure show. He ignored this, interrupting me. "Let's stick to the point. Here's how it is: If you want to plant crops and harvest them with the rest of us, you're more than welcome. Tomorrow morning I'll get the surveyor to do the measuring and I'll parcel out your land for you. But if you're going to do that, little fella, you'll have to take off these clothes you're wearing, and live like us, eat, drink, and sleep with us." He looked away, muttering to himself, "Of course you'll stay here with us. How else will you keep an eye on your property?"

He looked back to me. "And buy a donkey or two, and a little house big enough for you. The long and short of it is, will you farm the land? What do you say?"

He looked at me, then added, "And your good lady, she wouldn't leave you alone, would she? She's more than welcome here, to knead bread and bake it and sit at the ovens, just like our womenfolk."

I controlled myself with an effort. "And if I don't like one word of what you're saying, Uncle?"

"Now you're getting to the point. You'd have every right. You want to sell it, then. You wouldn't be wanting to rent it out, for sure! If anyone's going to rent it, we've more right to tenancy than a stranger. Or are you thinking of letting it lie fallow? That's a sin! Healthy land like that, left like that, with no one using it?"

Farid came back. He tried to find out what had taken place in his absence, but our uncle told him to keep his mouth shut. He said pleasantly, "Tell me what you're thinking of, and I'll make it all easy for you."

I ignored what my uncle had said. I turned to Farid, and repeated to him what had been said in his absence.

Farid's ire rose. "What kind of talk is this? It's his land, Dad, it's his. If he wants to plant it, let it lie fallow, set it on fire—he can do with it whatever he pleases!"

"What's that, you music man, you bleating singer? Go find yourself a drum to beat or a pipe to toot, that's all you're good for. But serious talk—"

It happened before he finished his sentence. Something made him fall silent immediately, and we hurried to him. His breath was coming in short gasps. His finger shook as he motioned to Farid to bring him the pill he put under his tongue.

Farid hurried out, and I came closer. He put a palm out, indicating I should stay where I was. In a few seconds, Farid returned, accompanied by an elephantine woman whom I took to be my uncle's wife. She handed him the pill, while I sat there, unsure whether he really was ill. Was he faking it, as Leila said?

"Easy!" shouted the woman. "Go easy on your uncle, Mr. Galal! And you, Farid, shame on you. Do you want to kill your father?"

With that, she collapsed in a heap at my uncle's feet, massaging them from ankle to knee joint. The leg was lean, no softness in it, no blood flow, nothing pleasing to the eye. Skin, bone, and the traces of a suppurating infection in the calf. As she massaged, she recited verses of the Qur'an and called out to God for protection against the Devil, against wicked, unjust people, and against every man who was rude to his uncle and made him ill.

This went on for fifteen minutes, until my uncle opened his eyes and stared at us in astonishment, as though he had been asleep, and now woke to find us by his side. After he had sat up, he indicated to his wife that she should go now and leave us alone together. After a moment's hesitation, she obeyed, exiting while still yelling, "Go easy on him, he's not strong enough for this! Do you want to send him to his grave?"

A while passed, my uncle half-closing his eyes and opening them by turns. Farid was worried, clearly feeling responsible for his father's sudden bout of illness, and remained silent.

22

THE LAST ROUND BEGAN.

My uncle looked darkly at me. "Don't be difficult with me, there's a good boy. Before we set to disputing, there's something important you have to know: A man who sells his land is no man at all. It's like a man who sells his women's chastity and their honor: people have the right to spit on him in the street."

I said, finding a smile to support my words, "What have honor and chastity to do with our conversation, Uncle?"

"I don't blame you for saying that. You're a city boy. You don't know how we are. You don't know our nature: what makes us laugh, what makes us cry, and you don't know what makes us small, what brings us down in other men's eyes." He let his voice soften. "Listen here, son. Our land is one plot, all one piece—ours, and the part you call yours. It's al-Minshawi the Elder's land." He modulated his tone. "We've cradled it for generations. We have farmhands who till it and harvest it, and plows to turn it over. Every season, it's filled with traders, coming and going, buying the crops. It gives us prestige. It keeps us fed and clothed in wool and cashmere. In short, our land is our honor, and it's the reason we're respected. When you pull off a piece, and someone else pulls off a piece, it slips out of our hands, and little by little, we'll end up as farmhands like everyone else." He leaned in. "Would you want that for us?"

He was silent for a long time, his eyes seeking a reaction to what he had said. Finding me silent and staring, he appeared to think he was on the right track, and that I was about to give in. He let his features soften. "My boy, I'll give you a fair price; you'll get everything you want. Just like your sister. Would you have wanted me to give the land to that good-for-nothing girl, and let her useless husband lay hands on the Minshawi family plot, in broad daylight, just like that?" He waggled his right hand in my face. "That could never happen! Heads would roll!"

"Uncle, it's God's law."

"Good Lord! Who ever said a word against God's law? Did I deny her her right? Did I say, 'I don't owe her anything?'"

He held up a palm, seeing I was about to interrupt. "If you're going to till the land with your own hands and the sweat of your brow, then take your land. If you're going to rent it out, we've more right than a stranger, and we'll give you all we owe you."

"So I can't dispose of it as I see fit, then? I can't decide what to do with my birthright?"

"Your birthright! My dear boy, despite all the schooling you have, land has rights too." I said not a word, letting him say everything he wanted. "It deserves for you not to squander it. Not to sell it off to some other folk, to let them gloat that they got our land, and lord it over us, and not to be split by some stranger's hoe or plow. If you want to throw it away, then sell it to the closest man to you."

I tut-tutted.

"Why the tut-tut? Did you earn it by the sweat of your brow, Galal, man, to tut-tut, or do with it as you please? After all, it's the Minshawi family plot, and who are the Minshawi family? My father and grandfather, aren't they?"

"Aren't I a Minshawi, same as you?"

"A Minshawi! You're only a Minshawi in name. You don't act like us; you don't live like us. You never attended a wedding or helped us bury our dead. You never helped us run for election, nor attended a council with the village elder. And now you come, sleeves rolled up, wanting to grab the land and run? Well, now I've seen it all!" He warmed to his subject. "Tell me, how many times have you come to this village? Who knows you here? Did you know the way to your uncle's house, or did you need someone to show you the way? My son, Sultan, bless him, said you didn't even recognize one another. Never mind Sultan; what about your sister Leila? Did you ever ask after her or send her a letter from overseas? Did we even know where to find you, so we could consult you about her marriage?" He leaned back into the couch. "You, who say you're a Minshawi, same as us, did you know you had a relative called Marzouq, killed by two shots by the wayside, a couple of months ago? His brothers want to avenge him, and I'm trying to calm them down and see how we're going to get out of this one. Or Yassin? He's related to you. Did you know he drowned, and we stood by the creek for three days waiting for the body to surface?"

His voice rose belligerently. "What do you know of us, or of this land you're here to talk about? Where is it? In which plot? What's planted there? And here you come, in a suit and spectacles and wearing scent, yet, saying 'Give me my land to do with it as I please?!' Wonders will never cease!" He stared me in the face, letting fly his final arrow. "Land, my city boy, isn't a qintar of cotton or an ardab of wheat you can buy and sell. It's like breathing—you hold onto it until you give up the ghost. We were born and raised on it; it gave us life. At my age, when I go out into the fields, I never forget when I was a child, running after my father, while he pointed here and there at the farmhands spreading fertilizer, the ones turning over the soil, or carrying out the crops on donkey-back. He probably remembered his own self, as well, walking in the shadow of his father and grandfather, as they came and went on the land. Wake up, Galal, wake up! If you can't take care of the Minshawi family's land, son, leave it to others to care for it as best they can."

*

We had reached a dead end. My uncle, one foot in the grave, was fighting me tooth and nail. He was nothing but skin and bone, in danger of expiring at any second, and yet, 'the land, the land' until his last breath. To my understanding, it came down to money and the profit I might make from selling the land; to him, it was honor, virtue, and life itself. True, he was greedy and grasping, wanting every scrap of Grandfather Abd al-Hamid's inheritance; but was all that he said now solely motivated by avarice, or was there a grain of truth in it? Was he truly defending what he thought was right, or was it covetousness and nothing else? There was no answer to this question without delving into his motivations: I could lean in, armed with a magnifying glass, an archaeologist's brush in one hand, a deep-sea lantern in the other, beam bright enough to split the murkiest waters; but even if I did so, how could I probe the psyche of this wily old man, who could, as the proverb said, lead you to water and bring you back thirsty?

My uncle was seventy years old. He listened only to himself, never deviating from his intent to swallow up my land, and I sat before him, crippled. This was a world to which I was a stranger, and I had no influential friends, no one to support me but a sister who could do nothing but talk, and a brother-in-law who was the same as nothing. Should I grow angry and shout at him? He would have accused me of disrespecting an elder, and thrown me out of the house. Should I go along with him and accept the scraps he threw me, as Leila and my aunts had done? Was I to allow my will to be broken and allow my birthright to be wrested from me? I could see no path before me; I was exhausted by this endless argument. In despair, I said, "Uncle, get to the point."

"Now you're talking! The point: if it's farming we're talking about, you're not going to farm the land, right?"

"Right."

"Rent; you'll rent it out to us, not to strangers, right?"

"Why shouldn't I rent it out to a stranger?"

"Because you can't. No one would dare set foot in the land unless I allow it. Anyone who set foot in it would get his legs broken. He'd be buried, him and his hoe and his plow, at the border of the plot."

"So?"

"You want to sell."

"And if I do?"

"Would you sell to us?"

"And not to a stranger?"

"Not a soul in the town of Mansouriya would dare to make you an offer."

"If I did want to sell it, what would you give me for it?"

"Ten thousand pounds a feddan. And I can only buy one feddan a year, so the seven feddans over seven years."

"But Uncle, I've heard that the price per feddan is thirty thousand."

"What I'm telling you isn't the asking price. Leila's talk, her and that husband of hers in his tight pants, isn't worth a penny to me."

"And if I don't agree?"

"Agree or don't, do as you please."

"And if I don't want to sell it, and demand my land?"

"Then you finish your tea, go on home, and we'll send you the rent every year."

"Is that your last word, Uncle?"

"Excuse me. I'm going to bed."

I went home to Leila. I said, as she buried her head in her hands, "There's nothing for it but to go to court."

She lifted her head to look at me. Her husband said, "Even if they rule in your favor, you won't be able to get an execution on the ruling. And if they do execute it, you won't be able to sell or rent it to anyone."

"Shut up!" Leila shoved her splayed hand into his face. "Shut up, you stay out of it. And you," she said turning to me, "Off to court you go!"

23

I RECEIVED A TELEPHONE CALL from Abul Saad Effendi. His words tumbling out in a hurry, he managed to convey to me that Fouad, Nadia's husband, was very ill and had been taken to the Military Hospital.

"Fouad?" I said, in hushed tones.

"He's in a coma. God help him."

I remained pensive afterward, thinking of the Fouad I had met in Zaghloul's grocery shop. He had the most amiable face, his eyes filled with human kindness. I found myself feeling very sorry for him and grieved at his ill health; he didn't deserve to suffer, and he seemed too frail to endure severe illness. Try as I might, though, I could not suppress a rogue thought, a traitorous glee at the news, whispering that I might stand to benefit: Fouad's departure from this world would leave the path clear for me. I pushed the thought away, but it persisted. I pushed it away all the same, overcome with shame, asking myself how I could think such things? A small part of my heart made me think it against my will: a piece of my self, yes, a piece that had made explicit what I desired. I dismissed it, refusing to go along with it, but it had a life of its own. I could not control it, nor stop it from speaking to me. It was a thought that crossed my mind, leaving despondency in its wake, to pile upon the despondency I already felt. I had just arrived back from visiting my uncle, and was overcome with the sensation that I was not a son among his family, nor yet a man whose possessions were held in trust by honest and virtuous folk, but rather one with a buried treasure that lay in the hands of hucksters and shysters.

I was overcome with the desire to go back home to Cairo. However, I decided to stay for a few days longer to see my late grandfather's valet and faithful servant Imam. I remembered him vividly from my childhood: he had been the first to teach me the words for things in the countryside. "This is a grain of wheat; this is a stalk of clover." He had washed mulberries and sycamore figs especially for me. He had always visited us at our home in Daher, either to deliver the monthly stipend that my uncle had kept sending at my grandfather's behest, even after his death, or simply because he was in town and stopped by to say hello. He had been sprightly, always on the move; whenever I had had a request, he had always fulfilled it with alacrity, and a "Yes, Master Galal," or a "whatever you say, son, you're a boy of good stock!"

He and my grandfather had been together day and night. He made him his tea before he knew he wanted it; if I ever found my grandfather by himself, I would ask in surprise, "Where's Amm Imam, then?"

My brother-in-law led me through a narrow street, past a drainage ditch, and into a small alley, where Imam's house was to be found. The house looked like some mendicant. Its mud bricks, partly worn away by rain, were like the threadbare gallabiya; the baking heat and dew had worn away the tips and corners, leaving holes deep enough for a chicken to roost within, accompanied comfortably by three chicks. The structure was unevenly roofed with palm fronds and tree branches, some sticking noticeably out from the edge, some barely reaching it, like the beggar's dirty, tattered shawl. Piles of dry wood and dried cowpats were carefully stacked outside; some were not entirely dry, still retaining the color and softness of dung. An unhappy palm tree stood nearby, visibly bowed, its drooping branches trailing unfortunate bunches of dates that had withered, still unripe, on the vine.

In this remote location, inhabited by Amm Imam and the surrounding houses, time had never marched on: it was as though I were watching a scene a thousand years old. But for a glimpse I could catch, from where I stood, of a car speeding by on the highway, and a television antenna sticking out from a roof, I would never have guessed that I was on the brink of the twenty-first century, and that we and the inhabitants of these buildings lived in the same era.

My brother-in-law knocked; we heard a hand lifting the bar from within. A man with a turban on his head looked out through the crack in the door. He broke into smiles, and held out a hand to shake ours.

"This is Sheikh Masoud, Amm Imam's son," said my brother-in-law. He went on to tell me that he had obtained his preparatory school certificate from the religious school in al-Azhar, and, deeming this quite education enough, had appointed himself the teacher at a kuttab, one of the traditional schools where rural children learned the Qur'an. He pointed at a mud-brick house a stone's throw away: I understood that this was the kuttab he meant.

My brother-in-law introduced me, whereupon Masoud's face became positively wreathed in smiles, and he let the door swing open. It gave a piercing creak as he stepped back, revealing the interior of the house. Masoud looked behind him as we entered, giving a series of warning coughs. The rays of my eyes followed where his head indicated: I caught a glimpse of some women sitting around a washtub, who, taking his warning, snatched their hands from the sudsy water, bubbles flying, and scurried away, barefooted, out of sight.

The doorstep was worn; inside was an open-air courtyard with a water pump in the center, a sink facing it, with some plates and utensils stacked upside-down around the edge. There was a clay oven, next to which sat a stack of baskets, a hoe, and some odds and ends. A buffalo was lying in a corner; she looked up at us with her large eyes, then turned back to chewing a few stalks that lay before her. A gaggle of geese, with some chickens mixed in, raised their eyes to us briefly, then continued to go about their business. The only creature who seemed uncomfortable with our arrival was the dog: his barking filled the air, and he tried to attack us—me in particular—until Masoud upbraided him. He only relented after Masoud kicked him away, and he slunk into a corner glaring at his master, resentful of the human's injustice and the way he stood up for strangers. The dog appeared to be giving some serious thought to the mandate of his role as guardian of the household.

At the end of the courtyard, on the right-hand side, was a waiting room, which we entered. Masoud heralded us in, greeting us loudly, almost cheering. "Dad! Dad! I've brought guests! Guests here to see you!"

Imam was lying on his bed at the end of the room. On each side of him stood two wooden couches, each topped with a mattress covered with a length of fabric, and a backrest in the form of a cushion resting against the wall. The room was vacant of any other furniture, save for the mat we trod upon. On the wall was a verse of the Qur'an in a frame, next to which hung a cheap paper calendar of the type where you tear off a page every day, indicating a day two months before our arrival. In the center of the wall opposite hung a photograph of President Nasser in military dress, the stripes of a bikbashi, the old Turkish rank for lieutenant colonel, on his shoulders—it was the old familiar picture that had gained such a wide circulation in the early days of the 1952 Revolution, hanging in every government office, and even in cafés and the modest shops that sold sugar-cane juice and beans. This one appeared to be a page torn out of an old magazine, glued to the wall with lumps, it seemed, of dough.

When Masoud opened the window fully, the sun's rays burst in on us, illuminating the room.

Imam looked like a man from another time. Masoud supported him into a sitting position on one of the couches, ignorant as yet of who we were. He motioned us to take a seat on the other couch, and went back to his father. He rested his back on the cushion behind him, and arranged his legs so they hung off the couch. They were bare to the calf and skinny. One of his slippers lay overturned on the floor; the other dangled from the tip of his toe for a moment, then fell to join its mate.

I only found his eyes after intense scrutiny. As far as I could tell, they couldn't see further than the hand in front of his face. "Father, this is Mahmoud Effendi, from the Agricultural Co-op!" his son said to him, gesturing to my brother-in-law; Imam nodded, indicating that he knew him. When my turn came, Masoud raised his voice slightly. "Galal, the late Mahmoud's son!"

Imam looked me carefully in the face, then leaned toward Masoud; the latter realized he hadn't heard properly, and repeated in a near-yell, "Galal Effendi from Cairo! Galal Effendi! Galal!"

His yelling was bootless, however, and he was obliged to repeat himself. What he didn't realize was that his father's attention was not on him, but wholly on me: he craned his neck toward me, still gazing intently, lost in silence. He seemed to be searching for me in some deep cavern of the recesses of memory, Masoud still calling out for all he was worth, over and over. When he grew tired of this, he apologized to me. "Begging your pardon, Galal Effendi. My father's hearing isn't what it was."

Imam appeared to have recognized me. He waved Masoud away, a reedy voice issuing from his lips. "Galal?"

"Yes, Dad, it's Galal."

He looked at me again. "Galal? From Daher?"

139

"Oh, for Heaven's sake! Yes, the one from Daher!"

"The son of the lady who was. . . ." He broke off.

"Yes, Dad," Masoud burst out in exasperation, "That's what we've been saying since we walked in here! Give me strength! Galal, Galal!"

Imam surged to his feet—I know not how—and so did I. He flung his arms around me, now patting me on the chest, now on the back, now on the shoulder. Masoud and my brother-in-law looked on in astonishment at this sudden expenditure of energy. Masoud left the room, returning shortly with a little girl bearing a tea tray.

There was no table to put our glasses on, so each of us sat, teacup in hand, sweet steam wafting off the mouths of the cups. Amm Imam lifted up one leg onto the couch. He laid a hand on his knee, the other occupied by the teacup. His constant motion eventually made his gallabiya ride up, revealing his underpants, whereupon Masoud would rush periodically to pull it down. And so it went: the gallabiya riding up, and an increasingly irritated Masoud preserving his father's modesty.

Imam glowed with simple joy whenever he bent over his cup to blow the steam aside. He did this repeatedly, like a child; Masoud looked on, disapproving, and silently urged him to stop. The glass felt too hot in my hand; I noticed him growing uncomfortable with it as well, and raising it to his lips to take a sip and reduce the risk of anything spilling over the rim. He failed, though, and some tea slopped onto the front of his gallabiya. His little granddaughter watched him, suppressing a laugh with her hand. He reddened and glared at her. She looked up at him, unable to keep from giggling. He snapped at her for her bad manners, telling her father to use the stick on her to teach her a lesson. Then he started to talk to us. "Ah, Master Abd al-Hamid! You died, and everything good died with you!"

I moved to sit beside him. "How's Sitt Camellia, your mother?"

I raised my voice loud enough for him to hear. "Fine, thank you."

We talked, and talked, and in the end, I told him all about what had taken place between me and Uncle Ibrahim. "What? And you stood for that?"

"We'd do better to mind our own business, Dad, it's a family affair."

The old man ignored him. "Your uncle Ibrahim's an old swindler! He's nothing but a con artist, who knows no religion but his own interests! Don't let appearances fool you: not his three pilgrimages to Mecca, nor that he touched the window of the Prophet's mausoleum, as he says!" He raised his chin. "You've the police station, you've the courts at your disposal—go and complain!"

"Dad!" Masoud remonstrated. "Dad!"

"Shut your trap! What business is it of yours? I'm talking to my guest!"

"Dad, why cause trouble? Have you forgotten what they did to you after Master Abd al-Hamid died?" He turned to me: "Sorry, Mr. Galal. This father of mine, you see—"

"What's this trouble you think I'll make? Why do you think he threw me out of the half-feddan I used to plant, you good-for-nothing? Wasn't it because I told him the truth to his face? I said 'Master Abd al-Hamid made you promise, before he died, to play fair with your sisters and nieces and nephews,' and I said, straight out, 'Don't do them out of their birthright, give them what's owed to them according to God's law, Master Ibrahim!' Or am I wrong, Mr. Galal?" He didn't wait for an answer. "My heart was breaking at what he did to your sister Leila! If I'd been able to, if I'd had the health to, I'd have picked up my staff and made him answer to me!"

"Dad!" Masoud entreated. "Dad! Oh, this will not end well!"

Amm Imam shushed him. "Just because her heart led her down her own path, was he entitled to take her land from her, and give her a pittance in return?" His cap fell off his head onto the arm of his seat in his enthusiasm, and he reached for it and jammed it back on his head, still speaking. "And as if that wasn't enough, he went around saying 'I won't put my hand in the hands of lowlife strangers such as these, and I won't marry my niece to some nobody, with no family to speak of!' Can you believe it?"

Masoud appeared embarrassed—my brother-in-law was, after all, sitting right there. He bit his lip, trying to alert his father to what he was saying, but his father was too engrossed in what he was saying. "You know what God says? The man who allows himself to steal an orphan's inheritance swallows live coals in his stomach. He ignored what God's law and His holy book say about rightful inheritance!" He held forth on Ibrahim's sins and his lousy reputation for close to an hour, saying such choice phrases about Leila and Mahmoud's marriage as, "And what concern is it of his if she marries a lowlife, or a no-account, or a stray dog? It's her choice and she'll drink the piss of it!"

Poor Masoud was beside himself with embarrassment, but had abandoned all hope, merely looking at his father despondently. My brother-in-law, next to him, was grey as ash, at a loss what to do or say. Amm Imam had found his stride, and wasn't giving anyone a chance to say a word. He only paused when he glimpsed a trace of mockery on his son's face. The blood surged to his cheeks, and he got off the couch, looking for a slipper to throw at him. I jumped up, taking hold of both his hands, and helped him back to his seat. Masoud was shifting carefully from side to side, wary eyes measuring the distance from his father's hand to the slipper lying before the couch, so as not to be taken unawares.

Naturally, the sounds of shouting reached the ears of the household: shadowy women passed outside and doors were pushed ajar. From where I sat, I could also hear children pausing in their play in the courtyard, coming up to the window to listen. One of them, bolder than the others, stood quite plainly on a perch made of several bricks he had stacked on top of one another, and stood at the window to see for himself what was going on, then ran like the wind to give the report to the women, then flew back to listen some more, and so on, coming and going without pause.

After a tense silence, Amm Imam subsided, speaking much more calmly. "Look here, my dear boy. The plot of land that adjoins the drainage ditch, that's the one that's yours. And the plot th—"

He didn't finish. Masoud took his attention, dusting his hands off in desperation: "Dad! For crying out loud! Dad, keep quiet! Men in glass houses shouldn't throw stones!"

"What stones, Mr. Sheikh? While every Friday you run off to the graveyard to recite a quarter of the Qur'an for a few cakes and some loose change!"

"Really, Dad!" Masoud fumed. "God forgive you, that's all I can say! But since we're talking plain, blame yourself before you blame others!" He burst out. "Didn't my grandfather Abd al-Azim leave you the house and three qirats of land, and you with two sisters? What did they get? Didn't they send everyone and anyone who knew us to entreat you to give them their due, and you with one ear of dough and the other of clay, as they say?"

Amm Imam glanced at me, then at Masoud, and yelled at him. "The house is theirs to come and go as they please! When they fight with their husbands, they come here and stay for months on end! Besides, what business do you have poking your nose between me and my sisters? They know how hard I have it, and they're happy and fine with it."

This time he managed to find the slipper, and threw it at his son. Masoud stormed out. Amm Imam's wife burst in, swimming in a too-large gallabiya, and yelling at him, "Imam! Is this any way to behave in front of guests, starting fights and airing dirty laundry? Every day it's something! Yesterday you bit Saniya in the ear, and the day before you crept out and milked the buffalo and drank all the milk yourself, and left the kids starving and crying with hunger the livelong day! Drop dead, may you never see another day! I hope I find you dead tomorrow morning, like a chicken in the coop!"

My brother-in-law and I fled, leaving the charged atmosphere behind us.

24

WHEN I CAME BACK FROM Imam's, I found my two aunts, my father's sisters, waiting for me. They rose from the couch as soon as I came in. We stood there for a moment facing each other, unable to do anything but stare. Aunt Hanem was tall and slim, and her reaction to seeing me was quicker and warmer. Aunt Umm al-Kheir, on the other hand, stayed where she was, one hand resting on the arm of the couch. Both wore a black malass, black scarves wound tightly about their heads, and an ostentatious gold kirdan about their necks. They looked nothing alike; you would never think they were sisters. Aunt Hanem had small, fine features, with a pink-and-white complexion, the freshness and glow in her eyes making her seem younger than my sister Leila, although she was twenty years older. Aunt Umm al-Kheir was the complete opposite. Her nose was broad, as was her forehead. Almost everything about her was as rounded as a panda; she even resembled that animal in her slow movements and expressionless eyes.

"Well, hello!" smiled Aunt Hanem, walking toward me. "Come closer, now! Why so surprised, dear?" She embraced me, followed by Aunt Umm al-Kheir. They sat, and asked me what the world was doing with me, and what diplomas I had, and whether I was married or still seeking a wife. We talked for a long time, without either of them saying a word about my mother, not even asking whether she was alive or dead. Leila sat silently, looking at all of us by turns.

Aunt Hanem monopolized the conversation: she rose, and sat, and pointed, and laughed. Aunt Umm al-Kheir sat with her hands in her lap, speaking only when spoken to. When my father's name was mentioned, I asked her the question that had been on my mind since I was little: What did he look like?

"Your late father and Hanem were like peas in a pod," said Aunt Umm al-Kheir. "The same height, the same face, especially the lips, and the shape of their eyes." She sighed. "He was the image, poor boy, of my sister Hanem."

I leaned closer to Hanem; she gazed fondly upon me, and rose from her sister's side to sit beside me and talk to me about my father. His favorite place had been the eucalyptus tree behind the old house, and he only liked to sit and read there. One day my grandfather Abd al-Hamid had made him give the Friday sermon at the Minshawi Mosque, when the imam had been absent, and the only thing he had managed to do once on the pulpit was to recite from the al-Zalzala Chapter from the Qur'an: "Servants of God, obey God! After all, anyone who has done an atom's weight of good shall see it, and anyone who has done an atom's weight of evil shall see it. Let us pray!"

And the day he had done this, and the day he had done that . . . until the last day she had seen him, the day he and his comrades left for Port Said.

"He was worried before he left," said Hanem. "He had a feeling he wouldn't come back. I told him that I thought he was worried about Leila's mother, but he said, 'My wife is safe with you here. The one I'm really worried about is the poor woman in Cairo. She's in her seventh month now, and has no one to help her. If I don't come back'—that's what your father said, as if he knew—'you visit her and see how she is, Hanem. If it's a boy, name him Galal, and if it's a girl, name her Ihsan.' He said that . . ."

She stopped to blot away a tear that had fallen on her cheek. "But I didn't! I was scared. My brother's marriage to

Umm Galal was a secret, and we weren't allowed to mention it. He and our father and brother Ibrahim were the only ones who knew, or were supposed to know, and we girls hardly knew a thing about it. We only talked about it in whispers. Neither I nor Umm al-Kheir dared to talk about it out loud or ask the grownups about it."

I thought of my mother, in her house gallabiya, at home in the old days in Daher, going over math problems with me, bending at the waist to push a chair aside and pick up a pencil sharpener or eraser I had let fall, standing in the kitchen, my shrill voice calling after her, saying how hungry I was and to hurry up. I stared at the carpet, not really seeing it, overcome with longing for my mother, and filled with self-recrimination at the unpleasant tone I had taken with her during our last telephone call. If I could have, I would have flown to her upon the instant, kissing her hands, her brow, and every part of her my lips could reach. Aunt Hanem appeared to notice that I had grown pensive. She bit her lip and said, "I've reminded you of things past, dear boy."

I looked up at her, the other aunt staring at us as she had been doing since the conversation started, only nodding or looking sad, or chiming in with pro forma responses such as 'amen' when forced to. Leila seemed displeased with the turn the conversation had taken, as though it were a waste of time. She came straight to the point, cutting across our impromptu tête-à-tête. "Galal had to go to Uncle Ibrahim quite a few times before he'd even let him in," she said, "and when he broached the subject of his land—"

"We know, my dear girl, we know," Umm al-Kheir cut her off. She added, talking to me, "Hanem and I had to be careful, you see. We didn't feel it was all right to come and see you until you were done meeting your uncle." She added, eyes on Leila, "We were afraid he'd say, God forbid, that we were egging you on, or had a hand in it somehow, or stood to gain from this business between you."

"My heart is with you, dear," said my aunt Hanem. "Do what you think best. If you want to sell him your land, do. If you want to take possession of it, that's your right as well. Do what you want to, but be careful of Ibrahim. He's my brother, and I know him. He's wicked, and he'd cheat the Prophet himself given half a chance."

Umm al-Kheir silenced her with a warning glance, then bent to put on her slippers, taking her leave, followed by Aunt Hanem, although her face seemed to indicate that she wasn't yet ready to leave and would have preferred to stay a little longer with me.

I had resolved to go back home to Cairo the next morning, so I made my excuses to Leila and went to bed early. Sleep evaded me, however, and I tossed and turned till midnight. I finally rose, taking a chair and going out to sit in the court-yard for some reason, although I had never yet sat there, not even in daylight. Perhaps it was because it was the only open-air portion of the house and I wanted to see the sky on this moonlit night.

The courtyard was still and silent; no sound, not a breath, no one moving. A few chickens slept in a corner, heads tucked under their wings. A sheep slept. A pump caught the moonlight; I had no idea whether it still drew water. There was a small washtub and two pots, exactly the same size; the telltale stink of food gone bad wafted about one of them. This was all they had. They lived more in the style of city folk: they had no clay ovens, no cooking hearth, and no cattle, nor even a dog to guard the house. The moon was in its full splendor, and the stars beckoned your heart to a kingdom far from the one beneath your feet. Nothing but a slight cough from my brother-in-law scratched the surface of the silence. Little Galal screamed out suddenly, then fell silent just as suddenly; most probably he had been hungry, and Leila had given him her breast.

A bird settled on the top of the pump, dipping his beak into its mouth; I think it was a hoopoe. He spent a while dipping his beak inside, and coming up empty, whereupon he hopped to the ground, looking around for a drop of water. I sat still and quiet, hardly breathing, so as not to frighten him, and let him get what he wanted.

He walked like a bird unused to walking, unbalanced on the ground, almost stumbling as he went. He was wary, looking all around. I watched him until, with a sudden flapping of wings, he flew away like the wind. Only afterward did I notice that he had caught sight of a weasel, sticking its head out of a hole in one of the walls. He circled the house twice, then flew off.

My thoughts turned to Uncle Ibrahim, in another round of wondering at this man who, as he said, wasn't denying me my rights, just wouldn't hand them over. My share was as clear as the moon that lit up the sky, as clear as the shooting star that had caught my eye a moment ago. I remembered my uncle's words: "If you, in your city dress, want it, then take less than what's coming to you: either in the form of a small sum, paid in installments, or else retain the title to the land on paper, on the books, and get a handful of pound notes every season as rent! But if you want the soil, the earth, to run about on your land and do with it as you please like the rest of creation, then no, and a thousand times no, unless you take up the hoe and plow! You must change your stripes, wear breeches and a waistcoat, ride a donkey and milk the cows."

And thus you keep me from my land, you unjust ignoramus of an uncle.

I thought of my cousin Farid. 'You met me at the door, Farid, and welcomed me, not frowning like the rest of the household,' I thought. 'You supported me in the face of your father, openly disapproving of his words. But, cousin, you accepted the unjust, unlawful division imposed by your father, and you still profit from a number of feddans that were rightfully mine. What would you say, I wonder, if I asked you to hand them over? Would you come down on the side of fairness and justice, or would you go along with your father?'

25

I HAD RECEIVED THE LION's share of gifts from Umm Hassan:
a watch, made in China, with hands that glowed in the dark,
and a ballpoint pen that wrote in four different colors. And
she hadn't stopped there. There were also two pairs of socks
and a bottle of cologne bearing the name "Pierre Cardin"—a
knockoff, naturally, the scent emanating from it closer to what
we call 'spice-store sweepings.'

She held out the presents to me proudly, then rapped on my
knee with her knuckles to get my attention. "And Galal, no sooner
did I land in the airport than I found the whole world waiting for
me! But I looked around for my son Hassan, and there was neither hide nor hair of him! That useless oaf." She dampened the
tip of her sleeve with her tongue and wiped the face of the watch
before proffering it to me. "The building was yelling and ululating
as I came in, all happy to see me, and his wife, that witch, who
should have been first in line, just sauntering in, the last on the
scene! All I got from her was 'Welcome home, Aunt! The building wasn't the same without you!' Well, never mind. I'm not going
to beg for affection, and that kind of thing can't be bought."

I asked after Fouad. "You don't think I just sat here, do
you? I went to see him in hospital at once! Nadia was there,
poor thing, her face all sunken. You could fold her up and put
her in a handkerchief, she's grown so thin."

"Shouldn't I visit Fouad, too," I asked softly, "as a matter
of duty?"

She glanced at me, her eyes seeing much. "Don't give me duty. You stay away."

Sitt Nazira, Abul Saad's wife, came to visit, bringing her daughter Hadeel. I was about to make myself scarce, but Umm Hassan insisted I stay. "What's this? You're not some stranger! Stay! And you, Hadeel, sit here, in the chair next to Galal's!"

She looked like a modern girl, in jeans and sneakers. Her face was attractive, although ever so slightly cross-eyed: it was not unattractive, as opposed to the rascally cross-eyed boy who worked for Uncle Ibrahim. Sitt Nazira was like a sentinel, one eye on us, the other on Umm Hassan, who commandeered the conversation, going on and on about the way her heart beat faster in awe the first time she had come face-to-face with the Holy Kaaba. She would not shut up about it, nor about the day they took her to visit the Mountain of Uhud, where al-Hamza, the Prophet's uncle, was buried. After she had come out of the sacred state of ihram necessary for Hajj, and gone to Medina, she had thought the holy moments had come to an end: but her body had been transformed, or so she said, into ether, floating through the air, the moment she had stood before the tomb where our beloved Prophet was buried. She brought the talk back to Mecca, to tell of the Yemeni man with a fabric store at the entrance to the market, who could not be beaten when it came to bargaining, and of the African who had bitten a man in the shoulder in a fight that had broken out from the overcrowding.

Meanwhile, Sitt Nazira had noticed the wedding band on my finger. "Are you married?" she asked.

I explained to her that this was my grandfather Zaki's wedding ring, which I kept for remembrance.

"Poor Galal," Umm Hassan said pointedly. "He's all alone! Ever since his poor dear wife."

We took a moment of silence to recite the Fatiha under our breaths, as is the custom, for all those who have died. "No children, then?" Sitt Nazira said as soon as we had finished.

"Children?" Umm Hassan cut in before I could answer. "There wasn't time, poor thing! They were only married for a few weeks!"

Sitt Nazira, obviously pleased, smiled. Meanwhile, Hadeel, while I was distracted, took the opportunity to look me up and down, scrutinizing me closely. I noticed, and she looked away, but I could sense that she was thinking about me. Maybe she was asking herself who I was, and how I measured up in the marriage market. Was I the eligible bachelor her father imagined me to be, or just any old match?

Umm Hassan noticed that Hadeel and I were not talking to one another in the manner she had hoped. "Shouldn't you tell Hadeel about the land you're planning to buy?" she asked. "She's a clever girl, an agricultural engineer!"

She didn't leave us alone and turn back to Sitt Nazira until we had started to talk. Well, I talked, and Hadeel listened, then said a few words of noncommittal agreement.

After a while, though, she began to become engaged as I entered into her field of expertise, discussing matters of soil and water, and what kind of crops were more suited than others to the land in question. She offered to make an appointment for me to meet another engineer who had been in college with her, a man who had been about to reclaim twenty feddans on the outskirts of Beheira Governorate, but proved unable to cover the costs involved. I could perhaps come to an agreement and buy the land from him.

Little by little, Sitt Nazira and Umm Hassan's voices subsided, and they turned their attention on us. "But Mr. Galal," Hadeel was saying, only to be interrupted by Umm Hassan.

"What's this Mister? Call him Galal."

Hadeel looked down shyly. I looked at Umm Hassan in reproach.

"Nazira chimed in, "There's no one dearer to Abul Saad than Galal. Little by little," she smiled gaily, "Galal and Hadeel will get to know each other, and there'll be no more shyness."

She rose. "Well, excuse us, we must be going."

Umm Hassan rose to walk her to the door. Hadeel reached out to shake my hand; her hand lingered a little in mine.

Month after month passed. Ten months since I came to Egypt, sitting around like a bum. I busied myself with errands for Umm Hassan, or went where my feet led me, to the places of my youth, now fallen into ruin.

Where was Amm Mohamed's store, where I had bought the beans as a boy? I passed outside, finding no trace of him, nor of his two vast containers of hot beans, nor the crowds that had thronged the shop; instead, there was a haberdash-ery. I stared at the nasal-voiced man who stood there now, then recalled Amm Mohamed with his vast belly, covered with an apron dotted with oil stains. I used to call his name, and he would look up from the falafel sizzling in the deep pan filled with boiling oil. His face looked odd as he smiled at me, as he wore a permanent grimace to protect his eyes from the heat that rose from the stove before him. "Just a moment," he said, then filled the dish in my hands from an awe-inspiring pot of beans by his side, experienced eyes taking in the coin I had placed on the marble counter at a glance, making sure I had given him a full piaster, the value of the beans he had given me, and not a five-millieme piece, as some boys did, only half the value of what they had taken.

And Amm Raafat, the owner of the watch store! I picked out the one I wanted, while my mother asked him to give us a better price. He submitted, whereupon she entered the sec-ond round, asking to pay by installments. This he would not allow, though, and took the watch from my hand, as she and I exchanged disappointed glances.

I had allowed myself to drown in memories, so much so that I felt I was living in the past, no longer in the pres-ent. And while there is pleasure in reminiscing, and memory brings sweet melancholy, what's the use, if you make it your substitute for reality? I had become like a man who smells the flowers and delights in their scent, never taking a bite of nourishment or taking a step forward. Ten months without work or accomplishment were wearying for a man who had learned that time is money, that every minute counts, and that wasting it is the mark of the ignorant.

I had had enough.

There was no longer any point in staying in Egypt. What use, after all, was the business venture I had wanted? I had no real desire to make a profit out of it, nor would it add anything significant to my homeland. From start to finish it was nothing but a big fat zero, a cipher on the pages of my country.

My intention, nothing else, had been to revive my links with my homeland: that had been my intent and desire, at first and last. But, as the proverb says, a demon awaits us in every abandoned house. This uncle of mine, Ibrahim, had come out brandishing his staff; in France was my business partner, Abul Shawareb, displeased, threatening to dissolve our partnership if I should so much as think about withdrawing a single franc from the company account. And at home was Umm Hassan, who could talk of nothing from morn to night but Hadeel.

This morning, I gave her a shock: I packed my bag and left, a ticket to Paris in hand.

26

THE PLANE WAS THOUSANDS OF feet high. Vast spaces spread out before me, immense, limitless void, drawing me into its fantastic bounds, losing myself in a world of questions. There were the old questions: yes, the old questions, for misery begets misery.

For the thousandth time, I asked myself: 'Who am I? To whom do I belong?' Why had I, of all people, come out of the womb of a Jewess and the loins of a soldier killed in battle? How long, when I approached my mother, would I be haunted by something I could not decipher, something that pushed me away, filling me with self-blame and regret when I drew away from her? These questions had eaten away at me since childhood. When I accepted my fate, I was comforted; when I fought it, the questions drained me dry. I had never accepted it, nor yet found a single answer.

The new question that nagged at me now was about this country to which I was fleeing, away from Cairo. This country had offered me shelter, companionship, and plenty of money. It had received me, unable to speak in the tongue of its people and with no education to speak of, and here I was—after a single decade—sitting pretty, partners with Abul Shawareb in a company worth millions of francs.

Had I been unwise, after all, not to take my mother's advice, when she told me to apply for citizenship here, where I lived and from whose bounty I made my living, and to the devil with Egypt and everything in it, uncle and inheritance included? "Investing in Egypt," I thought, "is a pipe dream. Business opportunities lie abroad, security lies abroad—*everything* can be found abroad! I was just a guest in Egypt, only passing through; neither my home, nor my business, nor my country lie there!"

Why had I stuck my nose in the air? Why had I not cozied up to this country like all my fellow immigrants? Had I refused because it was my mother and her husband who had urged me to, being stubborn for stubbornness' sake? What was I going to do now? Was I going back, never to return, or to raise the money and go back to Egypt?

I was in crisis, in a state of confusion. I remained in this state until the loudspeakers announced the Fasten-Seat-Belt sign was about to come on, as we were coming in for a landing.

Paris, ah, Paris! Your ancient buildings; your carved mosaics; your pillars and statues, all fill the eyes as one comes in for a landing. The airport corridors were decorated with posters advertising Samsonite suitcases, Du Maurier, Marlboro and Gauloises, and filled with people of every description: in safari suits, jeans, coats and hats. Here and there, a woman sparkled like a jewel in boldly printed African national costume, or ladies from the Maghreb, draped in burnooses or with sefsaris pulled tight around them. In a flurry of movement, noise, and laughter, a gaggle of beautiful girls ran past me. Posters for the latest perfume from Christian Dior, creator of beauty, surrounded us.

I slipped out of the airport gate. A chill breeze whipped at me, droplets of water clinging to my coat. My body felt light, a rush of joy suddenly overtaking me, a voice whispering to me that we had finally come back to the City of Light! To the cafés of Montmartre, to the Champs-Elysées, the Gare Saint-Lazare, to crepes and croissants. Yet something else awoke, turning my face back to Egypt: it urged me to raise the sum by any means necessary, and return to Daher,

Abul Saad Effendi, Umm Hassan . . . and Nadia, whose love had never faded from my heart.

Should I ignore the devil's blandishments, and return to my homeland, with all it held of beauty and ugliness, with its every frown and smile, and insist on having a living home-land with blood pumping through its veins, not buried deep in the corridors of the heart, in the darkness of a foreign land, in the diaspora?

It was still early: the company's doors would definitely be open. I went there directly. Outside the building on the Boule-vard St-Michel, I stood staring at the sign on the second floor, bearing my name and that of Abul Shawareb. I was filled with contentment at the sight of it, like seeing a brother or a lover again: it offered protection and refuge.

"Galal!" Abul Shawareb greeted me, beaming in delight. He hugged me tight, and I returned the embrace. "You light up all of Paris, and you have left Cairo dark with your absence, as the Egyptians say!" He launched into a monologue about the company, and its profits, which had risen to a sum that aston-ished me; he said that he had put my share of the profits back into the company's capital, as well as his own, setting aside a sum for each of us to cover our own salary and personal expenses. When I asked him how much he had deposited into my personal account, he tapped a finger on the corner of the table: "I thought we should give ourselves a raise, see, because of inflation. Prices keep going up. Instead of ten thousand a month, I've made it twelve."

I looked skeptical. He said, "How are twelve thousand a month not enough for you? Why this big spending, and you with no wife or children?"

"I needed a million francs."

"Good Lord! Not again, Galal! For this venture of yours in Egypt, of course! Look, son, we agreed right at the start not to withdraw a single franc from the company account for our own personal expenses, only for company business. You know that as well as I do."

He scanned the papers in front of him. "I got a great opportunity five days ago."

He raised his right hand, all five fingers splayed. "Five days, I swear. I've been waiting for you to come home, to tell you the news. And here you come with this nonsense. We're going to need every last franc for the good of the company. I'm even thinking of taking out a quick loan, because there's no ignoring this opportunity I'm telling you about. We'll never get another chance like this."

He must have liked the curiosity that showed on my face, for, eyes bright, he started to talk: "Traders from India, Galal. Naïve traders, with 'I'm a novice' written all over their faces. They seem to be new in this business. And oh, my word! All short. No, no—midgets. All with beards, and whiskers like a cat's." I smiled, and he smiled for my sake, leaning in to me: "Jacques, the middleman, introduced me to them, and I met them at Fouquet's. We talked and talked. Then I noticed that Jacques and I were talking, and they were looking and nodding like they understood, all puffing on their pipes." He looked astonished. "When I asked, I found one of them was wearing not one but two hearing aids, and the other two only spoke English, so I asked Jacques to interpret for us!"

I must have looked astonished too. "What, is that odd? Soon you'll see them, and know it's true. Do you know how much they want to spend on goods?" He leaned back in his chair. "Five million. Ties, suits, blouses, skirts, and on and on. This is the list of their orders."

With thumb and forefinger, he picked up a two-page list that lay on the table between us, waving it in front of me, then added, seriously: "You know, man, we have to have cash on hand in our business. The fashion houses don't hand over their wares until they've gotten every centime! I thought, here we've got two million in the bank. We can get a loan for another three million with the company as collateral, from the Société Générale. In a few months, the deal will be done, and we'll get our money. Then we can pay back the bank and make a profit." He added, running a self-congratulatory forefinger over his mustache, "in a month or two, we'll make a million, or two, out of those dupes!"

"Are these people secure?"

"Secure and a half! You know me! I'm Abul Shawareb, I know everything. I'm the smartest fellow around! The man hasn't been born who could put one over on me."

I drooled over the prospective deal and plunged into the conversation with him. The odd thing was that it didn't occur to me, at that moment, to use the profits for the Egypt business venture. Seeing me distracted, he said, "What do you think, Galal? Will you stay on here with the company, or are you still thinking of Egypt and your venture there?"

I didn't reply.

The employees all came to greet me, first of all Fouad, the Egyptian accountant, our Lebanese chauffeur, Harfoush, and Bu-Lehya, the aged Tunisian office boy, who whispered hastily into my ear not to stay away for months on end like this, because Abul Shawareb was a hard man and they could not abide the way he treated them. Abul Shawareb, sensing that he was the subject of the conversation, looked at him suspiciously. Mademoiselle Jeannette, the secretary, came as well, and kissed me on both cheeks, as was the Parisian custom, and joked with me, "Didn't you bring a camel to show us, then?"

I knew it was a joke, and Jeannette was known for being facetious, yet I felt the blood surge to my head. Abul Shawareb noticed, and said with reproach, "Camels are amiable creatures, and we Arabs, especially Muslims, hold them in high esteem. We don't like to hear them joked about in our culture."

She grinned, unrelenting, "How come you eat them, then?"

Abul Shawareb had not even known why I was upset: he had just wanted to stand up for me. My strange touchiness was odd to him, and even to me; why I had taken it as a slur on my country, I had no idea. I preferred not to show it, playing along. I said, none too pleasantly, "Well, you eat frogs' legs and horse meat!"

Abul Shawareb motioned her to leave us alone.

That night, I went home to my grandfather Zaki's apartment in Barbès. It was just as I had left it: the socks I had meant to put on and changed my mind, one sock lying by the bed and the other I knew not where. The half-empty cup of tea I had been drinking stood on the bedside table; the liquid that remained in it was a disgusting mire, full of tiny insects drowned and decaying. The glass of the poorly closed window appeared to have been blown open suddenly at some point, for it had knocked over a vase and broken it in two.

The apartment was silent, except for my grandfather's spirit and the sound of my footsteps.

All of a sudden, the doorbell rang. It was Monsieur Thibaud, who lived opposite. He was about my grandfather's age, and was very fond of us: not content with a mere handshake, he embraced me warmly, and we kissed on both cheeks. The man had lived in Algeria for a long time, and was familiar with our customs. When I asked him if anyone had come knocking—my mother, Aunt Bella, or Uncle Shamoun, for he knew them all—he said no: "I didn't see any of them. I thought they had left Paris for good."

We parted, a little disgruntled in my case; more to the point, it was as though I had been searching for a reason to be mad at them.

I spent that first night as I had spent it in our apartment in Daher: my grandfather's shade keeping me company, the only one in my heart, while my eyes, with or without my volition, were drawn to his picture on the living room wall whenever I passed by it. He was the master of both houses; he was my father and mother. I lived in his protection in my youth in the old apartment, and remained with him in this one, content in his company and he in mine, until he died.

The next morning, Sheikh Munji al-Ayyari, the father of my late wife, came knocking. He made a great fuss, as usual, and the apartment was not in the least lonely during the hour he spent with me. He left me, saying, "Since you're back from a long trip, you count as a guest—you're to have all your meals at my place for the next three days, the way our ancestors did with travelers!"

27

"ONLY NOW DO YOU THINK of picking up the phone to call? A week? A week, Galal?" Reproachfully, my mother repeated, "Where did you learn how to be so hard-hearted, my boy?"

I was so ashamed that I headed straight to her apartment on Rue Camille Martin. She met me wearing a headscarf. Her clothing smelled of tobacco and she seemed to have gained weight. I grew pliant in her embrace, as she said, "Come here, come here, my darling boy! You're all I've got in this world! No brothers or sisters, no company, not even the man I'm supposed to be living with day in day out! Oh well, God forgive him!"

I tightened my arms around her, hugging her harder than she was hugging me. My attention was caught by a photograph on the wall of the entrance, showing the face of a woman in a tall hat with the front coming to a point, her hair cascading out from under it in careful waves. Her naturally long, graceful neck was captivating, and from one delicate ear dangled an earring the size and shape of a pomegranate seed. The image was in black and white, engraved with the name and address of the photographer at the bottom: "Antoine— Ramleh Station, Alexandria."

As we broke apart, her eyes followed mine to the picture, and she said, "That was the start of all my troubles."

I took a step forward, peering closely at the photograph, as she gestured to it. "That's his first wife, Liliane. I came back from an errand to find it on the wall."

I remembered the first time I had come with my grandfather to meet Uncle Yaqoub. He had not yet married my mother; when my grandfather had broached the subject, I had developed an immediate hatred for the man. The photograph had caught my eye that day, but it was hanging inside, not on this wall. "I've seen it before," I said, telling her where.

"I'd never seen the thing," she fumed, "until His Highness sprang it on me." She went on ahead of me into the house. She wore a short robe, something like a nightgown beneath it. Thin, spidery veins stood out on her legs; I felt that her steps had slowed, no longer sprightly as they had been. She preceded me into an armchair in the living room, and motioned to me to sit opposite. The photograph was visible from where we sat, almost as though the woman in it were watching my mother from above, overlooking her space. After a pause, my mother lit a cigarette, and took a sip out of a half-finished cup of tea that had been on the table between us. I noticed dried flecks of coffee on her lips: she might have had a spoonful of instant coffee dry, as she used to do. The smoke rose above her in concentric circles. No sooner did I wave it away than it came back.

She yawned, pushing the scarf back; it came untied, and fell into her lap. Her hair, which had been the loveliest thing about her, seemed unhealthy: dull and frayed. Her once-magnificent mane had lost its luster; there was a finger-sized circle on her scalp where hardly anything sprouted. I watched her speak, the cigarette shaking with the tremors in her fingers.

"When I came back and found the picture hanging there, I didn't say a word." My eyes ran over her hair: she noticed, and bent her head, pointing to the nape of her neck. "Here's another bit where I lost my hair. All at once, just like that!"

I offered false sympathy. She went on, speaking less to me than to herself: "But I'm too young for this!"

I said nothing, amazed at myself. When I was in Egypt, I was filled with guilt whenever my mother came to mind. In fact, I was offended when my uncle and aunts failed to ask after her health. Now, I was uncomfortable in her company, and all I could think of was finding some excuse to go. Accursed curiosity kept me in my seat, though. "What's going on with you and Uncle Yaqoub?"

"Yaqoub?" She slumped lower in her seat at the sound of his name, bending her head and gathering her robe tighter about her knees. "Treatments, laser sessions, injections, intramuscular, intravenous, and none of it was any use. Now a twinge in my chest, and they say I need an ECG. The doctors said, 'Be careful what you eat, you have a lazy liver.'"

I remembered our early days in Egypt: she had been unwell then, too. Back then, she would put a hand on my shoulder and off we would go to the Sayyid Galal hospital in Bab al-Shaariya, where treatment was free. They would give her a handful of pills, or some medicine in a bottle, that they said killed parasites and worms. She would never take the doctors' advice, nor show her poor stomach any mercy; on our way back, she would take me to the first falafel restaurant she could find, or perhaps buy us large soft pretzels from some street vendor; each of us would eat one or two, and we would go home satisfied, stomachs full, and her healthy as a horse.

"But I know why Yaqoub hung that picture there."

I was annoyed by the picture, the woman in the picture, and the talk of the picture, but, realizing there was nothing for it, sat there and listened.

"He put it there to please Simon."

I said, sick of the whole subject, "Who is this Simon?"

"Simon! Simon, his son, who lives in Argentina. The VIP's been here for a week as a houseguest."

Still disgusted, I said, "A houseguest?"

She said nothing. In a moment, she rose and left the room, then came back pushing a cart bearing a teapot and a platter piled high with cookies and French pastries. I contented myself with the tea, while she set to with the pastries as though it were her last meal on earth. We spent maybe a quarter of an hour in each other's company without a word. I looked at my watch; she espied me doing so, then returned to the pastries. I tried to tell her silently to say what she had to say so that I could be on my way. She did nothing of the sort, and I sat there watching, until she had eaten all the pastries, leaving only a tiny piece the size of an olive. I was astonished that she had not eaten this as well, and urged her to finish it. She held up a hand, indicating she had had enough, and started talking of her husband Yaqoub, who had divided his share of the casino in Sharm al-Sheikh equally between his daughter Sarah, who lived in Eilat, and his son, Simon, who was here from Argentina specially for this.

"And while he's here, as Yaqoub says, they can visit together while he gets his documents in order. As for Sarah, he's going to send her her documents with a relative who's going to Israel, on condition she gives him a power of attorney to run the business, as he's doing with Simon, and then they get everything after his death."

"She's an Israeli," I said, "it's illegal for her to own property in Egypt."

"I know, I know. That's all taken care of. She has a French passport, and she'll use it when necessary. And if that doesn't work, the bag of tricks is full." She looked at the photo. "Do you think she's beautiful?"

I was obliged to flatter her. "There's no comparison."

"But it's upsetting!" She said more sharply, "By God, if I had a photograph of your late father, I would hang it on the wall too, and see how he liked that."

I showed my displeasure at the way she had dragged my father into a dispute between her and her new husband; she looked away, changing the course of the conversation. "And that means I'm not getting a penny from him."

I stared at her in silence. She seemed to see my disbelief, and said, "It's just the apartment we're in now that I own. I nagged him into putting it in my name."

I scratched my nose, eyes on her. "And he says he'll raise my share in the casino from seven to ten per cent," she continued. "At least, that's what he says!"

"What about the bank account he opened for you?"

"Oh, Galal! That's no more than half a million, that's my nest egg for the future!"

"That's more than enough."

"You think so?"

I got up, making my excuses; she caught me by the hand and guided me back down into my seat, saying, "You haven't asked me about Yaqoub."

"Oh. How is he?"

"He goes off to the St. Daniel Club every other day with Simon, and they're there from early in the morning until late at night." Nastily, she added, "He wants to be a big shot and make himself president of the club. Wants to meet ministers, and organize events in honor of important people. He wants to be somebody among the Jews."

"But," I said, "as far as I know, he's not an Alexandrine, he's one of the Jews of Cairo."

"What can you say? He's using his first wife to get in: she was from the Nadler family, one of the Alexandria Nadlers."

She looked over at the picture for the tenth time; I did the same. She fell silent; so did I.

28

THE SILENCE BETWEEN ME AND my mother lengthened. Her face was despondent, and perhaps mine too. I looked around at the elements that made up the room: a wall clock, pendulum swinging; a small brass menorah, whose seven arms, I had been told, symbolized the six days of creation plus the seventh day, on which God had rested, and whose seven flames, I had also been told, represented the eyes of God on earth. It is even said that it symbolizes the return of the Jews to their true homeland after long absence in the diaspora. There was also a framed photograph of Sarrouf Bey Abul Saad, Yaqoub's father, with an upturned mustache and in an old-fashioned suit; and some distance away from me, on a tall side table, stood a box of expensive wood with erotic illustrations on the side. I had no idea why Uncle Yaqoub (the well-bred, respectable man of good family) would have acquired such a scandalous object. Had my mother no shame, morning and night, looking at this naked pair, getting ready to—I didn't finish looking around. I glanced at my mother out of the corner of my eye; she rose and moved toward her bedroom. I watched her from behind, looking at her as though she were not my mother, but a stranger whose every detail I was familiarizing myself with. When she disappeared through her bedroom door, my heart recalled the day she had married Yaqoub.

That night, they had sat next to one another in the traditional wedding pose: he in full regalia of black tuxedo and bowtie with his dyed hair; she in a veil and a white gown that displayed her cleavage. The guests all called Moses their prophet; I was the only exception. She had looked around, smiling and laughing, as though that night were her first wedding, and she still a virgin. I could have died, and lurked in a corner where she could not see me, watching her.

He asked her to dance. One of his hands encircled her waist; the other lay on her shoulder. Transported by delight, swept away by the musicians' playing, he pulled her to him; she yielded, her lips meeting his. Oppression upon oppression, insult to injury. I watched in agony, while my father lay under the earth, bones swallowed by dust.

I came back to myself. She was coming back in, her light perfume heralding her approach. She had tried to do something with her hair, but it was no use: it still looked dismal. She said, returning to the place where she had been sitting, "So, aren't you going to come in with us on the gambling casino? Was that your final answer?"

I wagged my finger decisively, indicating denial.

"As you like, son. I've done more than my duty, and I've offered you a chance at partnership not once but ten times. If you'd agreed, I would have given you part of my own share."

I ignored her words completely.

"We've already divided it into shares. A share for Yaqoub's children, as I've told you, part for Haroun, the same for your uncle Isaac, and mine. We plan to give the management of it to a man from the Levant, called Naawas, who's worked in casinos for generations."

I cared not a whit for their shares, nor for this Naawas. "What a businessman, Galal! He's not just coming in all by himself. He has a big company here, all in this business."

Her fingers drew out a cigarette, while her eyes searched around for a box of matches. "At first, he suggested we start a gambling hotel, not just a casino. When we asked in Egypt, they said it was illegal; they only granted permits for casinos."

"Excellent. Good for them."

"We've already hired a firm of contractors, and they've shown us the plans."

I stared at the Persian rug, with its embroidered cocks and peacocks. "Of course, you're aware that Israelis aren't allowed to own real estate in Sinai or on Egyptian land. For us, it's not an issue; we've all got French nationality. But your uncle Isaac, my brother, only has Israeli nationality. So what does your savvy uncle Isaac do? He says, 'What do you say to me bringing in my brother Shamoun in my stead? A figurehead, you know.' What a bright idea! We agreed, and after all, it's all in the family, and relatives have first right to charity, since, as the Prophet Muhammad says, 'Charity begins at home.'"

Her final phrase caught my attention, and I smiled at her.

She noticed and smiled as well. "Phrases one learned in Egypt, and they never leave one's tongue! Anyway, your uncle Isaac asked, 'Is Shamoun trustworthy?' We said, 'He's a harmless fellow, and he has a family to raise. As long as you give him some money after he's done his part in preparing the necessary papers.' So we put it to him—Yaqoub explained it to him in person. And what does this hopeless idiot do but lose his temper, and leap at Yaqoub, about to butt him like a goat. He told him, 'I won't be some kind of figurehead for gambling and vice. I want nothing to do with such enterprises, and I won't do anything that displeases God.' That's what he said."

She dusted off her hands in astonishment at Uncle Shamoun's stupidity. "God? God damn you, Shamoun, and may your funeral be on a day where the snow is coming down in bushelfuls, so no one walks in your procession." Fearing I would interrupt, she held up her hand, adding, "No, and that's not all! You know what else he did? With no shame or and no manners, he says to Yaqoub, 'Finish your coffee and get going, or I'll be late for work.' Work! The man's a streetsweeper with the city! He must have been missing his broom and dustpan, or maybe his bucket and mop!"

I remembered my uncle Shamoun, embracing me at Orly Airport nearly a year ago, as I was leaving for Egypt. I hadn't told any of my mother's family I was leaving, just him. My mother had not even known I was at the airport until a little while before the plane took off. I couldn't forget how he had looked that day: he had come in his orange jumpsuit and cap, having taken two hours off work. I still remember his eyes, overcome with yearning, as he said, "I wish I could have come with you."

"Where?" I had said, frowning. "To Egypt?"

"Of course, to Egypt."

I reproached myself for not asking after him until now. My mind conjured up images of him, ignoring my mother, who said mockingly: "He loves his poverty so much, he'll stay poor, too!"

I was shocked to suddenly hear her say: "And did you visit Papa's grave?"

"Yes," I said, my eyes saying, "What's that got to do with you?"

"Could you arrange for me to visit, too, when I'm in Egypt?"

"I know Uncle Yaqoub has the first and last word over everything," I said. "Will he give you permission?"

"Permission?" she burst out. "He'll look around and find me gone! When I get back, I'll make him burn with jealousy. 'Oh, Yaqoub!' I'll say. 'Oh, I miss Galal's father so very much! I found my feet leading me there! I just couldn't stop myself from going to see him.'"

I made to go. She saw me to the door. "I want to see Egypt again," she said. "I want to visit Umm Hassan, and the neighbors, and the street where I grew up."

Her words fell on deaf ears. I busied myself thinking of visiting our company, or my uncle Shamoun.

After I had walked a few steps down the street, I paused. I thought of going back to my mother. There was no real reason for it: just a desire, maybe a prick of conscience, or something I could not fully understand. It must not have been true or powerful enough to drive me to respond, however; it just gave me pause, after which I went on my way.

29

I ENDED UP NOT VISITING Uncle Shamoun, nor Abul Shawareb; I went home, feeling down. It was always the same with my mother; the further away I was from her, the worse I felt when I did her wrong, but whenever we met, my heart would start to chew on things that could not be said.

The streets I was walking through now were flanked by stout, historic buildings. There were balconies with marble Corinthian columns in the corners, or topped with miniatures representing animal or human figures, the great wooden building gates adorned with paintings. Rows and rows of chestnut and horse chestnut trees lined the street, their proud branches cleaned of any speck of dust, free from thirst, the kindness of the skies and the generosity of the rain providing unbroken bounty. All was shining and broad, dotted with cafés, shops, and dogs walking alongside their owners. In the sky, heavy clouds parted, or disappointed us by showering us with rain.

The world had a heart, a soul, and lips that smiled. Why was I joyless, seeming so depressed? Was it because these were not my streets? Because I had not crawled on them in my childhood, nor experienced my youth? What was wrong with the streets of Egypt and its nooks and crannies, that they, too, no longer seemed like my streets? The first knew me not, the second was no more. Yes, I was depressed! But why now? Yesterday and the day before, I had not felt what I felt now. Was it my mother? Was it that whenever I saw her, my mood changed? An unfortunate mother, and an ungrateful, unjust son? Or was it a diaspora of the heart, not of our own making, hurting me and her in equal measure?

Sheikh Munji caught sight of me walking into the building as he stood at his window facing onto the street. He called me over, motioning for me to come upstairs. He ran to open the door for me, and I went inside, my mood black.

"What's the matter with you, Galal, my boy?" he asked, leading me by the hand into the formal sitting room.

I had not been in this room many times: I was family, so I always sat with them in the hall, which served as a living room, or the balcony. My eye was caught by a photograph of my late wife, Khadija, hanging on the wall next to a picture of her grandfather, Sheikh Munji's father. Her face was tranquil, returning the gaze of whosoever contemplated her picture. On her chest hung a pendant we had bought together. She wore a smile I was familiar with. We had had the picture taken in Nice, when we had visited that city a few weeks after our marriage. "Two or three days' vacation," we had said, "and then we'll be back." Only it was I who had gone back, alone on an airplane, while she lay in a wooden box. After the photographer had taken several shots of us together, we had wanted him to take a picture of each of us alone. I had been forever smiling in those days. But her face had been serious and sad; after trying with no success, the photographer had enlisted my help, asking me to amuse her somehow from outside the frame: this smile had been the result.

Sheikh Munji came in, and noticed me looking at the picture. "Recite the Fatiha for her soul, and have done. Don't let yourself fall prey to thoughts and delusions that might lead you to displease God." He sat down, asking me how I was, and what was preying on my mind and making me so unhappy. I unburdened myself to him, and talked until he said, "Heaven help us! Why all this? Why, my boy? Banish these black thoughts from your head. Your mother is your mother, no matter what she does. Your fate is your fate. It's not right, Galal, to fight so hard against the fate that your God and mine has dealt." He started encouraging me to start on the business venture I had planned, saying that it would banish my doubts and strengthen my ties with my homeland, which would make up for what I felt I lacked.

He took the opportunity to let himself speak freely about Abul Shawareb. He felt that my business partner was a rash fool, and was afraid his recklessness and bright ideas would lead me into trouble. When the conversation turned to my mother's family, however, he kept silent, only saying, "May they never prosper. Because I'm a God-fearing Muslim, I won't say the things about them I want to say."

"Even my grandfather Zaki?"

"God forbid! That grandfather of yours was a Muslim, and a God-fearing man!"

In point of fact, my grandfather had not been a Muslim; he had been every inch a Jew, descended from Jews, devout in his faith and proud of it. Sheikh Munji, though, had his own ways of seeing things: he classed anyone who knew right from wrong and had a good heart as a Muslim.

"What about my uncle Shamoun?"

He nodded in approval of him too.

I rose to go, but he would have none of it. "Today we've cooked a wonderful meal: couscous with allouch potatoes and grilled salad."

After dinner, I left him, and went upstairs to my apartment. I had not yet managed to get rid of the siesta habit I had acquired in Egypt. I flung myself onto the bed and dreamed of Nadia.

It was true that I had been sighing over Khadija's picture an hour previous; but it was Nadia who came to me in the dream. She did not come as I had always seen her, with her prettiness, her innocence, and her school uniform, but as I had seen her on my visit to Egypt: a woman, a body, and feelings that were no more. I was standing in my pajamas in the balcony of our old apartment in Daher; she was crossing the street below. I knew she was coming, so I left the door ajar. She knew I was waiting, and was careful not to meet my eyes or let anyone know or guess what was between us. I desired her, so I stood, unmoving, not wanting to spoil the moment.

She came in the door safely, without attracting anyone's attention. Her eyes glowed with desire, and she was getting ready to fling herself into my arms. I was more full of desire, and readier than she. I had never seen her like this in any of my dreams, nor had I ever seduced her, even in my wildest imaginings.

When I awoke, I was ashamed of myself, for in my dream, I had been ravenous, plunging into her like a caveman, as though I knew nothing of sex but its most primitive form.

30

I STARTED MY DAY WITH a call to Umm Hassan. I had been thinking of her since I woke up, so I went to the first public telephone I found and dialed her number. She seemed to have missed me, too, for she interrupted me several times, and herself as well, asking when I was coming back.

She gave me a bulletin about the neighbors: Umm Nabil had slipped in the stairwell and would have died but for the grace of God, Abul Saad Effendi had been shocked to learn of my sudden departure, and her son Hassan had dragged the store's reputation through the dirt when the inspectors from the Ministry of Supplies visited the place and found mountains of expired stock.

"Do you have al-Askari wool in Paris?" she asked, adding that if this highly-prized brand was available, she wanted me to bring her three meters for the husband of Sitt Fatima, who rented the room on the roof. She also urged me to buy an al-Ghafir coat for Bashandi the doorman. I told her I would ask; but if I did not find it in Paris, was it really necessary to purchase this most prestigious of all brands?

"Yes!" she said. "He said so himself. Al-Ghafir or nothing!"

She asked about "squares"—square cotton headscarves. I said they didn't use them here, preferring to wear hats. Would she like a hat?

"Am I the sort that goes in for hats? What kind of woman do you take me for?" she snapped. "Hats, indeed!

I'm a respectable woman, and I've never done anything to be ashamed of!" She explained, "The squares aren't for me, anyway, they're for Umm Abbas' maid."

The call was almost wasted on these trivialities; but at the last moment, she remembered that a man in a turban, calling himself Sheikh Masoud, had come calling, asking for me.

"Masoud?"

"Yes, that was his name. He said he was the sheikh of the kuttab in your village, the son of old Imam, who used to carry you on his shoulder when you were a baby."

"Ah, yes, of course."

She cut me off. "He was bringing a message from your sister Leila. She said she wanted you for something important." I hung up as she said, "How long are you planning to stay there, anyway? Come back—I'm waiting for you!"

The call cheered me up; I felt there were people in the world who cared what became of me. After a while, though, I asked myself: Why had I forgotten to ask her about Nadia, and why had she not asked how my mother was, as she usually did?

I set off for the 20th Arrondissement, a poorer suburb of Paris, where my uncle Shamoun lived. His son Labib, God help us, was nothing but a wet blanket. He even had the same name as the first man who came to ask for my mother's hand after my father's death—another Labib, smooth, cold, and disgusting! I had hated his name and the way he looked; to this day I had reservations toward anyone with that name or any face that looked like his.

The youngest son was Saul; the middle one, Isaac, was about my age. We had always liked each other and had often gone for walks or sat together at some café or other. I would complain to him of my feelings of alienation, and he would complain to me of his father's poverty; he had had to quit school and work as a bartender in a Pigalle bar to help out with the household expenses.

My uncle was in a deplorable state, sick in bed. He called out in a quavering voice to his wife Sarah, as she led me in, "Who's at the door?"

As soon as I came in, he was completely overcome with surprise. His face went completely blank for a moment; then he pulled me to him, and I bent to let him embrace me. He hugged me tight to his chest, then pressed my shoulder with the palm of his hand to coax me down to sit on the bed, by his side.

"Here's Galal, come to see you," said my aunt Sarah, the smell of her cooking clinging to her clothes. "Happy now, Shamoun?"

The apartment was the size of a pack of Cleopatra cigarettes. No sitting room, nor even a passageway leading inside: the hall was right on the door to the apartment, and no larger than three by two-and-a-quarter meters. A Western-style couch sat between two termite-riddled chairs; the walls were pitted, lined, and covered with scribblings from a felt-tip pen. There was nothing worthy of note save a painting of a crow licking at an egg with a cracked shell, and an elderly cat who never stopped staring at me from the moment I came in. Then was a room with a closed door, and the one I found myself in now, the bedroom of my uncle and his wife: a matchbox of a room, nothing imposing whatsoever. The only tools that could conceivably improve it, in my humble opinion, were a can of gasoline and a match.

I knew that my uncle was the poorest among his siblings, but I hadn't thought it was that bad. I couldn't help remembering his old apartment in the Sakakini district: four big rooms, a hall, and a balcony that looked onto an intersection big enough to count as a square. Each day, he had come and gone to work with great pride in the car that he had bought in the Nasser era on an installment plan. I looked at his room now: the bed I sat on creaked incessantly and the bedstead had two scratches, I think from the cat I had seen a while ago.

On the wall before me was a photograph of my grandfather Zaki, and next to that, another of an old man in a smocked gallabiya, an old ink pen sticking out of the top pocket, and an abbreviated tarboosh with a white scarf around it. His face was depressing, with a big nose and a large Adam's apple. I knew he was Muallim Zikri, Aunt Sarah's father, which made him Uncle Shamoun's father-in-law.

On another wall, only much larger, was a picture of the Pyramids at sunset. At the bottom of the photograph was a mixture of tourists, people in western dress, and men in gallabiyas with jackets over them. A camel sat still on the ground, although a small boy stood behind it, clearly yelling at it, brandishing a stick. Another camel was kneeling, getting ready to let off his passenger, a foreign woman in a hat and pants. The poor woman was clearly apprehensive, and clung to the saddle with both hands as though she were landing a Mirage. The entire photo seemed very old: it must have been one of the tourist posters printed in the era of the late King Farouk.

No sooner had we started talking than the cat came in. In the blink of an eye, he had hopped up onto the bed, and slipped under the blanket next to my uncle Shamoun. My uncle tried to push him off the bed several times, but he would have none of it; finally, Sarah picked him up and lifted him off the bed, cursing him and his mother and father and all his feline ancestors into the bargain.

Uncle Shamoun asked me any amount of questions about Egypt and the people he had known there. I answered some of the questions with information I knew for a fact and made up all sorts of answers and flights of fancy for the others. No matter the variety of my answers, they could be summarized as follows: "Everyone is fine. Everyone says hello. Everyone misses you. Everyone's asking if you're not coming to visit sometime soon."

He nodded happily as I spoke, occasionally interrupting me to correct a name. Eventually, I asked after his health and how they were doing. He said that everything was "fine, thank the Lord." His words lacked conviction; Aunt Sarah's face made it plain that they were as far from fine as it was possible to be.

We talked desultorily of other topics; but no matter what we talked of, even if it was not even remotely connected to Egypt, he would interrupt me with a sudden, "Heavens above. Hajj Abd al-Rasoul from the feed-store still remembers me and says hello? He's a good man, I swear!" He slid the pillow that had slipped out of place back into its position behind him. "But he'll be old now, and his health will be failing."

It came upon me that I had indeed told him that Hajj Abd al-Rasoul sent his greetings; now, only now, did I remember that that worthy was no longer in this world. Umm Hassan had told me so when we were chatting one evening. What did it matter, though? Alive or dead, it was all the same. I did not think that my uncle would check up on it, and I was stuck, so all I could say was, "He's healthy as can be, and all day he sits outside his store, sunbathing!"

Then my uncle asked, "How is the Azhar Mosque? And the shrine of Saint al-Hussein?"

I knew that my uncle loved these places, so I was careful not to let my enthusiasm run away with me and allow me to give false information. "I'm sorry, I didn't get a chance to visit."

"Really? When I called you in Egypt, you told me you'd been there, not once but several times!"

"Yes, yes, I remember now!"

"You see, in *Al-Ahram*—you know, the international edition we get here – I read that they expanded the area in front of our saint al-Hussein's mosque, and added gardens and paths, and made the place more attractive for tourists."

I had read that, too, so I answered him based on what I had read, while he nodded, as though I were telling him something new. Since attack was the best form of defense, I thought I should start asking him questions to get him off my back. "How's Labib doing?"

"Labib? Labib's in Canada now."

"And Saul?"

My uncle smiled. "He's in school."

"He's the class Alpha!" his wife chimed in. The unfamiliar term 'Alpha' caught my attention. I turned to her. "What else should I say?" she continued. "My late father always said it about my brother Malaak." She turned to the photograph of Muallim Zikri, calling down the Lord's mercy on his soul; as though catching the bug, my uncle and I turned to do the same with my grandfather Zaki's photograph.

I eventually asked about Isaac. "Isaac?" My uncle's voice was filled with misery, as though I had broached an unwelcome subject. His eyes went to the photograph of the Pyramids.

Aunt Sarah avoided my eyes as well. "I'll be going," she said, but my uncle asked her to stay.

It was as though Isaac had died. They told me he had moved to Israel two months after I went to Egypt, and almost instantly been granted nationality and citizenship. "And not only that, but they say he's joined the army over there! While I sit here, knowing nothing. When he left, I said to him, 'Why move away from us? I'm sure you'll get a better job soon. If it's the money you give me every month, I don't want it, just stay,' I said." His voice subsided into a whisper. "He made me swear not to go see him off. It was Sarah who went to the airport, only to find out he was going to Israel, not to Brazil as he'd told us."

I wondered if they were truly pained by Isaac's actions, or if it was just for my benefit. My aunt stared at me, but avoided my eyes as soon as she noticed me looking toward her. A tear slipped from my uncle's eye. "He was fooling me. Since I found out I've been asking myself who was behind it?" He turned to face me fully. "I don't trust Isaac. My heart tells me it was all him."

My aunt Sarah had tears in her eyes, too; but my heart told me it was all an act, all pretense, and that she had been in cahoots with Isaac from the start and knew that he had taken El Al Airlines, and that my uncle was the only dupe in the household.

On my way home, Isaac's face came to me. I asked myself whether his actions were motivated by desperation or by conviction? Whatever the reason, this was a wedge between me and Isaac. I thought, too, of his brother Labib. My old resentment toward him seemed to be fading.

31

I MET THE MERCHANTS FROM India. They met us at the Carré d'Or, on the Champs-Elysées. I recognized them immediately: you couldn't miss them. A trio of very short men with identical goatees and upturned mustaches, they sat smoking identical pipes, wearing immense wristwatches bursting with buttons and dials.

The smallest of the trio, a fellow in thick spectacles, was their leader, and he monopolized the conversation from start to finish. His companions watched in silence, their only means of communication with him being their eyes. On the table before them sat three empty glasses, foam still on their rims. Each had a pouch of tobacco.

Jacques the middleman went on ahead of us and greeted them first. Then it was my and Abul Shawareb's turn. I was struck by a strong feeling that they were not as naïve as they looked, and had lied to Abul Shawareb when they told him they didn't speak French; for when a waiter approached and we insisted on buying them another drink, one of them almost gave his order in French, but caught himself just in time and used English instead.

They sat opposite us: their leader talking, Jacques interpreting what he said into French, while the others looked us over, their eyes going back and forth in the course of the conversation. I was now firmly convinced that I was facing three dark horses, certainly not green businessmen as Abul Shawareb had given me to understand. Jacques gestured to me, saying I was an Egyptian living in France and Abul Shawareb's partner in the deal. They appeared satisfied, and suddenly jumped to their feet and offered me their hands to shake all over again. To try and win me over to their side, they launched into a friendly conversation about the long and deep friendship between the Indian prime minister, Jawaharlal Nehru, and Egyptian President Nasser. We spoke of the Bandung Conference and the war of 1973.

Abul Shawareb was losing patience with this 'empty talk,' and wanted to 'talk business' and 'get down to brass tacks.' He produced the list of orders they had given him: with the interpretation of Jacques, he pointed to each item and its wholesale price, the trio exchanging glances and nodding, seeming to like the prices.

Their leader, Kumar, said with all his strength, "We're agreed," despite Abul Shawareb's truly inflated profit margin.

I was mystified. Who were these people? Did such simple businessmen exist? Or was there something fishy about the whole business?

When the talk turned to delivery schedules, they insisted on a delivery date no later than two months from today. We agreed. Abul Shawareb, leaning back, then asked for a down payment of two hundred thousand francs. Kumar looked at him, looked away for a moment, then back, giving me to think that he felt it was too much. Finally, he said, articulating his words precisely, "Two hundred thousand?"

Abul Shawareb looked at me, then at Jacques, pulled out a cigarette, and lit it. Then he took a puff, then another, and another. The poor fellow suffered from the misconception that this delay was a crafty business tactic. Finally, he raised a forefinger, saying, "Yes, two hundred thousand, and not a franc less."

Kumar smiled, pulled out his checkbook, and signed a check for a million francs. "Cash the check first, so you can be sure that our money is ready. We don't want a receipt or anything to prove you have taken the money; we are people whose watchword is 'Trust your partners, and put your faith in God.'"

We all gaped at him. The other two Indians watched silently, giving no indication of pleasure or displeasure.

What was apparent only to me was that they were gauging our reactions, waiting to see how appreciative we would prove of their elder Kumar's gesture. Abul Shawareb, trying to return goodwill for goodwill, so as to appear as respectable a businessman as Kumar, assumed an air of friendliness and courtesy. He frowned, saying that this was too much, and that a hundred thousand as a down payment was sufficient. He turned his face away from the check. At this point, Kumar placed a hand over the check and took it away, asking him if he was serious. Abul Shawareb immediately took it back when Jacques kicked him under the table.

We took the check. Abul Shawareb could barely contain his joy and placed it in his wallet, muttering under his breath. I think he was reciting the Fatiha. I, too, was reciting it in my head. The Indians, like us, were absorbed in reciting their own charms, muttering with their hands on their chests. Jacques stared at us in astonishment, as though watching a handful of madmen.

The check was made out to the Société Générale Bank, and as luck would have it, to our usual branch. We thought this augured well; we had no idea, back then, that it was a deliberate plot by the Indians.

The next day found us at the gates of the bank; we went to the businessmen's counter, and met our usual teller François. In minutes, we had done the task and received the money. Before we left the teller, Abul Shawareb motioned to me to keep an eye on the bag with the money in it, while he tried a ruse on the teller. He tilted his head sideways, putting a hand into his jacket pocket, blurting, "Just a moment, Monsieur François!" Then he asked if Kumar's account would allow him to withdraw another check for the sum of four million francs.

The man looked impassively at the computer screen. "Show me the check."

"Hold on . . . just a minute," said Abul Shawareb, still rummaging through his jacket pockets, then his pants pockets, then through his wallet in search of the imaginary check. He huffed, cursing his haste and forgetfulness. To reinforce his ruse, he roundly rebuked me for having distracted him with trivialities back at the office, making him forget the more substantial check. I played along, apologizing. François bought it and said: "Not to worry, the account is still solvent for that sum."

We sighed in relief: that was all we wanted to know.

We exited the branch, a million in hand, Abul Shawareb puffed up with pride. "This is good, isn't it? We bamboozled our friend François, and now we know they're all set to pay up. The main thing is to get them the stock now, get our money, and expand our business." As we passed through the door, he said, "I told you! We've struck gold! As the saying goes, this is the blessing of our mothers' prayers." Overcome with lust for profits and proceeds, I listened as he said, "So, what do you say now, partner? Will you stay, or are you still hankering after your venture over there?"

"Egypt?" I said, my sister Leila suddenly on my mind. I was angry at myself. She had wanted me for something important. How could I have forgotten? I should have called her back immediately, not now, when a week had passed.

I crossed the street in a hurry, making a beeline to a pay phone. "Where are you going, man?" called Abul Shawareb. "Hey!"

Leila's sad tones informed me that Uncle Ibrahim had passed away. Nearly crying, but containing herself, she said, "Two days before he died, he sent for me. I kept thinking, 'Should I go or should I stay?' I kept on like that until my aunt Hanem came and told me, 'He's in a bad way, you have to go to him.' That's what she said. . . ."

I knew my sister Leila: she would talk all day. "Leila. Long-distance line, cut to the chase."

"The chase? I'm coming to it; I'm coming to it. So there he was, lying in his bed, all of them around him. He reached out and gave me a bagful of money and said, 'Count it, niece.' I counted, and counted, and all of them scowling. Then I said, 'This is twenty thousand pounds, Uncle Ibrahim.' And there the bag lay in front of me, and me not knowing whether what was in it was mine or somebody else's. Then he said, 'I know it's not enough, not nearly enough to count as compensation. Count them as a goodwill gift, and forgive me.' I—"

The line cut off, of course. I called back.

"I nodded, thinking to myself 'I forgive you.' He said, 'I want to hear it.' I repeated it, over and over, and I said it at the top of my lungs: 'I forgive you! I forgive you!' He asked, 'Is it from the heart?' I said, 'By this illness and this trouble, I forgive you.' And—"

"Did you take the money?"

"Take it! Of course I took it, you didn't think I'd leave it, do you? And I ran straight home." She laughed. "Then, a couple of days later, I bought a cow and a bull, and sent them over to Imam's to have him raise them for me. And I had the house painted, and there's still a few thousand left over." The emotion crept back into her voice. "He asked after you, Galal. He said, 'He's my nephew, after all, and you can't separate the fingernail from the flesh, as they say, blood is thicker than water.'"

"But how shall I get my inheritance?" I asked.

"You don't think I'd forget you, do I? After the wake, I brought it up with your cousin Farid. He said to me, 'When he comes back safely, then we'll see.'"

I hung up, feeling much like Leila: grieved and joyous all at once.

32

NOT TWO DAYS LATER, AN ad appeared in *Le Monde* announcing that Kumar Ramadas Bros., based in Calcutta, was desirous of importing a consignment of French jackasses for heavy lifting, and tenders were invited. The phone number in the ad was the same as the one we used for Kumar; the same name, Kumar Ramadas.

Abul Shawareb and I looked at each other. We said to each other, in the same breath, "It's them! It's them! Quick, let's get in, before anyone else beats us to this deal!"

We met them again, with Jacques. The same tobacco, the same pipes, the same beards and mustaches. They did not wear coats and suits this time, but came in casual attire, jeans and running shoes. I was puzzled, wondering where Kumar's spectacles had gone. How could he read the figures on the document in that tiny print without his glasses?

Abul Shawareb took the opportunity to assure them that he was capable of procuring what they required: not only jackasses, for this was an easy task, but also any rare or prized breed of cat, dog, or fish; goat's cheese, if they wanted; or even, as they say, sparrow's milk. He could also provide them, he said, with nails, screws, Michelin tires, spare parts for Renaults and Peugeots, and everything in the great land of Gaul, from a needle to a rocket.

I was a little abashed by all this hyperbole. Jacques interrupted him several times, urging him to cut it short and get to the point. Kumar nodded every minute, without showing us his reactions: his eyes were well hidden by his Ray-Bans, while he could see our faces clearly. When he had had quite enough of Abul Shawareb's yarns, he tapped the table, saying that he was waiting for the result of the clothing deal he had already made a down payment on, and that he viewed this as a first deal and something of a test: if we proved our worth, and delivered the goods on time and according to specification, he promised that the deal for the beasts of burden would be ours as well.

Silence reigned, followed by Kumar scratching his forehead. He then huddled with his colleagues, and they conversed in their native tongue. It was a short conversation, yet there appeared to be some conflict. As we understood it, they yielded to his counsel: he surprised us by pulling out his checkbook, and writing us out another check for half a million. Abul Shawareb and I both thought this to be a new installment on the clothing deal, and waited for him to explain, but he was busy murmuring some more charms. He looked up at us. "You're good people to deal with," he said. "It's a pleasure doing business with you. We came across the sea thinking we might be unlucky, and fall prey to merciless businessmen, but God has answered our mothers' prayers, and the women and elderly folk who gave us their money to invest." He let out a comfortable sigh. "I've discussed the matter with my colleagues, as you just heard, and they have agreed to give you the contract for the jackasses. This check, Mr. Shawareb, is not for the old deal, but for the new one. Take it as a down payment.

"From now on," continued Kumar, "I shan't deal with anyone else. With all confidence, I can say, I have honorable brothers in this land."

Abul Shawareb was holding the check in two fingers in disbelief. I couldn't believe it myself. Jacques was punching the buttons on his calculator to see what his commission would be on this new deal. Kumar seemed to notice that Abul Shawareb was the decision-maker, and that I was a mere makeweight, of no real importance. Accordingly, he pulled Abul Shawareb aside, talking to him about life in general, while Jacques interpreted. When they went on for too long, he wearied, and began to skimp, translating only one sentence out of every three.

Eventually, they were done. When they had gone, we gave thanks for this check that had come at just the right time; Jacques was still there, refusing to leave, and asking after his commission on the mule deal; Abul Shawareb and I responded together, "Have some manners, man! We're not going anywhere, and this deal with the jackasses is nothing but talk, as yet."

What French beasts of burden had to do with Brother Leithi's fruit and vegetables, I have no idea; be that as it may, I thought of him during the session with the Indians. I remembered the day I had gone through the gates of the Rod al-Farag marketplace in search of him. The way he had exhaled smoke from his mouth as he said he had nothing against becoming partners with me in selling produce, but that he only traded in traditionally grown produce without hormones or artificial stimulants. The smell of the profits I expected from these Indians had encouraged me, it seemed. "Why not start gathering information about the state of the market here?" I said to myself. "It will be useful when I start the venture."

I left Abul Shawareb and Jacques and hurried home to see Sheikh Munji: it was his day off, and he had promised to help me with the project. He didn't disappoint, and immediately telephoned a tradesman of Moroccan origin, by the name of Sheikh Bu-Miknas. We headed off to the wholesale produce market to see him.

He was certainly an impressive figure: a sight, as the saying goes, to fill the eyes. From his cashmere coat and Cartier sunglasses to his Clarks shoes, he looked more like a jeweler than a produce salesman. He had a large store on one floor, with an attic above. Crates were stacked around: oranges, tangerines, kiwi, zucchini, peas, and other evidence of nature's bounty of every conceivable type: free-farmed, greenhouse, hybrid, and still full of grime and looking just as God had created it. The floor was immaculate: no rotten produce, not a stalk of arugula, no onions and garlic fallen from their sacks, no spittle, no paper littering the floor, no insects wandering about. A man sat at a computer set up on a wooden table, calculating what came in and out, expenditures and profits. The market was crowded with various scents, noises, and people rushing about and arguing. Occasionally, an argument would develop into a quarrel, and curses would be exchanged. In the pathways, carts came and went, laden with fruit: dates, pomegranates, quinces, and more cartons and crates than the eye could see. It was as though all the food in the entire world had come together in this place.

The man greeted us warmly, and showed us to two seats against a wall upon which hung a portrait of King Hassan in Moroccan national costume. He offered each of us a glass of milk with dates chopped into it, the customary welcome drink of Moroccans. When we had finished these, he followed up with green tea. Before we started our talk, Sheikh Munji pointed at me and started singing my praises. "Listen to me, Sheikh Bu-Miknas. This man is like a son to me. He was married to my daughter Khadija, may she rest in peace. Please do help him—if you do him a favor, it's like you're helping me personally."

The man tapped his white cap. "I shall carry him upon my head," he said, in the old-fashioned phrase, meaning he would hold me in high esteem.

I poured out what I was thinking of doing and launched into an explanation of the project I had in mind: of planting my country's earth with vegetables and fruit for export to France, and of needing an importer, who I hoped might be he. If he was amenable to the idea, I hoped he would give me information as to the requirements and criteria for produce in France, as well as what sold well, so I might benefit from his experience before I set to planting and exporting.

"Advise him, Bu-Miknas," Sheikh Munji chimed in, "Give him the benefit of your advice, bless you."

I spent nearly an hour explaining to the man, and suddenly noticed that my enthusiasm had led me into the trap of repeating myself: I was saying the same things I had said before in the same words and even the same phrasing. The man had infinite patience and was still politely listening. When he was sure that I had nothing to add, he finally spoke: "Do what you want, my boy, but don't forget that Egyptians are notorious for making a hash of the produce business. I've seen many of them crash and burn, and I don't want you to be one of them." For Munji's sake, he said that his store would be the first to buy my wares. He leaned in to me, giving me advice about proper packaging, and that the produce should be fresh, and as uniform in size as possible. "And if you really want to stand out, you need to provide produce completely free of any artificial additives, just water and fertilizer. Not just any fertilizer, but natural fertilizer made from dung: that kind of produce is highly prized here. It's always in demand in the best restaurants and in five-star hotels." He gave me a sheet with his contact information, and how to contact him as an importer.

33

WE ALL MET AT ORLY Airport, to leave for Egypt. Uncle Yaqoub wore a shirt with gold thread at the cuffs, and a suit and tie.

My mother wore jeans and a hat; she listed slightly to the left, as though something were wrong with the leg on that side. The poor woman, no matter how she put on foreign airs and graces, and spoke in a foreign language, was still Camellia: daughter of Zaki al-Azra, who saved his pennies, the girl who used to go to the grocer's, the butcher's, and the spice store, and every Saturday to Cinema Misr on al-Geish Street, or to Madame Rathle who taught her crochet. Her head, beneath the foreign-style hat, was still largely stuffed with the words of Umm Hassan and Umm Nabil, and those of Safiya al-Muhandis, the radio presenter, who had a daily program every morning for housewives.

Next to them stood my aunt Bella's husband, the scoundrel Haroun, with his big proboscis and false teeth. I detested him; he was unpredictable and behaved like a gangster—not a gang boss, but more of a low-ranking crook. He had changed his clothes, trying, the rascal, to improve his image: but try as he might, he looked like nothing so much as a retired criminal.

I was the last to arrive; everyone was surprised to see me in the company of my uncle Shamoun, a suitcase in his hand as well. They greeted him with astonishment. My mother, far from glad to see him, said, "Galal, I get. We said we'd go together. But you, what are you doing here?"

He avoided her and moved closer to Uncle Yaqoub. She dusted off her hands. "Do you think you're still a spring chicken, Shamoun? You need a hospital and doctors, not all this traveling about!"

Ire started to rise on his face. His eyes took in Haroun, sneering at him. Just then, the airport speakers announced that the EgyptAir flight to Cairo would be delayed. Yaqoub and I looked up to check the new takeoff time, while Haroun added fuel to the fire. "Your sister pities you, Abu Labib. She's too kind. She means to tell you that you're a decrepit old wreck. Forget about traveling, there's a good boy."

"Stay away from me, Haroun." Shamoun held up a warning finger. "You of all people, stay out of my business." He turned to Yaqoub. "Did I ask your opinion? Abu Simon. A man misses his country. That same man doesn't ask anyone to pay for his ticket. He doesn't want anyone to cover his expenses there. Does anyone have the right to interfere?"

Yaqoub nodded in agreement, indicating that no blame could attach to him.

"Right, then!" Shamoun stood surprisingly erect as he spoke. "Have this man with you," he motioned to Haroun, "not overstep! And tell your good lady to leave me in peace!"

"His good lady?" my mother muttered. Uncle Yaqoub motioned to her for silence, and said he would buy us all something to drink while we waited for our flight. My uncle hesitated, looking at me; I indicated that it was all right. He walked alongside me, quiet and docile: the poor man saw me as a benefactor, not to say a guardian, since I had paid for his ticket, and took my advice on all matters great and small.

I took my mother aside, asking her not to be so hard on Shamoun. Then I asked her what was wrong with her leg. "What a day that was!" she replied. "I'm glad it's over. The day Simon left—he might even have still been taking his bags down the stairs with Yaqoub—I pulled up a chair and climbed onto it, to take down the picture of that Liliane. I'd just reached out to touch the picture when I simply fell sideways, right off the chair! The frame broke in two. When Yaqoub came back from the airport, he lost his temper, and we had a huge fight."

"What became of the picture?"

She looked around, wary of her husband. "What picture? There's no picture any more. I scratched it and crumpled it up. I told him, 'That's the end of its natural life. Or are you more upset about an old photograph than your wife's sprained ankle?'"

We boarded the plane. They went to the first-class compartment, my uncle and I to the rear of the plane in economy class.

I had brought no book, newspaper, or anything to read. I had been stupid enough to think it an opportunity to chat with my uncle on the way; he let me down, though, and was snoring contentedly before the plane had even left Paris.

When we landed, we looked at each other; my uncle pulled out his cigarettes and lighter. I pointed out that the 'No Smoking' sign was still on; he nodded, putting the lighter back in his pocket, not noticing that the pack of cigarettes had slipped to the floor and landed somewhere beneath his feet.

His face had changed. It was not the same face I had seen in the airport, nor even an hour ago, when he had woken and talked to me about his son Isaac. The change was something to be felt, not described. His face bore a remarkable aura of repose: on second thought, though, I realized it was less repose than an inability to express what he was feeling. It was not the type of peaceful expression that allows one to understand the wearer's feelings, nor even a mysterious type of stillness. It was different, a mixture of this and that, expressive and inexpressive all at once, speaking and silent. I imputed it to his state of mind: he had longed for this moment, yet found it strange at the same time. He might have been worried, even wary. Above all, it was clear to me that his nervous system was not equipped to handle the initial rush of feelings that had over-come him in the moment of his arrival.

I smiled at him before he could do anything; he returned my smile, then looked out the window at a group of airport workers putting up the ladder at the side of the plane. My eyes roved over him. His face, from the side I could see, was worn and pale; his clothing was threadbare and noticeably poorer than those around him; and even his face was unevenly shaven, showing patches of stubble. His whole being was frag-ile and weightless, a man of no importance. There was no way to avoid classing him as anything but a poor unfortunate.

He looked back to me. He raised his eyebrows: I thought it signaled that he was about to say something; he didn't, though. He pulled a comb out of a top pocket, then proceeded to do nothing with it. Turning it over in his hand, he looked at his watch. "What time is it?" he asked, a moment later, "Can we catch the EgyptAir bus to Opera Square, and then catch any-thing going to Daher?"

"EgyptAir discontinued that service years ago," I said. "We'll get a taxi."

"Why a taxi? I want to ride the bus." He jumped to his feet. "Let's go! The passengers are leaving the plane!"

No one had disembarked as yet; the speakers admonished us to remain seated until the doors were open, but everyone was ignoring them and getting their things ready. When my uncle made to get his bag out of the overhead bin, he found that the comb was still in his hand, making it difficult; he stared at it as though it were some strange foreign object. For a moment, he appeared to think about combing his hair, then changed his mind and put it back into his jacket pocket. Remembering his pack of cigarettes, he started to look for it. I pointed to where it lay, under his seat, and he bent and retrieved it.

The gangway was filled with baggage and people. A fat woman, weighing two qintars, got stuck in the middle, the passengers behind her helplessly cursing their bad luck. My uncle achieved the impossible, however: he overtook everyone, while I was still stuck in my seat: a push, then another push, and he was at the head of the queue of economy-class passengers still standing at the stairs, held back until the first-class passengers in the front had disembarked.

At the bottom of the stairs, the rest of our party was already waiting. Haroun, catching sight of my uncle, waved to him from below: "Watch yourself, man! If you're not careful, you'll fall on your face and roll right down those stairs!"

Shamoun gestured at him from above to shut his mouth. My mother, and Yaqoub beside her, looked pensive: when I stepped off the stairs, she hugged me hard, a tear gathering on her lashes. She hugged Shamoun too, and asked him not to be mad at her. Yaqoub shook my hand and my uncle's warmly, as though we had not been together on the same flight; then he took a deep puff of his cigar.

The daylight was just fading; things were just being born inside our hearts.

A plane, with a mighty roar, sped like the wind, preparing for flight. Another was gently descending to earth, people inside looking out of the windows. All around us was movement, and a breeze more gentle than the air conditioning inside the plane. The sunset prayer call. rang out; I instinctively looked about me in search of the nearest minaret. My mother's ears seemed to welcome the sound, as well.

At the same moment, I saw in my mind's eye the minaret next to our house, and my mother telling me that she scheduled my days by the prayer calls! When the afternoon call sounded, it was time to do my homework; no sooner was the evening prayer done than books closed for family dinner; then back to homework. Was she thinking the same thing I was as we stood there?

We only came to when the bus driver sounded the horn; a security officer told us we couldn't stand there and had to get on the bus. We looked around in search of Haroun, but he wasn't there: he had preceded us onto the bus and was fighting with the fat woman over a seat!

We parted at the airport gates. My mother and her husband rented a limousine to take them to Shepheard's Hotel on the Nile; it was his favorite spot, and many was the time he had told me of his childhood and youth there, of the Lycée Français school bus he had always taken on the corner of the old Semiramis Hotel. Haroun was a native of the Birkat al-Rathla district, adjacent to Daher. He made his excuses, as he had a reservation at a boarding house near the railway station.

My uncle and I hurried to Umm Hassan, whom we had notified of our arrival in advance.

34

UMM HASSAN WASN'T AT ALL embarrassed to stay in the apartment with my uncle Shamoun. With welcoming delight, she said, "Shamoun's no stranger! Shamoun is like a son to me, or a younger brother!" She sighed deeply. "Where are the days when he used to go to the Khedive Ismail School, or when he got his high-school degree, and his mother, God forgive her, Sitt Yvonne, would have it no other way but that she'd hire a band and have a celebration on the roof! And Amm Zaki, may he rest in peace, wonderful man!"

Uncle Shamoun sat on the couch, suitcase still at his feet, his face showing pleasure at her words. After a few moments, his eyes went to my grandfather's room. The door was slightly ajar, just a crack. His eyes leapt into that opening, even though the room was dark and he could see nothing from where he sat. He tried again, craning his neck forward: with this motion, our eyes met. Umm Hassan smeared a tiny amount of ambergris on a match head, which she subsequently stirred into our tea. Shamoun seemed unable to control himself: his eyes seemed ready to sacrifice all future sight for a glimpse of his father's room or a touch of one of the things inside it.

A street vendor's call floated up to us from the window. A woman on a balcony nearby yelled to him to hold up. My uncle's eyes bugged out at the sight of the sewing machine: he might have been seeing his mother, Sitt Yvonne, sitting at it in her house gallabiya, bending to bite off a thread with her teeth, or to run the hem of a dress beneath its needle. His gaze moved upward, to her photograph on the wall, the one where my aunt Bella stood next to her in school uniform. He rubbed his knee: "I remember this photo so well!" His voice lowered. "Like it was yesterday." His eyes roved over us, voice changing with emotion as he spoke. "Darwish, the photographer, had just opened up his shop. Mama was going to have her picture taken when Bella met her on her way home from school and just insisted on coming with her! I was playing ball in the street, and I said, 'Where are you going? I want to come along.' Mama said to me, 'Come where, all covered with dust like that, like a street sweeper? Go play ball or go mind your goalposts! The other team might score!' That was what she said."

"You're so right, brother, you're so right!" Umm Hassan said, remembering too. "That was in '35, to be exact. We moved into the building in '33, and Darwish Effendi opened up shop two years later." She added, her voice softening, "You know, I miss Bella. How's she doing now with Haroun?"

We both said, "They're doing fine."

She asked after my mother, and we said that she, too, was fine; neither of us wanted to volunteer the information that my mother was here in Cairo, lest Umm Hassan take offense that she had not stopped by to say hello. We decided to leave it to chance, especially as we knew nothing of my mother's plans and whether or not she was going to visit.

Days passed. Umm Hassan, old as she was, came and went, cleaning and tidying the apartment, cooking for us and doing our laundry.

She had added a few layers to her clothing: her hair was covered with a veil or scarf day and night, although she had not been so careful of this when she and I had been alone in the apartment. She also wore socks all the time, and she didn't roll up her sleeves when cooking or cleaning: her cuffs were always buttoned now. She always cleared her throat before coming into the room where we sat; nor did she bathe, wash her hair, or raise a foot into the sink for ablutions, unless she had taken a thousand precautions beforehand to safeguard her privacy. She stayed on in my mother's old room while my uncle and I shared the bed in my grandfather's.

I had thought that sleep might elude him the first night, since many people are unable to sleep in a strange bed; he proved me wrong, though, appearing comfortable in this new place. He dropped off at once. This proved a curse. No sooner did I close my eyes then he took to snoring and kicking about. Once, talking in his sleep, he cursed Haroun loudly.

We left it to him to choose the menu. One day he would ask for mulukhiya with chicken; the next, boiled meat with fattah, made with vinegar and garlic; in addition, he would request Oriental sweets such as lukma, kunafa, baklava, and other heavy and unhealthy fare. Umm Hassan was always obliging, crying out "Of course! Whatever you want! Your wish is my command!"

After he had eaten everything on the table, she would bring him a pot of coffee or a great mug of tea. Hand on my heart, I would pray daily, "Please let him survive this meal!" My uncle was riddled with disease, and the French doctors had strictly forbidden him to eat anything but breadsticks, boiled vegetables, and four spoonfuls of rice only at each meal; if he absolutely insisted on meat, they said, then the smallest of chicken breasts every other day.

Meanwhile, I would leave the house for half the day, returning to find him and Umm Hassan sitting on the balcony, or sitting on the floor on the sofa cushions, deep in conversation about the Turkish cheese that had been sold at Khawaga Kafouris', and gossiping about the day the policemen and the officers had come in their tarbooshes and surrounded Sakhawi's house and found two pieces of hashish in that girl Enayat's closet. And how about the Sayyid Galal hospital? It had started out as a two-room clinic and was now blessed with a five-story building.

I stared at him, sitting there in his pajamas, the pack of Cleopatra cigarettes before him, alongside bagfuls of sunflower seeds and peanuts, or coming out of the bathroom, the popular magazine *Akher Sa'a* or the newspaper *Akhbar al-Youm* in hand. "Isn't this man, born and raised, kneaded and baked in the alleyways of Daher, properly at home now?" I thought. "Or is he, as the papers and files say, merely a stranger, soon to return whence he has come, his stay in this land counted by days? If something happens to him or because of him, must we turn to the French consul? For what a difference between our truth, and the 'facts' of the passport officials."

35

ABUL SAAD STARTED COMING TO visit. He and my uncle had been friends; I found out later that they had been corresponding, albeit sparingly, and Abul Saad had even sent him some books from the Iqraa series and some novels published by Dar al-Hilal. My uncle, on the other hand, had only sent him two parcels: one with makeup for his daughter Hadeel and another with a reference book on agriculture, also for Hadeel. Now, they spent most of their time in each other's company.

They would disappear all of a sudden, then saunter back, saying they had been to Hussein, and had "slammed down a proper meal of calf trotters" at al-Ahd al-Gadid Restaurant, then walked through the old quarter of al-Ghouri, through the old al-Metwalli Gate, which in ancient times had been one of the four portals of Cairo, and then on to al-Khalig Street. Other times, they'd tell us that they'd been taking a walk downtown. Sometimes they wouldn't tell us where they had been. They would often sit together in Abul Saad Effendi's sitting room, listening to taped recordings of Mohamed Abd al-Wahhab, my uncle's dreamy eyes taking him back to the good old days as Abd al-Wahhab sang: "When evening comes, the scattered stars do shine / Across the sky, then ask the night, which of the stars is mine."

They dreamed along with him as he sang: "Gallop, gallop, gallop! Take me to where my sweetheart is waiting!"

I had a suspicion that Abul Saad, who chose the music, was turning everything he heard to his old romance with Aunt Bella. If I could have seen inside his head and gone where his imagination soared, I would probably have seen her posing for him in her dress with the spaghetti straps, or perhaps in his dreams the naughty fellow had gotten her alone in a side street and was even now planting a kiss on her lips! My suspicions were confirmed when he got up to put on another tape, and Abd al-Wahhab sang, "Oh love, traveling far away, leaving me all alone! Why go far away, why make me think of you? My tears tell of my love. . . ."

The poor man's memories must have been all stirred up; I could sense his disappointment, and his frustration, every time he looked at his wife, Sitt Nazira with her squat body, coming and going carrying trays of sweets and tea with milk.

Hadeel came in to say hello to my uncle Shamoun; she shook his hand, then mine. I'm not sure which of us started pressing the other's hand: I think it was she, and I went along. Sitt Nazira, at the kitchen sink, was blissfully oblivious to both her daughter and husband.

One day, I accompanied my uncle to the street they called Jews' Alley, a narrow shopping passageway where most of the stores had been Jewish-owned. He wanted to say hello to an old Jewish friend called Hazzan, who still kept a store there. 'Why not?' I thought, and we went in by way of the crowded shopping street of Moski.

It wasn't an alley, as the name suggested, but a maze. Its spinal column was a tiny, insignificant passageway, from which other alleys, footpaths, and passageways branched out and intersected. The whole of this, small and large paths alike, was known as Jews' Alley; alley by name, labyrinth in reality! Each of these alleys—the spine and its tributaries—was shaped like a snake with its tail in its mouth, the end the same as its beginning! Any unsuspecting pedestrian trying to navigate the area according to the rules of familiar streets was deluded, making himself a willing victim. For no sooner did you think you had arrived than you found your poor duped self at the starting point once more. In this fashion you kept looping until you arrived—either at your destination or back where you started!

As for the breadth or width of the streets, please, don't even ask. The most capacious of these passageways was barely enough to accommodate three people, and they would need to crowd almost shoulder-by-shoulder. It might possibly be wide enough to accommodate a Honda or Suzuki mini-truck, the type specially designed for tight spaces, or a motorcycle with a goods platform attached, the type we call a tricycle. The narrowest was barely enough to allow two people at the same time; the houses set so close together that their inhabitants could converse while at their windows, or even from the comfort of their beds! They were close enough for neighbors to reach out and easily shake hands through the windows.

Shops, shops, nothing but shops. The big ones were the size of your hand, wares arranged in stacks like soap at the grocery store. Some sold nails and screws, some children's clothing and toys; needles, thread, and other tools for sewing and embroidery; soap and bath things. People came and went, pressed close together, while vendors spread their wares on the ground. There were workshops making chandeliers, warehouses, accessories, and all manner of small stores.

Three old landmarks still bore Hebrew inscriptions and a Star of David. I asked a passer-by if there was still a store that sold silverware and jewelry. For some reason, my uncle shrank back, retreating several paces. The man answered, pointing, "You mean Hazzan's? You'll find it over there, at the top of Qarabin Alley."

We looked at each other, unmoving, allowing the man to think what he would of our hesitation. He probably thought we were shady characters, especially my uncle, who was so apprehensive and nervous that he really did look quite suspicious. "Go on, don't be nervous. Amm Hazzam is a good man: he doesn't overcharge and he has tons of customers."

We finally headed in that direction, the busybody still calling instructions after us.

36

No sooner had my uncle and Amm Hazzan laid eyes on each other than they launched themselves into each other's arms in a tearful embrace. So keen was he on giving us a proper welcome that he led us through streets and passageways to a sitting area set out in a blind alley. It was just a place to sit, not a café nor even a smoking corner. An old woman sat on the ground, making cups of tea on an iron cooking ring, supplied with gas by means of a length of tubing attached to a butane-gas cylinder. Next to her was a bucket of water, in which she dunked the cups and pulled them out again, by way of washing. Three glass jars sat in her lap: one held sugar, the other two coffee and tea. The sugar spoons were strewn all about on the ground. However, in the interests of hygiene, the old woman did, I must admit, wipe them on the hem of her gallabiya before each use.

All this took place in a small courtyard outside the doorstep of a building. From one of its windows a woman sat, gaping at us. Of her face I can only say: God help us! She stared incessantly at everyone who sat there. There were some bricks set out to serve as seats, and two wooden chairs, which we avoided, as they bore the ravages of time and looked about to collapse at any moment; I doubt that anyone who sat on them would escape a nasty fall. Why the old woman kept them, I had no clue. Perhaps they served her as some form of prestige or as window dressing.

When we were comfortably settled on our seats of brick, Amm Hazzam inspected me, asking my uncle warily, "Is the gentleman . . . ?" He didn't finish.

My uncle, taking his meaning, said, "Not exactly. He's one of us, but the seed isn't." He patted my knee, saying, "He's Galal, my sister's boy. But his papa is Muslim. Been resting in peace for years now."

I was astonished that my uncle, after all these years, during which I had prayed, and fasted, and married, and divorced all according to Islam—and the Hanafi School at that—still counted me as one of them! Angered, I bit my lip, looking away, but I didn't overthink it: he was my uncle, my kind uncle. I doubted he meant anything by it; it was just words, hot air. I let it go, telling myself I was just being oversensitive, as I had been before with Mademoiselle Jeannette, taking her joke about camels as a personal insult. However, I couldn't quite help looking at him in disbelief.

Because he hadn't meant anything, he didn't interpret the glance the way I intended; he must have thought me upset by this odd brick-seat excuse for a café, as he said, "Sorry, Galal, about all this!"

"It's all right," I said shortly.

"So Mr. Galal is your nephew?" said Amm Hazzan. "Yes, yes, I remember! Isn't he Bella's boy, the one whose father died in '56?"

My uncle nodded: "Yes, yes, that's right. Only it was Camellia, not Bella."

"Camellia?—Oh!" Then he gave a "hmm" as he remembered. "And how's Bella?" he said eagerly. It sounded as though he too had a special fondness for her, for he started to talk about her, and it appeared he was about to wax indiscreet, but stammered and got himself under control. My uncle told him, rather shortly, that she was fine and doing well.

I was astonished at this aunt of mine, who had everyone's tongue wagging! Hazzan was saying to my uncle, his eyes on me, "Oh, Shamoun! How many of our girls married Muslims! Some stayed Jewish, some converted." He looked at me again. "Their kids, bless 'em, are all doing well. Living in the wide world: lawyers, engineers, and doctors." He turned to me: "What do you do, then, young Galal?"

I hesitated. "I own my own business."

"Business?" He shook his head in disbelief.

Meanwhile, he took a last drag on his cigarette, talking with my uncle about what was left of the Egyptian Jews. "Some here, some in Alexandria, and a handful in Mansoura—not three hundred and fifty, all told. Most of them are either old, or ill." My uncle listened avidly, curious as to what had become of the people who shared his faith. "This thing is driving us crazy, Shamoun. And the young men can't find girls to marry. My son Khaled got out of the predicament by the skin of his teeth, managed to find a girl from Alexandria. The second boy's the problem! The youngest bride we can find for him is over sixty." Suddenly, he said, "I wish you hadn't left, Shamoun. What good did it do you?"

He called for three more cups of tea. "I really couldn't," I said. To tell the truth, that last cup of tea had been so disgusting I was thinking of giving up tea altogether.

Hazzan wasn't finished talking, not by a long shot. "I don't mean the Ashkenazi; they think they're better than everybody. I'm talking about the Karaites, the modest folk like you and me, Shamoun. No sooner had you left than we heard all kinds of heartbreaking stories—the first was about Amm Zaki, may he rest in peace. I heard he got sick and miserable and never quit complaining about being away from home till the day he died. Is that true, Shamoun?" Grief appeared on my uncle's face: I could tell he didn't want to talk about this. "And you, Shamoun! Look at yourself! Worn, and ill, and looking ten years older than you are. If you would just tell me why you left?"

My uncle looked down unhappily. Hazzan continued, relentless. "You don't somehow think that that foreign passport makes you a foreigner, do you?"

"A foreigner?" my uncle muttered. "Foreigner. What garbage."

I cut in, trying to lighten the mood. "Ease up on him, Amm Hazzan! My uncle's an Egyptian through and through. He talks like an Egyptian; his blood's Egyptian. He even thinks in Egyptian when he's abroad, and that's landed him in trouble lots of times!"

"If that's the way he is, then why did he leave Egypt? He had a respectable job in the government. He was the boss, with salespeople at his beck and call. He had an apartment, his own car, and his kids were schooled for free. And he knew everyone; he had friends." He pointed out a passing man in a long-sleeved vest and breeches, pushing a cart piled high with cartons full of things he was selling. "That man over there, or that woman walking with a bunch of kids in tow, and that one standing in front of his shop, the one opening a pack of Cleopatras—what difference is there between us and them? We walk the same streets, ride the same bus; our kids get the same degrees, we read the same newspapers: we share what makes us happy and what makes us sad."

He took a sip of his tea. "That's why I didn't leave. Where would I go? It's all I know." His voice lowered, as though he were talking to himself, not to us. "I put up with the ill-treatment from the men of the revolution, and from the Jewish bunch who turned Zionist and started saying Israel this and Israel that. Those revolution officials wanted to make it so hard for us that we'd have to leave, but they wanted to make it seem like our choice. And the Zionists were worse, trying to make Israel seem attractive, saying it was the promised land, and good things await you there, and come on, come on, sell your assets and put your name on the list." He leaned back, spreading his hands: "I was blessed with an ear of clay and an ear of dough! Neither the first ones nor the second managed to have any effect on me."

He looked at my uncle. "I don't know about the others. The ones who packed up and rushed off."

Hazzan's words were bitter. I tried to distract him from his rebukes of my uncle. "Didn't you ever think of leaving, too, and going to Israel?"

"Me?" He gave a derisive smile. "If I'd wanted to go, I'd have gone in my youth. You come to ask now, nephew?" His face reddened. "What exactly are you driving at?"

"I don't mean anything! It's talk, just talk."

"Oh. Right."

He looked at my uncle, who appeared to be nodding off. Hazzan pulled a sheet of paper out of his pocket, looking at the numbers on it, counting something or other on his fingers, as if I weren't there.

My eyes went to the woman at the window who had been watching us for an hour straight. She appeared to have no cooking, cleaning, or housework to occupy her time. She was cracking sunflower seeds in her teeth and spitting the shells out the window; they fluttered down to land on the gallabiya of another man sitting there, who appeared not to notice.

Amm Hazzam put the paper back in his pocket and yawned. "The people I admire the most are the Arabs who stayed in Israel after the partition in '48. They never left their homes nor their land, and the Zionists can't do jack about them now."

"You're absolutely right," I said, and started talking with him on the subject. At the end of it, he looked at my uncle.

"We're the idiots, I'll tell you that much," he said. I tried to interrupt, but he wouldn't let me. "I know, I know what you're going to say. It's not just us, those poor guys in Palestine who were driven out of their country. Maybe if all of us had held on to our land and our homes, the world would have been different."

My uncle's eyes opened. The rest of his tea sat at the bottom of his cup. He drank it and readied himself for another round of sleep. I patted him lightly on the shoulder, letting him know it was time to go. A boy in trousers and a tattered jersey came and collected our empty glasses, the woman dusting the seed shells from her hands and closing the window. My uncle and I took our leave, while Amm Hazzan—as a matter of course, for he was a good Egyptian host—paid for the drinks.

37

My UNCLE WOKE UP ONE day to find me dressed to go out. I told him I was on the way to my village to pay my respects for my uncle's passing and finalize my inheritance, and that I might spend a night or two there.

"Galal! Breakfast's ready!" called Umm Hassan. The nine o'clock news was blaring from my grandfather's old radio, which was still working. This was followed by a long piece on the president and his achievements during his first term, now drawing to a close.

My uncle leapt out of bed. "Wait, wait! I'll find a hotel to stay in!" he cried out. It went without saying that he couldn't stay alone in the apartment with Umm Hassan.

"I wouldn't dream of it!" said Umm Hassan. "I'll just spend the night at my son Hassan's, or at any of the neighbors'."

"Umm Hassan, don't do any such thing—"

"I shan't be a bad hostess, nor do anything other than my duty to my guests! If you make him leave this apartment, Galal, I shall never speak to you again as long as I live. It shall be a sin for me to speak to you, till Judgment Day."

In the face of such vociferous oaths, I was forced to relent. As she strode toward the door, she called behind her, "And every mealtime, Shamoun, you'll find your meals on a tray at the door! And if you need any washing done, just give it to the boy who brings the tray. Don't you dare hold back out of shyness! We're family! We've broken bread together!"

I was more grateful to her than I could say. I made the journey, finally meeting my sister Leila, who was in mourning. At the door to her house, she said, "We'll go at once. News of your arrival will have spread, and every minute you delay will count against you."

We left, she walking two paces behind me. "Come and walk by me," I said.

"Stay the way we are," she said under her breath, "That's the village custom. People would hold it against us otherwise."

"But what about when we went to the graveyard?"

"Then we were in the fields and it was mostly women. But now we're walking past houses and there are a thousand eyes on us."

I thought no more of her, and let myself think about my grandfather, my father's father. I saw him in my mind's eye, placing me behind him on his mule, on our way back from visiting my father's grave. "Put your arm around me tight so you don't fall!" he said. My arms had been tiny and would not reach all the way around him, but I reached around him as far as I could. "Not like that! Tighter! Tighter!" he warned. "If you don't hold tight, the mule will throw you off her back!"

It wasn't as he had said, of course: the mule had nothing to do with it, and besides, she had been a good-natured animal and knew I was only a child. He was only trying to trick me into giving him a hug.

I thought beatifically of my old grandfather, and felt that I was a child of none other than this place: although I had not grown up here, nor had my seed taken root here, it was enough that it had been shaped among these houses, among these winding streets. Through the streets we walked until we knocked on our uncle's door. The cross-eyed boy, who had played cat-and-mouse with me for so long, opened the door. He recognized me, of course, and seemed programmed to continue our previous encounters. "You want my grandfather Ibrahim?" he said. "He's dead."

I cursed him under my breath, while Leila simply pushed him aside and let us in.

We ascended to the room with the couches. In a few moments, the trio of cousins came in: Sultan, Farid, and al-Shahhat, in woolen gallabiyas and felt caps. The sounds of the Qur'an being recited came to us faintly from inside the house. My uncle's wife arrived, fat and grim-faced, all in black. She sat a distance from us, next to Leila, silent, half-asleep. At least, that was how she seemed: but I soon realized that it was not as I imagined. She was silent, true, but her head and her whole nervous system were at the height of activity, and her eyes, that I had thought sleepy, were roving over each of us in turn without a movement of her head. Whenever I argued with Sultan over something, and he wanted to take a decision, he caught her eye secretly, and she sent him "Yes" and "No" messages in silence.

We started by exchanging condolences. At the request of my uncle's wife, we recited the Fatiha, so that we might banish any ill will, act like God-fearing men, respect our family ties with one another. We all recited it, putting our hands together at the forehead and running them down the sides of our faces afterward, as was the old-fashioned custom. Each of us had his own intentions: Leila and I had put our trust in God, hoping to rise vindicated, with minimal losses. As for them, I imagine they prayed for us to leave naked, or barefoot at the very least.

We eventually got to the point, after a discussion punctuated by periods of silence. The silences, in their turn, were punctuated by the eldest brother, Sultan, clearing his throat. This was no regular cough: it was modulated and meaningful, followed by a string of coughs or perhaps a throat-clearing from their brother Shahhat. As for Farid, the friendly, amiable fellow looked from me to them, and smiled. All of this—even the smiles and the throat-clearing—was dialogue, with my uncle's widow holding the tiller.

I doubt that anything would have gotten done without this old witch's approval and blessing.

We sat haggling until the sunset prayer, circling, maneuvering, attacks and counterattacks. Finally, we agreed that I should sell them my land for a price approaching the market price, in two installments: the first tomorrow or the day after, upon signing of the contract, and the second next year, "may it find us all in good health," when they had sold their harvest. I was unable to get my share in the house, though.

"What about God's law, Sultan?"

"Heavens above, whoever said a word against God's law? It's a large house, cousin, and there's room for everyone. Get your things and come and live here, by all means!"

I remembered Uncle Ibrahim: it had been his favorite phrase. "Live here?"

"Of course! If you want to live with us, then you're most welcome. Just say the word, and we'll build you an apartment above Shahhat's."

Shahhat didn't like this, though. "But Hajj Sultan, the house is barely big enough for us!" I looked at this Shahhat, who they were recommending should be my neighbor. A thick mustache and a face like a highwayman's, his meaty fist resting on a thick staff with a crook handle resting between his legs. It wasn't a walking stick that people used to walk or lean on: this was something else entirely. The accursed thing was lethal: if this criminal were to strike a dog on the head with it, it would be dead before it fell.

I was drawn from my contemplation of the staff by my aunt's shrill voice. "Shut up, Shihta!"—this was her nickname for him—"He's the son of our dearest boy. If only he would!" She turned to me. "But, my dear, if you want that, then we'll need you to leave us about fifty thousand out of the first installment, for the building works." Her voice dropped to a whisper: "Oh, yes. Building works are expensive! They cost money."

Shahhat caught her. "He should pay his share of the foundations, too. Would the apartment have been built on thin air?"

Leila burst out. "What is this, Aunt? After he left them the land, you want him to come live on top of that lousy Shahhat, who goes around head-butting people? And charge him fifty thousand for the privilege, and more for the foundations too?"

Shahhat surged up in rage. His mother silenced him, saying to Leila, "Hush now, girl. Be a peacemaker, and don't add fuel to the fire."

All eyes turned to me. I said, to end the conversation: "We're agreed on the land. As for the house, let me think about it, and I'll get back to you later."

With that, Leila and I left.

38

I SPENT THREE DAYS MORE there, as Leila's guest. When it came
time for me to return, Leila's husband sent for his uncle, who
drove the Toyota truck, and they both insisted that the man
drive me to Cairo, for it was too risky to travel by public trans-
portation carrying all that money.

We set off. The truck flew over an asphalt road filled with
bumps and cracks, tall willows on our left; the ground sloped
gently down from them to the banks of the stream. I thought
of what had happened the day before, when Sultan and
Shahhat had come to see me at Leila's house. Al-Shahhat
was carrying the bag of money; Sultan had the contract in
hand. The coward found it insufficient for me to sign every
page of the contract; he insisted that I also place my thumb-
print below my signature. Even the thought of them irritated
me; I pushed them from my thoughts, alongside Haroun,
who had come to join this irksome pair in my mind. Shooing
them away, I set all annoyances aside and looked forward to
the future.

Overtaken by this feeling, I asked the driver to take me
first to the Rod al-Farag market. I met with Leithi. I told him
of my visit to Paris and my meeting with Sheikh Bu-Miknas,
and the advice he had given me if our produce were to stand
a chance at Parisian wholesalers. Then I told him of what had
taken place in my village, and that I had the cash ready. "I'm
with you," he said simply. "Fifty-fifty."

From Rod al-Farag, I went on to Daher, where I passed by Abul Saad Effendi's first. He was just on his way back from his village, Osim. He took me into the sitting room; Hadeel was with us. I had complete confidence in him and asked him to meet with Hadeel's agricultural-engineer colleague in my stead—the one who had managed to reclaim the twenty feddans he had taken possession of.

"Are the deeds to this land of your friend's clear?" Abul Saad Effendi asked.

"Yes, and the land's registered too," Hadeel affirmed. "No worries on that score."

"In that case, let's go ahead," I said, "and arrange a meeting at some café."

"Café? You can't be serious, Galal! Maybe they do that kind of thing in Paris, but here, you meet in the field itself. Furthermore, I'm calling al-Shahhat and having him come over immediately."

"Al-Shahhat?"

"Yes, al-Shahhat. He's my cousin, and I trust him. He's been working in land all his life. He's the one who can value the land, and tell us how much it's worth." He turned to his daughter enthusiastically. "Where is this land, anyway, Hadeel, kid? And what's your friend's name?"

She appeared embarrassed by him calling her a child. "Really, Dad! Really! We've got company!"

"Company? It's only Galal! Soon you'll be thick as thieves, and there won't need to be any shyness between you!"

"Next Friday," Abul Saad continued, "you come along with us, and I'll call al-Shahhat and find out how we're going to meet. That day at dawn we'll all set off. But where to?"

"A place called Abul Matamir, Dad. The man's called Husam. Here's his number."

I went upstairs, only to get bad news: my uncle Shamoun was sick in bed, Umm Hassan nursing him. I sat on a chair by his bedside. "He's been ill ever since you left," she said. "He only improved a little bit today."

"Bless her, she was with me all through my troubles," said my uncle.

"Has a doctor been in to see him?"

"Of course! I brought the doctor from the clinic by the house. When he examined him, and looked at the medicines Mr. Shamoun brought from abroad, he said he should take the same medicines, no change, just be careful what he eats, and prescribed him bed rest for a week or two." She raised a hand. "The thing is that I wasn't aware of it on the first day, as I was busy with Fouad's funeral."

"Fouad? Nadia's husband?"

"Yes, God rest his soul. We got the news not two hours after you left. Everyone in the building went and got his body from the hospital, and we all prayed for him at the Shaarani Mosque. They held the funeral there, too, for men and women both."

"How's Nadia doing?"

"Nadia?" She stared. "She's up in her apartment, with the neighbors coming to visit all day." Pityingly, she added, "Poor thing, she's never had any luck. She'll be leaving us in a few days, anyway. You see, Sheikh Mustafa al-Subki, her father-in-law, doesn't think she should stay there alone. He gave her a few days to pack her things, then come live with him with her daughter."

"Sheikh Mustafa?" I muttered. "Is she going to do what he says?"

"Well, why not? He's her uncle—her mother's brother—and the girl's grandfather, isn't he?"

The bad news never stopped: in the middle of the night, I got a telephone call from Abul Shawareb.

He was beside himself. He babbled, and cursed, and repeated himself, and cursed again, calling down damnation and ruin on the Indians. "I'll chase them down to the ends of the earth! To Judgment Day!"

He couldn't believe that he, Abul Shawareb, the canny businessman, had been taken for a ride, and was the laughingstock of the business world. Those little scoundrels had led him on and convinced him that everything was fine and dandy, until he had given Kumar the stock and signed the export documents, while they still owed him two million francs.

They had conned him, delaying and delaying, and Kumar had not signed the final check for two million until the cargo flight had left, bearing their merchandise. They had told him to cash the check and meet them that night at the Moulin Rouge to celebrate. Along with the check, Kumar had given him a gold Rolex, "As a token of their friendship, he said, and lifelong partnership. And I believed them!"

When he'd gone to the bank to cash the check, the account had contained four francs. He had rushed to the Rolex dealership, whereupon they had told him it was a copy, albeit a good one. They had done their business, and flown the coop.

"But what became of the other deal?" I asked. "The one with the jackasses?"

"Jackasses?" groaned Abul Shawareb. "We're the jackasses!"

39

NO ONE HAD ANYTHING BAD TO say about Sheikh Mustafa al-Subki. He had loomed large in my life in my early youth: Nadia had often spoken to me of his financial support for her and her mother after her father's death, and that her mother never did a thing without asking him. He was awe-inspiring, with his height, his turban, and the fact that he knew the complete Qur'an by heart. He never stopped saying, "O Lord!" whenever he ascended the stairs of our building on a visit to Nadia and her mother, as was the custom of lower-class people when entering a private residence so as to announce the presence of a stranger, giving its residents time to get dressed or take cover.

I had always thought that this was the man whom I would ask for Nadia's hand in marriage; this only increased my respect for him, and I would stop to greet him warmly. He noticed my enthusiastic welcome, not attributing it, of course, to the purpose I had in mind, which remained unknown to him, and he always nodded and smiled at me. In the days that preceded my departure with my mother, he had taken to looking away when I passed, and I had the feeling that he was silently muttering prayers for God to protect him from me.

This man, without meaning to, was one of the reasons behind my suffering: after my affections for Nadia had come out, and he had found out, he had insisted that Nadia and her mother quit their apartment and come to live with him in

Abbasiya. He would not allow one of his womenfolk to ally herself with the likes of me; he might even have disapproved of the very concept of love, and all that nonsense that people like us clung to. My mother had been pleased by this development: in those days, she had been seeking a means to get me away from Nadia. Sheikh Mustafa had provided it.

As if that weren't enough, he had married her off, against her will, to his son Fouad, who now was no more. Since then, my life had changed, and here he was, taking her from me once again.

I saw him in my mind's eye, frowning; with him came the image of my mother, who had been maneuvering like mad in those days. They flitted past, filling me with resentment and regret, and left.

Umm Hassan came to me as I sat on the couch in the hall. She sat by me, a tray of rice in her lap; she commenced picking over it. I asked her to come upstairs with me so that I could give Nadia my condolences.

"Now there's really no need for that!" she said. "The men paid their respects at the Shaarani Mosque. You were out of town, and that's that."

Overcome with childish ire, I rose to the door. "Then I'll go by myself."

She set the rice aside and put on her veil, looking around for her shoes. Wagging her finger, she caught up with me. "Just quickly, mind! Then we'll come straight back down."

We went upstairs. We were surprised when the door opened to reveal Sheikh Mustafa himself. No sooner did I see him than I took a step backward in shock. I stood there nervously, apprehensive as to his reaction. He, too, seemed surprised to see me, then looked me carefully in the face. I think he was doing his best to search for me in the black books of his memory, while Umm Hassan, who had been dreading just this moment, stood there in embarrassment, coughing and wedging herself between us to force him to look at her. He knew her, and nodded a welcome, then motioned her inside. He ignored me completely.

His staff, and his hand on it, caught my eye. They were in an offensive position. I thought of taking another step back. Prudence dictated constant vigilance and wariness: who was to say, after all, that he would not bring his stick down upon my head? His eyes said that he recognized me: the frown was the same frown as before. I was the uncouth boy who had interfered with his niece, I was the reason they had had to leave the apartment, and here I was, seeing my way clear, knocking on her door without shame.

"It's Mr. Galal," said Umm Hassan in my defense. "He was away and couldn't pay his respects at Shaarani, so he's here to give his condolences." With that, she darted inside.

The man said nothing. He looked me over carefully again, then turned and went into the house, leaving me unsure whether to follow him inside or turn and go back whence I had come.

Finally, I followed him in. We sat there looking at each other for a quarter of an hour in almost complete silence, broken only by routine phrases: "Thank you for your condolences."

"May your sins be forgiven."

"Are you married, then, or single?"

I didn't let him know one way or the other; I gave a motion of my head that could have been interpreted either way.

He pulled a pocket watch from his pocket and looked at it. "Huh. It's time for the sunset prayer already."

I looked at my watch.

I was afraid that, in his resentment of me, he might throw the ashtray at me; so I rose and said my goodbyes. He rose along with me, saying he was on his way to Sheikh Khalaf's prayer nook. "Are you coming, or do you not pray like normal people?"

"Of course I pray!" And I turned and fled.

I never saw Nadia that day, nor again afterward.

*

Nadia was gone. She had gone, leaving behind a discontent with life and a heart that beat in vain.

One day, when I was at the height of my brooding, Umm Hassan pulled a note out of her bra, and handed it to me. It was a scrap of paper, unsigned and undated. It seemed hastily scrawled. But it was in Nadia's familiar handwriting.

> Galal,
> The Nadia you knew doesn't exist any more. Find your-
> self another path. I'm a mother now, all I care about is
> my daughter Reem, and I'm a woman whose husband
> is dearer to her in death than he was in life. Plus, there's
> my uncle Mustafa. Your visit to our apartment made
> him think things, and he's started dropping hints.

I read the note as Umm Hassan said, "What was I to do? I saw you wanting her, and unhappy, so I went upstairs. I thought I'd beg her to say a few words to set your mind at rest, so you could make a decision and do what's best for you."

I asked her to let me keep the letter; she snatched it out of my hand. "She made me swear, anything but that! She made me swear by God Almighty to burn it after you'd read it."

I tried to insist.

"Galal! Would you have me offend God by breaking an oath?" She lit a match, and the paper curled and twisted, blackening in the fire. Pieces of it rose into the air, then fluttered to the floor as ash. What was left, she threw into the ashtray.

I went to see my mother a few days later. I took the elevator to the ninth floor at Shepheard's Hotel, where she and her husband sat overlooking the Nile. Her cheeks were rosier than they had been in Paris; it was the first time I had not smelt smoke on her breath or on her clothing.

234

Uncle Yaqoub was talking about Sitt Amina, who had been the housekeeper at the home of his father, Sarrouf Bey Abul Saad. She was now over eighty-five. "She recognized me as soon as I walked in, and I bent and kissed both her hands." His eyes were dreamy. "Forty years she spent in Papa's house! She kept so many of my secrets—why, she knew more of me than Mama did!" He turned to my mother. "So, what do you think of extending our visit for another week, or fortnight?"

"I'd love that," she said, sounding relieved.

She told me that she and Uncle Yaqoub were leaving tomorrow for Sharm al-Sheikh, and that Uncle Isaac had arrived from Haifa the day before yesterday, and he and Haroun were already there. She asked how Umm Hassan was, and told me she planned to visit her before she went back to Paris. "Not just Umm Hassan. I want to see our street, and our building, too, and roll about on my own bed like old times, and go calling on each and every one of the neighbor women."

She didn't ask how Uncle Shamoun was, not once during my entire visit; for my part, I didn't tell her of his illness.

When I got home, Abul Saad Effendi showed me a map of the land that he had obtained from the Planning Authority; he told me that his consultant, al-Shahhat, had inspected it, and found the soil sandy, suited to growing vegetables and fruit. About half of it was already planted, while the other half was in need of reclamation.

"And if we work hard at it, it will take a little more than six months. But I need you to make me out a power of attorney, and we'll go to the fellow tomorrow and make the down payment."

I did so; two days later, I took my leave of Umm Hassan and Uncle Shamoun, and went to Sharm al-Sheikh, to see what my family was doing there.

40

IT WAS STILL EARLY MORNING. The bus for Sharm al-Sheikh was getting ready to leave Abbasiya. The passengers were chattering, panting under the weight of their luggage, frowning for no reason, and glaring around as though at enemies and not fellow travelers. The driver wore a blue jumpsuit and a cap, yelling orders and bossing everyone around outside the baggage compartment in the bottom of the bus. What made me stare at him, I wasn't sure: it might have been his prominent nose, or the way he lorded it over the porters, the passengers, and everyone there, and his insistence on rearranging the bags for the twentieth time to allow an elderly woman to place a basket and two bundles inside. "What was wrong with him?" I asked myself. "Was all this shouting and screaming to make up for some sense of inferiority, or genuine sympathy for the old lady?"

The passengers finally settled in, and he climbed up to the driver's seat. He seemed to me—not for a moment, but for the entire journey—to be far greater in stature than the seat he occupied. He should have been captain of a battleship or leader of a fleet of tanks. After a few moments, he tapped the microphone and informed everyone that the bus radio was out of order and that only the tape player was working. "To entertain you on your journey, I've brought some tapes with me to play on the way." His voice had the ring of finality that accompanies military announcements.

Nobody noticed, and those who did had nothing to say. Only one man dusted off his hands in exasperation. "Oh, no! I'm always coming and going on this service, and I know this driver well. I know his name, too; it's Abd al-Alim. And believe me, nothing's out of order—he just wants to play old-time songs!"

The sheikh in the neighboring seat adjusted his turban as his neighbor added, "Heaven help us, every time the same story, every time the same songs."

Our driver, Abd al-Alim, slipped the first cassette into the player. The man stared at him, raising a finger to his neighbor. "Now, sir, you're going to listen to 'The Tugboat!'"

The sheikh blinked: "Tugboat?"

As if to corroborate the passenger's words, there were the scratchy sounds of an ancient recording, and then the voice of Mohamed Abd al-Muttalib wafted out of the player. "Cross the canal, tugboat skipper, cross the canal! Talk to us before you cross the canal! It was my grandfather who dug the canal."

The man was fuming, but he took care not to let the driver see him in the rearview mirror.

We only started to eat after we had left the Autostrade: most of the sandwiches were beans and falafel, but some had gone so far as to bring eggplant and spring onions. The ones who had eaten at home took out thermoses and started pouring tea. The man whispered into the sheikh's ear that we were about to listen to "The Pigeons." And so we did. "O Pigeons, flap your wings! Fly, take wing! On the shoulders of free men stand, and pluck the grain from their hands!"

At this point, a group of young men in the rear seats surged up, having reached their limit. They seemed to be barmen, waiters, and entertainers who served the tourists of Sharm al-Sheikh. "We've had enough of this drivel! Here, driver, we've got Michael Jackson and Bryan Adams!" Or anything else, they said, that they listened to with the tourists in Sharm.

The driver pooh-poohed the suggestion. He did, however, rather pointedly, I thought, swap out "The Pigeons" for an Umm Kalthoum tape, in which she sang, "O Weapons, I have missed you! I have missed you in battle! Remain vigilant, for it is a long time since I have waged war!"

I wanted to see outside and double my pleasure, so I opened the curtain at the window. No sooner had I done so than the sun's rays pierced the interior of the bus, falling across my lap and that of my neighbor. Displeased, he informed me the curtain should not be opened all the way.

"Like this?" I asked, returning the curtain to its original position, only opening it a slit; my fellow traveler still didn't like it, for the sunlight skipped my lap, and settled completely on his; some even rose to the top button of his shirt. He looked at me; I looked back. I took pity on him: he was clearly a day laborer, eyes red, face darkened with misery and poverty. I was obliged to pull the curtain completely closed until the sun had set and the light had gone.

Soon he began to yawn, and fell fast asleep. Little by little, sleep gained ground, and this unfortunate fellow began to snore loudly. It was painful to the ear. Also, he murmured and flailed about in his sleep. He seemed to be arguing or fighting with someone in his dream.

Suez appeared before us. The bus then took us into the Shaheed Ahmed Hamdi tunnel. When we came out, the passengers had been struck down by sleep. My neighbor's head fell onto my shoulder every couple of minutes. I pushed him off in self-defense; it escalated into a fight, and I once slapped him in irritation as he snored on. Oddly, he seemed not to notice at all, merely leaning his head back onto me and starting over. I would gladly have strangled him.

Taking advantage of his slumber, I opened the curtain. Sinai lay spread before me: sand dunes on the side of the road, and a winding road, leading to Oyoun Mousa, Ras Sidr, then Abu Zemeima, with its hairpin turns and looming mountains. Far off, we could see Abu Rdeis, and Tor Sinai.

All was empty. Land, horizon, and in between vast emptiness. All was silence, but for the sound of the wind and the occasional horn of a vehicle heading in the opposite direction.

The land was barren of foliage or water; a lone tree stood here and there, scraggly and solitary, no birds on branch or trunk. Litter, old tires, and tin cans were scattered about on the sides of the road. The lighter items, dry sticks, and especially tumbleweeds, were sometimes whipped up by the wind to run alongside the bus, or fly up into the air in little whirlwinds. Grains of sand, fine as flour, would suddenly fill the air, reducing visibility to a few meters, which forced Abd al-Alim, our driver, to slow down and honk his horn to avoid any unpleasant surprises.

The Bedouins, who inhabited this region, were with us: they stared at us travelers. There was an old man in a gallabiya and ugal, a boy herding a few goats, and another man keeping pace with our bus in his Jeep, stirring up a whirlwind of dust. Under a tree, a group of men had built a fire in a kiln improvised of mud and were drinking tea and coffee. They stilled as we drove by, watching until we had passed, then returning to what they were doing. There were children who seemed to have been waiting for the bus, waving madly at us. Some had readied themselves with stones, and threw them at the bus as it passed, while the hardy passengers slept on.

I had heard much about Sinai as a child. At school, they had always promised us a trip to Sinai, where we could see Rafah, Gaza, and al-Arish. "The Ministry of Education demands it," they said, "they want you to see your fellow citizens there. If you don't want to go, you can take the trip south, there's one to Luxor and Aswan."

Sinai had its own charm, and we would have all preferred to go there; but our dream dissipated with the outbreak of war

240

in 1967. When liberation finally came, I had grown too old for the trip. And here I was, surrounded by sleeping strangers, entering Sinai for the first time; not to see its people, as our schoolteachers had said, but to see my own family, there to build a casino!

41

When we arrived in Sharm al-Sheikh, I immediately headed for Neama Bay, to the Helnan Hotel to be precise, where they were staying.

The hotel was bursting with foreigners. These were divided into two kinds: businessmen like my family, and others who had come in shorts and sandals for sun, sand, and sea; some wore their hair in braids or adorned themselves with an earring, carrying copies of *Time* and *Newsweek*.

The fairer sex were as I had always known them: sweet and serious, but their conception of what constituted modest dress differed markedly from ours. I asked at the reception desk about my party, and was told that they had been out since early morning.

It was only with great difficulty that I managed to secure a room. With no view to speak of, it was more like a wooden crate than a room, or a kiosk like the ones that sold cigarettes, tea, and workmen's supplies. Some distance away, built of stone, with a decorated façade, was a boutique selling papyrus and other souvenirs in the style of Ancient Egypt: jewelry, statues, and scarabs, among other things. This seemed to be popular among the hotel guests.

Past this, everything was vacant and empty: vacant lots, fenced in, bearing signs that proclaimed the owner's name, or cement foundations poking out of the ground. It was impossible to tell whether they were for a hotel or a casino. Builders, bearing their equipment and wearing breeches, loitered about, washing their faces at the tap, or lying down for a nap. It was siesta time: time for rest and sleep.

The next morning, I met my family, who took me to the site for the casino, on a road they called Salam Road, still being paved. We spent most of the day there, looking at the girders being placed, and huge trucks dumping loads of sand, stones, and other building supplies. My attention was especially drawn by Isaac and Haroun: they took the most interest in the proceedings and made the most observations. A chair was brought for Uncle Yaqoub, in deference to his age, and my mother continually brought him soft drinks.

We returned. We had rented a four-wheel-drive vehicle for the trip, driven by a garrulous Bedouin; Uncle Yaqoub sat next to him in a safari suit, my mother and I behind them in the center seat, and Uncle Isaac in the back, accompanied by Haroun. They whispered to each other and laughed the whole time.

Haroun broke the silence. "It's still early. We have time to go up the Umm Sayyid Hill today. When I suggested it yesterday, you said you were too tired, and the day before you said it was nighttime and it would be better to visit during the day. Any excuse this time?"

We offered none, and up the hill we went. To my right, on the way up the hill, I saw buildings with several stories and small windows. They didn't look like any style of building I had seen before. Next to these were one-story buildings that looked like the old British-style townhouses built by the Suez Canal Authority, of the type still standing today in Ismailia and Port Said. I only glimpsed them, but everyone else stared at them, especially Haroun. He must have heard about them before; they might have been the reason for his insistence on coming. The driver, noting our interest, slowed down, saying, "They're the houses of your relations. The first were for soldiers; the others for the officers' quarters."

My mother gave a small cough, while Uncle Yaqoub shooed away an imaginary insect from his forehead. His eyes searched for me in the rearview mirror as he said to the driver, "You mean they were residences for Israeli soldiers? Never mind that. They're no relations of ours."

The driver, not understanding, said, "But I thought you were from—"

"No. We're not," Yaqoub cut him off. "And keep your eyes on the road, my good man, it's bumpy and dangerous."

Haroun, the scoundrel, seemed to be enjoying the conversation. He started asking questions, all of which were vastly annoying, the naïve Bedouin answering him, and they talked and talked until he said, "And that's not all, Mr. Haroun! There's still a graveyard for Jewish soldiers near the port, and a synagogue, too."

"A graveyard and a synagogue?"

"And between Taba and Dahab, a monument to the Israeli architect who built this road."

My mother coughed again, trying to change the subject.

"Isaac! Isaac!" Uncle Yaqoub called, sounding at the end of his patience. Isaac seemed to get it, and nudged Haroun, whereupon he finally shut up.

The driver, though, had not gotten the memo, and was still talking. I rapped him on the head with my knuckles, asking him to hold his tongue.

We went for a drive around the plateau, after which we got out of the car to observe Sharm al-Sheikh from above. Uncle Yaqoub stayed in the car, complaining of a headache, while Haroun and Isaac stood aside together. I moved toward the cliff, my mother in her lemon-yellow dress, sunglasses on top of her head, calling to me not to stand so close to the edge.

The view from above was relaxing. Mountains, hills, bays; waves breaking on the shore, their foam lingering as the water receded. The Red Sea lay in a waking dream, all of Sinai in its arms. Above us was an awe-inspiring expanse of sky, a few greyish clouds dotted on the edge of the sky, the ones closest to the sinking sun borrowing its scarlet hues. The island of Tiran was on one side, and on the other, although I could not see it from where I stood, the island of Shadwan. How our hearts had beat listening to the news about it in 1967.

In the midst of this unspoiled wonderland, another world was springing up: roads were being paved and foundations laid for rest houses, hotels, motels, and casinos. Bulldozers frolicked here and there; there was sand, concrete, and iron girders; there were people in workmen's garb filling the place as far as the eye could see.

Haroun hadn't had enough. He insisted on visiting the graveyard and the synagogue, so we went to the port. There it was: a featureless plot, covered with metal plates. A man standing nearby volunteered the information that it had been a funeral home or a sort of morgue for the invading soldiers who died on the land of Sinai. A stone's throw away was a two-story synagogue, with bars over the windows. Both synagogue and the graveyard were nothing but ruins: monuments, nothing more.

Leaving them to go to the old market in Uncle Yaqoub's company to arrange a trip to the desert, what they called here a "camel safari," I felt this place was unworthy of my presence, and took the night bus home. I hoped the driver would be Abd al-Alim, but I found another driver who hugged the steering wheel, with a deep voice and a round face that hid his cunning beneath a mask of stupidity. "Where's Abd al-Alim?" I asked.

"After he drove yesterday's bus here, he fell unconscious. They took him to hospital in an ambulance," he said.

"Dear God!" I said, and climbed into the bus, saying, "God help us. It's you, then, who will take us home."

42

THE ANGEL OF DEATH DESCENDED upon us. He would not leave until he had taken Uncle Shamoun.

We were having dinner, followed by tea. Then, we started watching the movie *Return My Heart*. Umm Hassan was nodding off, then waking, by turns, asking what the aristocrat in the movie had done to Inji and Ali. We had not realized that an uninvited guest had opened our door and was eyeing my uncle, all unseen.

When the film was over, my uncle asked me to buy him a copy, and a copy of *Among the Ruins*. Then he yawned. "This is such good company, and I've got to leave in two days!"

"Stay another week, do!" Umm Hassan entreated him.

"If only I could," he sighed. "My vacation is over. Next year, though, I'll plan for a whole month."

"You'll light up the whole place, and we'll be glad of your company," beamed Umm Hassan. "If God grants me life and health, I'll be waiting." I went into my room for evening prayers, leaving him fumbling with his matchbook and getting ready to light a cigarette.

I never finished my prayers. I ran out to the sound of Umm Hassan screaming, and my uncle slumped over. His cigarette, still alight, had dropped onto the front of his gallabiya. I rushed to him, followed by Umm Hassan with a glass of water. Abul Saad Effendi ran upstairs as well. We screamed, shouted, and turned him over, to no avail; nothing was any use. It hadn't been another attack, which was what we had thought at first. He had simply passed away, as we floundered between grief and hope.

Umm Hassan went inside, weeping as though he had been her own son; Abul Saad and I stared at one another, paralyzed by death. Uncle Shamoun had left us and gone away. Only the flesh, the clay, was with us now.

After we recovered from the shock, Abul Saad pressed my wrist. "God give you strength, Galal! As the proverb says, 'Burying the dead does them honor.'"

I was at a loss. "You mean. . . . "

"Yes, of course, here! Doesn't Amm Zaki have a family grave here?"

Umm Hassan interrupted. "Yes, he does! It's in Basatin. I used to hear Sitt Yvonne say that their grave was shoulder-to-shoulder with Samaan's. If you go and ask after it, you'll find it there."

Abul Saad didn't seem to think these were good enough directions, but he didn't say anything.

"Just get started," he said. "And ask your mother what to do. You said she was here in Egypt, didn't you? As for me, I'll get you the death certificate and permission for burial. Don't worry about the arrangements or finding the grave, I'll take care of that."

Meanwhile, Umm Hassan was staring at me. "Camellia's here? Here where?"

And the interrogation started.

Things went more smoothly than I had expected. The certificate arrived; Abul Saad Effendi got directions to the gravesite; my mother, Amm Yaqoub, and Sarah were perfectly all right with him being buried in Egypt. We didn't consult Haroun or my uncle Isaac.

We held the wake at our apartment. I had wanted to play tapes of the Qur'an, but Abul Saad Effendi protested. "Tapes?

What tapes? Do you want the evening to be a flop? We have to have a reciter!"

"And another for the women's side," Umm Hassan chimed in. "Else they'll set to gabbing, and give me a headache."

I hadn't expected it, but people came flooding in, and Abul Saad Effendi was more or less the man of the hour. He saw everyone in and out and provided them with drinks. When I tried to help, he motioned me to sit where I was and leave him to take care of things. He passed cigarettes around to the mourners, his lips constantly moving as he received condolences in the traditional manner.

As usual, there where whispers everywhere, especially from the older mourners who had known my uncle as a young man. Suddenly, someone would remember a moment with him, and they would whisper the anecdote into the ears of whoever happened to be sitting next to them. Some kept it in, for post-funeral gossip. Some had not known him well, and had come for form's sake or out of curiosity. They could hardly believe what they were seeing: a dead Jew, and a Muslim funeral.

What was annoying, though only at the start of the wake, was the noise coming from Morgan's Café. It was so close that its din pierced our ears. Tonight was not a night like any other; there had been live broadcasts a while ago, for they were inaugurating the president for his second term. Now was the time for songs and anthems. Morgan had strong ties with politicians and insisted that everyone must share his triumph. However, the reciter, bless him, raised his voice to a ringing crescendo, effectively pulling the rug from under Morgan's feet. He was blind, with a moving voice; he paused in exactly the right places. The only thing about him was that he cleared his throat often, and grew miffed if his glass of hot aniseed was late. Abul Saad finally told a boy to stand there exclusively to serve him. He could not stop praising him, and the sheikh searched for the direction the voice was coming from, and nodded gratefully.

Uncle Yaqoub was sitting next to me, and stood to shake hands whenever a group of mourners arrived. That unpleasant Haroun sat opposite us, next to Magdi, Muallim Habib's son. Hardly anyone reached out for a cup of coffee from the tray that was making the rounds. When it was offered to Haroun, he refused it in disgust, and asked for 7-Up. Nonplussed, the server looked around for Abul Saad Effendi, and whispered Haroun's order into his ear. Abul Saad hurried to Haroun and whispered hotly to him, "7-Up indeed! Have you no shame, man?"

He said to me, "He'll be ordering milk pudding, mahallabiya, and ice cream next! He should know only coffee and water are to be served!"

Yaqoub, overhearing, glared at Haroun to have a little self-respect or leave.

There was no shortage of women, either. They came out of respect and affection for Umm Hassan; she received them at her old apartment, a separate sheikh, as per her request, reciting the Qur'an. Everything went normally, except for little things—too-loud murmuring, a woman whispering into her neighbor's ear, another hiding a giggle behind her palm, or incessantly going to and from the bathroom.

Umm Hassan, in control of the occasion, issued polite rebukes or pointed with a finger to the man reciting, indicating that it was our religious duty to listen in silence. Sitt Nazira backed her up, playing the same role that her husband was filling in the men's apartment. Despite her portly figure, she served the women mourners continuously, and supplied the reciter with cup after cup of hot cress-seed tea.

The situation deteriorated only when my mother arrived. Umm Hassan and the neighbor women who still remembered her were stunned, then leapt to greet her. There were hugs and kisses, and tears mingled with declarations of how much she had been missed. There was a scramble as the women each tried to take her by the hand, wanting her to sit by them; but she finally sat by Umm Hassan.

Naturally, the reciter paused in his Qur'an, watching them, dusting off his hands and muttering that, as the Prophet said, women really were "lacking in common and religious sense!"

There was so much of an uproar that even the women who had never so much as heard of my mother before leapt up to greet her, with embraces and kisses. When they returned to their seats, they couldn't wait an instant longer: they had to know everything on the spot, and find out the whole story, from start to finish. Chaos reigned: the women stayed like that for an hour, with nothing and no one to control them, Umm Hassan having abandoned her position at the metaphorical tiller and immersed herself in welcome rituals.

The Qur'an reciter had given up, and sat there watching gloomily, cursing the fate that had landed him among these hopeless women.

43

My MOTHER DIDN'T STAY LONG. After the women had left, she went upstairs to her old apartment, caressing it with her eyes. She even stood staring at the kitchen sink, turning on the tap, then turning it off. The frame with my grandfather Zaki's picture had listed a little to the left; she straightened it with a touch of her fingers.

Before she left, she gathered what traces remained of her. They were insignificant things: a hand mirror; a kohl holder; a wristwatch with no hands, no longer of any use. When she added to these a spectacle case that had belonged to my grandfather, I drew it gently from her hand and set it aside.

There was a black-and-white photograph of us underneath the glass of the dressing table: she in a sleeveless dress, I in her lap. She performed impossible feats in her attempts to get it out, but the photograph refused to budge. Time had welded it irrevocably to the glass, so that they now formed a single unit. At that moment, she seemed to me to be the mother I had known as a boy, not the mother whom the world had led to Uncle Yaqoub and to a foreign country. I almost succumbed to temptation and asked her to stay, but for a glimmer of sense that made me hold my tongue.

When she stood there, saying goodbye, I couldn't control myself. I burst out crying, all at once. Was it our grief at my uncle's death? Our meeting in the apartment of long ago— was I grieving for that lost time? Was it simpler, an outpouring of grief in a moment of parting, that would soon pass? If it was this last, then why the bitterness that filled my weeping? Why was I so unmanned, disappointed, bereft, as if nothing meant anything to me any more? Why was my insistently suspicious heart on the verge of plunging me into a world of what-ifs? "If this had happened, then that would have happened . . . . And if it hadn't been for this, then this wouldn't have been. . . . " I chewed on truths that were immutable, rebelling against them and asking questions that had no answers.

As I wept, I sought refuge in her, not knowing that she was no better off than I. We shared our tears. "It's like time's gone backward," she choked out through her tears. "I can see you crawling on your hands and knees toward me. Your first day of school, going off holding your grandfather Zaki's hand, I on the balcony looking down at you . . ."

We took a step toward the door. Her lip trembled. "Visit your uncle Shamoun. Don't leave him all alone." Her eyes roved over the room. She tried to speak again, but she was crying too hard.

Umm Hassan went to her, trying to comfort her. "That's quite enough of depressing talk! Go join your husband downstairs, do, he's driving us half-deaf with that car horn of his! And you, dear, why are you crying?" She patted me on the shoulder. "Your future will be sweet, God willing. The land you were worried about is in your possession now. Your bride is waiting, just for the asking. Put your trust in God, and give it to Him."

My mother told me she was going to leave tomorrow morning for Paris. "Are you going to join me?"

In a low voice, I said, "If God wills it."

"Leaving again!" Umm Hassan remonstrated. "What about your business here?"

To please her, too, I said, "If God wills it."

I tried to walk my mother to the car, but she wouldn't let me, not wanting her husband to see me crying.

She took a step down the stairs. Then she turned back and said, in the old-fashioned way, "Health and success while we're apart."

We watched her from the balcony. Night had fallen and the street was almost silent, save for a lone passer-by and a shadowy figure leaving his house in the distance. A car passed, then another. The third car was my mother's. She waved to us out of the car window. The car drove down the street and disappeared into the distance, her hand still waving goodbye.

The shops were closed. Hilal, the spice shop boy, stepped on the lock of the sliding metal door of the store until it clicked. Hassan stood by him, stretching and yawning. He took the keys from the boy. Morgan's Café was the only place that remained open: a handful of men sat at scattered tables on the sidewalk. Umm Kalthoum was singing to them and to us, the song "Ruins," from a poem by Mohamed Nagi, mourning his lost love. I imagined her singing to me.

Umm Hassan leaned over the railing, chattering to distract me. "Hadeel's a great girl, bless her. So pretty she lights up the room! And clever, with a university degree yet. Why are you dragging your heels?"

I looked silently at her. Disliking my attitude, she changed her tone. "To tell you the truth, her mother's been dropping hints. I don't know what to say to her. If you're not interested, let me know one way or the other."

I looked toward the horizon. I thought of Nadia and the moments we had shared; moments I was reliving even now. Hassan arrived at the entrance to our building. His mother peered down from above. "Wasn't that my boy Hassan who just walked in the door?"

I paid no attention. "What's wrong with you?" she urged, trying to get me to speak. "You must be sad about your mother leaving. Never you mind, I'm sure you'll soon meet again." Meanwhile, Abul Saad Effendi was leaning out of the balcony, entreating the boys at Morgan's Café to be neighborly and turn the radio down. "Poor fellow, who can blame him?" said Umm Hassan. "His girl Hadeel's exhausted!"

Abul Saad got what he wanted. The boys didn't just turn the radio down, they turned it off.

The last thing I heard that evening was Umm Kalthoum's voice:

How to forget a love that is gone?
Burning coals, to lie thereon!